THE IOWA SCHOOL OF LETTERS AWARD FOR SHORT FICTION

Fly Away Home

EIGHTEEN SHORT STORIES BY
MARY HEDIN

UNIVERSITY OF IOWA PRESS   IOWA CITY

ACKNOWLEDGMENTS

The previously published stories in this collection appear by permission:

"The Loon," *Great River Review* (Spring, 1978), as "Devourers."

"Plastic Edge to Plastic Edge," *McCalls' Magazine* (February 1978), as "Staying Married."

"Tale of a Mountain Place," *Brushfire* (1969).

"Oatmeal," *Descant* (Spring, 1971).

"The Peculiar Vision of Mrs. Winkler," *Redbook Magazine* (May 1969).

"The Followers," *South Dakota Review* (Summer, 1970).

"October," *Southwest Review* (Winter, 1971) as "Pookie."

"Ladybug, Fly Away Home," *Southwest Review* (October 1975); *The O. Henry Prize Stories 1977,* Doubleday.

"Places We Lost," *McCalls' Magazine* (October 1965); *Best American Short Stories, 1966,* Houghton Mifflin.

"Tuesdays," *Shenandoah* (Spring, 1977).

"The Middle Place," *Southwest Review* (Summer, 1978); *Best American Short Stories, 1979,* Houghton Mifflin.

Library of Congress Cataloging in Publication Data

Hedin, Mary.
  Fly away home.

  (The Iowa School of Letters award for short fiction)
  I. Title. II. Series: Iowa. University.
School of Letters. Iowa School of Letters award for
short fiction.
PZ4.H457Fl   [PS3558.E317]   813'.54   79-28524
ISBN O-87745-099-4
ISBN O-87745-100-1 pbk.

University of Iowa Press, Iowa City 52242
© 1980 by The University of Iowa. All rights reserved
Printed in the United States of America

CONTENTS

The Shadow In The Pond

At least twice each year as long as Anna could remember the family had made this journey. On a given summer Sunday they all climbed into the car at dawn with tins of cookies, boxes of outgrown or cast-off clothing, newspaper packets of peony or iris roots, the inevitable chocolate cake — all of which they were taking to the Monson family.

Always before, the journey had been an adventure. They planned and anticipated it, started upon it joyously. But this trip was different. The difference was there from the very beginning, the moment when Anna's mother read the letter and gasped, *Yvonne! Yvonne has died. Drowned in the little pond!*

Anna, sitting alone in the back seat, her hands folded severely against the bodice of her white dress, felt the journey's difference in the quietness in which her mother and father sat the entire long way. Difference showed in the way her father drove. Ordinarily, he drove the country roads leaning toward the open window's rush of air and sun, his bare arm on the edge of the car door catching the flickers of white summer sun. On this Sunday he wore his dark-blue suit and drove with his elbows properly at his sides. Anna's mother looked straight ahead at the stretch of tan road. She was not dressed in her flower-printed voile, but in the black crepe that whitened her skin and darkened the red of her hair.

Then, too, Kristin, Anna's sister, was lying at home in a quiet bed in a shade-darkened room, recovering from nosebleed. Her absence made Anna feel lonely and even apprehensive. She wished she were home, safely convalescing.

Anna's sigh shook with the joggling of the car. This, the last part of the journey was familiar to her. Studiously she observed the narrow corrugated road on which the car lurched as if it were hooved and breathing; the low clusters of tree and shrub, dust-dulled, heavy-shadowed, at road's edge; and soon, even then, visible at the end of the narrow road, the small white house set in the middle of stretching fields, the place where the Monson family lived.

The road turned abruptly. The car spun in its flume of dust, dragged to a stop in the patchy shade of a spindly elm in the grassless yard. Before the sound of the motor died on the country quiet, and before the rising cloud of their dust had begun to disperse, the screen door of the low house opened and closed. Hilma stood on the stoop, her shoulders sharp inside her black dress, her eyes and brows black in her long thin face. Her hands hung at her sides and she did not come to greet them.

But Bert darted down the path from the barn in his peculiar, jerking gait, leaping toward them like a grasshopper. Under the hard sun, his white shirt dazzled the eye, and his wide tie flapped out over his shoulder as he came. Before they could climb out of the car, Bert was leaning in the open window where Anna's mother sat, shoving his white-sleeved arm and stained, horny hand across to her father.

"You're welcome as the flowers in May," he cried, and the sweet sharp alcoholic smell of his breath blew over them all. His pale eyes were fired with red and his face with its great knob of a nose, twisted. "Welcome as the flowers in May," he repeated, excited and sad. He pulled open the door and stood like a cabby, holding it wide, his white, sunburned lips looped up in a toothy smile.

From the stoop of the step where she stood in shadow, Hilma called. "Stop that foolishness, Albert Monson." She did not move. The words seemed to come of their own power from her mouth and stood as if printed, large and black, on the summer air.

Anna's mother slid from the sticky front seat. She ran across the gravelly earth to Hilma and put her arms about the taller women. Hilma laid her cheek against her friend's forehead and shut her eyes. Anna's father climbed out and ran his long fingers through his hair, pulled at the knot of his tie.

"Come along, come along, Axel," Bert cried, nodding and grinning. He waved his thick arms vaguely at house and yard and the dry far fields. "Come out of the heat now. Rest yourselves."

Anna's father squinted up at the blurred sun. "It's going to be a real hot one, all right," he said and followed Bert across the yard and into the house where the women were already shut from view.

Forgotten by them all, Anna slowly got out of the back seat. She stood by the dust-covered car and looked at the things about her which were strange with elapsed time and were also familiar and apparently unchanged. The wide yard with its burned weeds sloped up toward the weathered gray barn. The warped wooden trough ran from the black pump and the high windmill to the fenced pigpen. Open fields stretched west to the remembered woods and east were the high shabby chicken coop, the woodpile, the rickety stand that supported the honing wheel. Everything was the same. Yet nothing seemed the same at all. In the shade of the chicken coop a few chickens pecked at the hard earth. But the pigs were were not in sight, nor the cows. Not even the old dog, who was devoted to farm business and never paid attention to them except to bark fiercely at their arrival, was around. The windmill was still. The sun pressed down into the empty yard, focused on Anna's head.

"Welcome as the flowers in May," Anna murmured. She brushed at the flecks of dirt peppering her white skirt. Bert, too, was different. Other visits he stood apart from them most of the day, red-faced, awkward in his Sunday clothes, his shyness and quietness slowly wearing away as the hours of their visit passed, as if he were so unused to company that he only got used to the feel of them being there when it was nearly time to go home. But this time he grinned and chattered and gestured like someone in a play. And where was Elsie?

Anna went slowly to the small house. She opened the screen door and stepped into the small kitchen. The big gray cat lay on the sill of the window, flat-sided, asleep, its thick tail curved around the base of a pot of pale geranium. Kettles simmering on the wood stove added heat to the hot air. The smells, too, of chicken and biscuits, corn and coffee, seemed hot.

Through the doorway to the other room Anna saw her mother and father and Hilma and Bert. And with them Elsie. Elsie sat on a straight wood chair. Her spine curved like a shell. Her elbows leaned on her parted knees, her heels hung on the chair's rung. Her brown hair lay in a flat curve over her cheek, and all Anna could see of her face was the pale, heavy downward curve of her mouth. Elsie was older, eleven, and she never played with Kristin and Anna and Yvonne.

Anna crossed the plank floor and stood in the doorway. From under dropped lids, Elsie glanced at her and did not smile. Anna's mother observed her absent-mindedly and listened intently to Hilma's low grieving monotone. The men stood by the window gazing out at the failed crops, the fields full of withered spikes of corn.

"Rain," Bert was saying. "Haven't had a drop since April. Worse than last year. Well's going dry, too." The bony humps of his shoulders rose and fell, his hands spread open toward the opposing walls of the room. His face twisted into a helpless grin. "Yessir, it's bad for everyone, all the way around."

Anna's father shook his head. "Too bad, too bad," he said, "More trouble than a man can stand. When it rains, it pours," he said and stared at the dusty fields. A fly circled the room, buzzing fiercely.

"Lunch," Bert suddenly announced. "Let's get these folks a bite to eat, Hilma!"

At the long, narrow table they sat as if they were in church. Sometimes Bert sat in bleak silence; then with a shake of head, a sheepish smile, he broke into a rush of talk. Then suddenly he was silent again. Anna's father ate methodically. Sometimes he looked up, cleared his throat as if to speak but said nothing and went on eating. Her mother murmured, now and then, something inconsequential, and ate nothing on her plate.

Throughout the meal, Anna felt herself the object of insidious attention. During his sudden speeches, Bert's hot glances darted toward her. When Hilma was not hurrying back and forth between the kitchen and the table, she sat with her dark gaze fixed on Anna's face, as if she wanted something from her. Even Elsie, her pale face unchanged by anything that was said or done during the entire meal, slid long mysterious looks at Anna that made her shiver.

With the whole Monson family watching her with strange expectation, Anna could not eat. She tried the creamy milk, but it had an odd flavor. She looked at her mother, but the look her mother gave back warned against rudeness. To avoid their glances then, Anna kept her eyes on the colorless chicken, the gray mashed potatoes, the large green peas stuck in yellow cream sauce. It seemed a very long time before Hilma brought the gray enamel coffee pot and the green glass dish mounded with oatmeal cookies, and long again before the men pushed back their chairs and strolled outdoors and the women began to clear the table. The task released them and they took up their usual chatter. Elsie pushed aside her plate, got up and disappeared.

Anna sat where she was at the littered table. She pushed the crumbs from her oatmeal cookie into a heap. One by one she lifted a crumb on a wet forefinger, took it on the tip of her tongue, crunched it between her front teeth. A fly buzzed around her. Anna kept waving it away.

After a while Hilma came and stood in the doorway, her knobby hands wrapped in the skirt of her apron. She leaned forward a little so that her narrow feet in the black heavy shoes seemed fastened to the floor. In the shadow of her frown, her eyes were like a stray dog's, hungry and pleading. Her thin lips parted and it seemed she would ask some important question. But she only leaned in that precarious way, gazed at Anna and said nothing. When Anna's mother questioned from the kitchen behind her, "Hilma?" Hilma did not seem to hear.

"You wait here, Anna," she suddenly ordered.

Hilma clumped away, up the stairs and back down. She came back to Anna at the table, her ropy arms cradling some object against her flat chest. She leaned over Anna and lay the thing she held in Anna's arms. "Yvonne's," Hilma said in a shaking voice. "You take it, Anna. You can have it now."

Anna looked down at the doll. It was old and not pretty and Anna did not want it. But a downturned smile shook across Hilma's face. Her eyes filled with tears. Anna held the doll stiffly and tried to smile.

Anna's mother came and took Hilma's arm, turning her away from Anna and the doll. "Go play now, Anna," she said too brusquely. "You get Elsie and find something to do. Like good girls, now, Anna."

"Elsie," Hilma nodded. "Elsie needs company. She's lonesome now."

Unconvinced, but unable to stay where she was, Anna went with the doll in her arms in search of Elsie. She climbed the high stairs to the low, loft bedroom. The tan shades were drawn to the sills. In the brown air, Elsie lay on the bed, pinch-nosed and slack-mouthed. She lay rigid, as if unable to move. Elsie always frightened Anna. Nevertheless she tiptoed up to the bed, leaned close, plucked at the chenille spread. "Elsie?" she whispered.

Heavy lids half-covering her eyes, Elsie only stared at the bars at the foot of the bed. She didn't move. Not even her lips moved when the sounds came. But the words were clear, sharply sibilant.

"What are you doing sneaking up here, spying on people? Go away, see? Go away, Nasty-nose. Your sister didn't drown, did she?"

Slowly Anna backed away from the thin girl who lay with her eyes fixed on the metal bedstead, giving no sign that she had said anything at all. At the doorway Anna dropped the doll on the floor, then fled down the stairs. She crept past the women at the sink, past the cat still sleeping on the window sill, out into the bare chicken-scarred yard. She stood under the blast of sun until she grew too hot. Then she went to the north side of the house.

There in a square of shade Bert and her father had spread a blanket. Her father lay on the blanket, leaning on one elbow. Bert sat near him. There was little talk between them, but that was not unusual. Whenever they were visiting it was like that. After the men discussed the weather, the crops, the state of the union, the state of the economy, they rested in silence. In a short time they would lie back on the blanket and permit the summer warmth, the Sunday quietness, the luxury of idleness to carry them into napping. It was meant to be so, just as it was meant that the women were to visit unremittingly, and the children knew they must stay very quiet or go far away to play their games.

But there was no other place to go, no other human comfort, so Anna came quietly and settled herself on a corner of the blanket. Her father hardly noticed. Already he was lying flat on his back, a wedge of the Sunday newspaper tenting his face from the flies. Bert sat with his white-sleeved arms hooked over his knees, his red tie drooping away from his craning neck. He looked sadly into the distance, his red eyes vague. He did not seem to notice Anna at all.

Anna sat very still, grateful to be near them but careful not to attract their attention. Even when one of the bold flies landed and bit her, she was careful to make no noise. Despite her caution, just when she grew sleepy, Bert's great-nosed face turned toward her. He looked at her with steady concentration. When at last she had to return his look, she saw that the profound sadness that had occupied his face was gone. A big smile looped under his nose. He unhooked his arms from his knees, leaned toward her. His fumey breath made Anna's breath stop.

"Where is Elsie, Anna?" he whispered. He glanced at the newspaper covering her father's face, but steady snores blew the newspaper up and down. "Won't Elsie play with you, Anna?" Bert persisted.

Anna felt her face turn red. She shook her head.

"Ah," Bert sighed. His thin hair lifted with the shake of his head. "It's just her way, Anna. She means to be nice. She just doesn't feel good." He frowned, looked uncertain and helpless. But then his eyebrows flew up and his big smile came back. He began to whisper rapidly. "Anna, sweetheart, how would you like to go for a ride? A ride on old Betsy, like Yvonne used to do? Just you and me, up there to the woods?"

Bert got up and leaned over her, holding out his hand, smiling with remarkable happiness. Anna could not refuse. She looked once at her father, sleeping under the paper, then let Bert fold her hand in his rough hand. She walked with him the long dusty path to the barn, once more doing something she did not want to do, not understanding why she had to do it, having no name for what reddened her cheeks.

In the barn the old smell assaulted — dung, hay, ammonia, mash—sweetness and rottenness mingled. Bert took Anna past dim dusty bins and empty littered stalls to the one occupied stall. Betsy, the great round-haunched bow-necked plow horse whinnied at them, tossed her head and tail. Anna watched while Bert bridled the horse and backed her out of the stall, shouting, "Hey, Betsy, back up there, hey!" slapping her shoulders.

Then he bent down, swooped Anna up, his big hands hard against her ribs. He swung her high and set her up in the broad hollow of Betsy's wide back. "Hold on to her mane, Anna. Here we go." He laughed and led Betsy out the barn doors and down the ramp into the brassy light and heat of the afternoon.

Anna clung with knees and hands to the animal lurching and rocking beneath her. The ground seem immensely far away and she felt her posture there on the horse's back completely rootless, as precarious as if she sat on an over-turned boat in the middle of a choppy lake.

"Now isn't that fun, Anna?" Bert shouted up at her.

Anna swallowed. Words wouldn't come to her dry tongue, and she was afraid, anyway, to protest. They started along the edge of the field, rocking and lurching beside the split log fence. Suddenly Bert paused. Betsy came to a stop beside him, bobbed her huge head, waited. Bert stood under the hot sun, looking at the ground, thinking. His frown dropped a shadow that screened his face. At last he jerked his chin, glanced up at Anna where she sat on Betsy's back. "Wait," he mumbled.

He threw the reins over the top rail of the fence and ran back to the barn and disappeared inside. Anna hardly breathed. Why had he left her there alone? She didn't know about horses. What could she do if Betsy started to move, to gallop away? Betsy, as if impatient, snuffed at the turf. She lifted her head, stretched her neck. Her ears went flat to her head, the wide nostrils dilated, black lips parted. Under the high fierce whinny, the air shook. Under Anna's legs the hot flesh shuddered.

As if in response to Betsy's complaint, Bert plunged out on the sunlit ramp. "All right," he called and came running crookedly toward them, a white and blue bobber on waves of light. "Here we are, all set," he panted and laughed. "Now we'll have a nice little ride, just the thing for a nice girl like Anna!" He wiped his brow on the sleeve of his shirt and took up the trailing reins. On his shoulder he hung the coils of the rope he had gone back to the barn to get. He clucked his tongue, Betsy shook herself into motion. Anna opened her mouth to protest, and did not.

They followed the fence along the edge of the fields where dead seedlings stood in yellow rows. Once across the vast sky a few crows arced. Betsy's flanks grew wet, and her rough hide scratched Anna's thighs. The sun seemed to lay a hot hand on the top of her head. As they went Bert lifted his face, making speeches to Anna. His right hand flew out in sweeping gestures. His face was red and drops of sweat fell from his nose. On his shoulder the coiled rope swung, a heavy pendulum.

"Yvonne loved to ride," Bert declared. "Sometimes she didn't even ask. She figured I'd say no. She'd just sneak out there to the barn and take Betsy out all by herself." He gave his looping grin, shook his head. He swiped his forearm at his sweaty brow. "She was a lively one, Yvonne. She'd try to make old Betsy gallop. She'd smack away at Betsy's rear with her bare hand. Like a butterfly spanking a turtle." He laughed, coughed. His open hand swept at empty air.

Dust rose from Betsy's hooves and hung in a low cloud about them. Her head sawed up and down, her haunches rolled with each step. Anna's fingers ached from clenching the wiry mane.

"You're like her, Anna," Bert said and suddenly seemed very sad. But then he laughed and his eyes were strange. "Yep, just like her. The same size. Your hair, that's the color Yvonne's hair was. And eyes. The same. Blue."

Anna tried to remember Yvonne, her bright face, her shouts of laughter. Were they really alike? But Yvonne was

dead. She, Anna, was alive. She, not Yvonne, rode on the beast
that heaved and lurched, full of power, full of fleshy life. But
because Bert's eyes were full of remembrance and forgetfulness Anna still did not cry out that she wanted to get down,
to go back, to find her mother inside the distant small house.

Even before they stopped in the blue shade of the first tall
oaks, Anna knew where Bert would take her, so when Betsy
stopped beside him with a mild stomp of heavy hooves and
a deep shudder of spine, Anna shuddered, too.

"Well, here we are," Bert said. He shifted the rope on his
shoulder, knotted Betsy's reins over a fence post, reached up
for Anna. She slid down into his arms. On the ground she
wavered like a blown flower.

"Steady there," Bert laughed, his hand at her back.

"Where are we going?" Anna asked. She wondered if her
voice showed that she already knew.

"A pretty place, where it's nice and cool." Bert ducked
through an opening in the fence where one rail was gone. He
held out his hand to help Jenny through. He was taking her
to the pond where Yvonne had drowned. As she climbed
through the fence Anna's skirt caught on a rusty nail. The
fabric gave way in a small tear. Anna hardly noticed, merely
brushed at the ruined place, and went with Bert, her hand
held by his.

The trees arched over them and their green shade cooled
them. The ground was soft under their feet. Birds twittered
at their passing. Bert walked slowly, parting the branches of
the leaning shrubs. He was quiet there in the quiet woods.

Once Bert stopped. He dropped Anna's hand and stood
studying her face, his own face drawn to a knot. Then he
turned away from her and stepped off the path. Anna watched
him pull down a limber branch of sumac. He slid the coil of
rope from his shoulder and hung it over the tip of the branch.
The slender branch did not spring up when Bert let go, but
curved toward him under the weight of rope. Carefully Bert

arranged green branches around it, hiding the rope from view.

Then he came back and smiled foolishly at Anna and grasped her hand. A little farther they stepped into a clearing where sunshine dropped through a lacy roofing of leaf. The pond lay before them, ringed with a wide border of spiky green grass. Its water shone a deep blue-black. Along the muddy shallows lay the flat dark green of lily pads. The flowers, creamy white, lay open upon circles of green.

Inside Anna's ears a voice said flatly, Here. It happened here. She stared at the still pond. Its dark shining seemed as impenetrable as mirrors. Anna left Bert's side. She took the marshy footpath to the weathered pier stretching over the shore grasses and muddy shallows to the clear water. She walked the pier's length and stood over the water on the very spot from which, on a recent summer day when heat and dust had made that dark still pond a marvelous escape, Yvonne had jumped — happy, laughing, alive. And had not returned. Anna thought perhaps somewhere in that depth of quiet water Yvonne still lay. Or drifted. Or moved about with the slow motions of swimmers under water.

Then she saw something actually there in the dark water, a body, its vague limbs shaking slowly with the water's imperceptible motion. Anna's breath stopped in her throat. For a moment she froze in horror. Then she understood. It was her own reflection, only the ghostly echo of herself in the mirroring water, nothing to be afraid of at all.

And when she knew that, she became aware that a second shape was shimmering in the water below her, that of some-one taller, someone familiar, grown strange as her own reflec-tion was strange down there. It was Bert. Bert was beside her in the reflecting pond.

Anna turned to look at Bert who was leaning over the water, his white shirt gray with sweat, his red tie swinging free. He was wholly absorbed, and his face was so changed it seemed made new. It was full of light, a kind of red shining. Dampness and rosiness made a look of joyous worship, and the look sprang from his vision of the child wavering in the water below. He saw in the deluding darkness of the pond, Yvonne, the child he loved.

"It's only me," Anna cried so loudly a startled bird flew from the reeds. "It's my shadow down there."

She stepped back from the edge of the pier to make the reflection disappear. Bert turned then and looked at her. He shook his head. Color flared across his cheeks and he closed his eyes. His head dropped so that his chin rested against his tie. Anna turned and led him back, away from the pond, back through the shady woods the way they had come. When they passed the place where the rope swung on the sumac, something cold tocked in Anna's mind.

Betsy waited at the fence. Once again Bert swung Anna up on the horse's back. This time Anna rode without panic, watching the stocky man who rocked along beside her like a worn-out clown.

At the house the women watched for their return. They looked at Anna's muddy shoes, the torn, soiled white dress. Their faces were stiff but they did not scold. "Bert," Anna's mother said. "Are you all right?" But Bert turned away and Anna's mother took her to the sink, filled the enamel basin with cool pump water and bathed her. Hilma placed brown bread and a glass of milk on the table for her supper.

From the other room Elsie in the creaking rocker watched, the book in her hands raised high enough to almost hide her eyes.

Then at last they started the journey home.

In the gathering dusk Anna sat in the back seat of the rushing car. Up front her mother and father sat watching the spinning road in silence. On the seat beside her lay the doll Hilma had found and thrust upon her. Anna pushed the doll away. She wanted to forget Hilma and Elsie and Bert and even Yvonne. Resentfully she looked at the heads of her parents, dark and without contour against the darkened sky. Did they love her, she wondered, as much as Hilma and Bert loved Yvonne?

Anna lay down on the wide back seat, pulled her sweater close, and gave herself up to the bounce and sway of the speeding car. She watched the jerk and shift of stars on the purpled windshield and then finally grew sleepy. She sighed with gratitude. In a little while she would be sound asleep, and in sleep, she foolishly thought, she would forget them all, even the secret rope that waited in the shadowy woods that circled the pond where Yvonne had died.

The Loon

All summer long the old lake house shuddered with the noise of raucous young voices. The kitchen was always occupied. The refrigerator door opened and shut constantly. The toilet flushed every five minutes. The cesspool overflowed. Books, papers, games, jackets, and shoes were scattered about the living room. Balls, rackets, fishing gear, cans of bait, jars of bugs, torn wrappers from candy and gum cluttered the yard.

During the long winter months Winston Berg waited for the abrupt fury of the Minnesota spring and the sudden arrival of summer when they would come. And so did Ellen his wife. But now in the August Sunday evening at the dinner table, Winston felt entirely out of tune. His fidgeting grandchildren—Rob, Barney, and Teddy—gulped, chewed, babbled. Carrie, his daughter-in-law, came through the kitchen door carrying two cups of coffee. Her faded shorts showed too much of pale, heavy thigh. Her hair, loose and straight from swimming, fell thickly about her face and neck. She looked unkempt, rather wild. Even if Robert were there, she would not have bothered to fix herself up. She leaned now past Teddy, set one of the cups of coffee by Winston's plate. She dropped down into her own chair.

"There's coffee in the saucer," Winston snapped. He lifted the cup and saucer from its place and held it out toward Carrie. "I can't stand a cup dripping from the bottom the whole time you try to drink from it."

Carrie's lips swelled. She took on a passive, offended look. The three boys turned suddenly quiet. They watched him carefully. Was he scolding their mother? Angry at her? They were stiff with apprehension.

"Everywhere you go these days," Winston said, "there's coffee in the saucer. Every time I go to the Puritan Cafe for lunch the waitress slops coffee into the saucer. Send it back, I do," he looked from one boy's face to another, smiling, offering amusement. No one smiled. "Yes sir, I send it back. If there's one thing I can't stand," Winston finished gamely, though he perceived that his efforts to placate were without grace, "it's sloppiness."

Carrie's chair scraped. She lurched up. She took the cup from Winston's hand. Ellen came from the kitchen carrying a glass bowl heaped with raspberries.

"For Heaven's sake, Win," she scolded, "Can't you simply wipe off the saucer?" She took the cup from Carrie, a paper napkin from the holder, polished off the spilled brown liquid, handed it back. "There," she said and laughed, and Winston, though chastened, was grateful for the rescue.

But Carrie sat poking at her fruit, lowered eyelids hiding what she felt. Winston knew she thought him arbitrary, demanding, and resented his criticisms. Well, he was what he was. He believed he was right in what he expected. But his difference from them made him feel solitary, even lonely. He turned his attention away from them, did not listen any longer to their chatter, their disputes.

After dinner Winston sat in his rocker on the screen porch. He studied the folded newspaper he held in one hand. The small clatter of women at dishes came from the kitchen. In the stained sky over the hackberry trees, the martins wheeled in the ritualistic patterns of dusk flight, and their high cries mingled with the calls of the children running in the rituals of their evening games. An odor of sweetness and decay, of zinnias, petunias, and phlox, and the musty decadence of the lake's shore, rose into the deepening lilac of evening air.

Suddenly out of the shadows rimming the gleaming quiet

lake, a long call sounded, shaking, wild, lonely, mad. It was
the cry of a loon. Winston got up, put his paper in the wicker
rack beside his chair. He went out the screen door, down the
steps. A tall, lean man with a shaggy, forward-thrusting gray
head, he ambled over the wide lawn, down the slope to the
water's edge. He stood on the bank and looked out at the
gold-streaked shimmering water. The loon's cry wavered
again, and to the watching, listening man it seemed the spaces
of water and air grew strangely large, filled with a great
nameless desire and chilling portent.

Then a speed boat crashed around the bend of shore. Its
motor's roar cracked across the stillness. The lake's surface
broke into repeating shudders.

Winston shuddered also, as if abruptly cold. The calm of
the dinner hour was over. From then on, till nightfall, the
motorboats and water skiers would churn across the lake. He
turned away. Near him, on the grass flanking the rocky shore,
the minnow net still lay where the boys had stretched it to
dry. Muttering at their forgetfulness, Winston stooped,
straightened the net, rolled it to a neat bundle and took it to
the pumphouse and stored it inside.

He saw that the minnow bucket still hung from the pier's
first pole. He walked out onto the pier and pulled at the
bucket's rope, the bucket came up heavily, water pouring in
a thick ring from the perforations near the top. He set the
bucket on the pier, unclamped the lid. A dozen or more
minnows floated in limp white loops on the water's surface.
Darned kids. They netted the minnows only for sport, always
took more than they needed for bait. They seemed not to care
for those they let die. He corrected them, scolded them,
taught them, trying to keep them from becoming like those
city-bred men who came pouring into the half-wild lake
country he loved, wasting its resources, spoiling its beauty.

Winston glanced once more at the softened, bloated
corpses. Then he swung the pail in a shallow arc and sprayed

the contents over the lake. He rinsed out the bucket and set it upside down to drain. He walked heavily over the creaking planks to the end of the pier. He stood there, scowling, not at what he saw of water and shore and sky, which was all the rich color of stained glass, but at the darkness and bitterness in his own heart. He stood considering his own life. He was pretty lucky, according to any man's judgment. He still had Ellen. His old friend Norb had lost his wife years ago. And Ozzie's wife was dying now, a long agonizing death. Winston still had his own life, and his health. Many of those he had loved were already gone, and if their going had taken from him a large sum of what he had been and known, still he was here. And he had these others taking up their places in his time and thoughts—his daughter and his son, six grandchildren. So should he not, he chastised himself, attach himself with gratitude to what was left? Why, then, did he stand there, full of grief and vacancy in the August sunset, an ache in his being as acute as disease?

As Winston so instructed himself, the boy Teddy came running down the bank at full speed, his legs flashing against the dark grass, his face lifted up on the thin neck, his dark hair (too long, Winston thought, for an active boy of six) blown back by the parting air.

Of all the grandchildren, he preferred Teddy. But he knew that preference grew from the fact that the boy was most like him and only reflected his own pride and egotism, and so he never indulged it. He watched the lad come, unwilling to move again into that relationship of giving which the young demanded of him. Already Teddy was shouting *Grandpa, Grandpa* at the top of his voice so that the sound rang clear and full up into the glowing bell of the sky and rocked out over the water in mocking repetitions. *Dr. Berg* he was called in town, *Win* by his friends. Out here *Grandpa, Grandpa, Grandpa,* as if his only identity were progenitor to these all-important young.

The boy's feet hit the pier in quick hard beats. The whole length of the pier trembled. "Grandpa, let's go trolling," he cried. "I want to fish. Can we go fishing, Grandpa? It's not too late, is it Grandpa? The sun's just going down!"

"Now slow down, Ted," Winston admonished. "Slow down a little. Where are your brothers? Where have they got to?"

They'd gone to the mill, the boy reported. They hadn't wanted to go fishing. But he, Teddy, did. "Please Grandpa," he repeated. "Let's go trolling."

For a small fellow, Ted had a lot of patience for fishing. Every day he spent hours on the pier, tending his pole, changing bait, trying for something big enough to keep. And Winston admired that. But trolling. Lowering the boat from its rack, filling the tank with fuel, getting out all the fishing gear, putting it all in order again on coming in, perhaps fish to clean, besides—he didn't feel up to it. "No, Ted," he said. "Not tonight."

The loon called out again, a high harsh warble. For a moment Winston turned to the sound. But he felt the child look at him, and he turned again to face him.

The boy's eyes were dark with understanding. "Are you too tired, Grandpa?" he asked. Winston looked down at him almost resentfully, but nodded. "Yes," he confessed. "I'm tired tonight." The boy nodded also, his eyes narrowed and bleak as if he himself were in that moment sixty-eight years old and felt precisely the oppression of body and mind that had taken hold of his grandfather. But it was only a moment and then the child returned.

"Well, then I'm going to fish from the pier," he announced. "You can sit there on the bench and watch, Grandpa."

He ran to the pumphouse and came back carrying his pole in one hand and his green tackle box in the other. He squatted beside Winston and opened the lid of the box. The last flat rays of the sun burnished his skin to a bright gold. "I think

I'll catch a bass," he said, sober as a judge. "I think there's a bass right under the pier, big as your arm, Grandpa."

He pulled a snarl of lures from the bottom of his tackle box. He tugged at the lures, unable to separate them. Winston reached for them. "Here, I'll do that, Ted," he said, and the boy leaned against him as he maneuvered the hooks locked intricately together.

"So you think there's a bass under the pier," Winston said, simply for the recognition of what the boy had left in the air between them.

"Yep, big as your arm," Ted confidently repeated, his brows drawn together in an absurd, scholarly frown.

"Never did see a bass big as my arm," Winston said, his long fingers deft in the snarled metal. "Got a pike, once, near as big as my arm, though." And regretted at once that he had said it. Always the boy seemed to do that to him, to spring some catch in his mind, opening up a time of the past which he himself would not have brought up. So he was in for it, the questions, the story-telling. He gave up a deep sigh, unfastened the last two linked hooks and handed the boy the red and white plug he wanted.

"When?" Teddy had already demanded. "When did you catch a pike that big, Grandpa? Where? Here in Green Lake?"

Sometimes it seemed to Winston that the boy believed all the years of his living had been gone through only for the purpose of providing tales for a small boy's amusement. He seemed to want everything in Winston's head, to consume in bits and pieces everything Winston was. Winston felt himself almost devoured by the boy's curiosity, but still as if he could not keep from giving himself away, Winston gave up the words.

"No, it wasn't Green Lake." His voice deepened and slowed as he moved far back into his mind to pick up the sights and sound and events of the day on which he had

caught the massive fish. Nineteen-thirty-five. No, nine-
teen-thirty-six, that was it. He and the gang — Norb, Ozzie,
Al, Cappie, all of them — had gone to Norb's cabin on
Alexander Lake. And all of them young then as he himself
was young, all full of the ridiculous confidence that seemed
to assume in those sweet repeating days that because all was
well then, all would be well with all of them forever, as if
they were immovable upon that point of time on which they
stood.

The lake in the past time was quiet. No speed boats tearing
at its surface. No traffic of automobiles ringing it. The water
was then pure enough to drink right from the spring-fed
lake, and the great pure depths teemed with bass and crappie
and pike.

On that particular Saturday of the big pike, Winston had
gone out with Norb to try his luck at trolling. It was one of
those pallid July days when a milkiness to the light seemed
to draw all color and sound from the world. They pushed out
from the rotting pier in Norb's old leaky boat, Norb rocking
his great muscular body in the rhythms of stealthy rowing,
and the quietness was so complete they did not want to talk.
Beneath the boat the water was darkened and green. The
shoreline trees were swollen with heat and shadow. They
skirted the lake's shore for some time, their thoughts coming
close enough at times for a muttered word or two, then
drifting back into silence that preserved the stillness about
them. There had been a loon that afternoon, too, its startling
cry rippling out like a celebration. They caught a glimpse of
the bird, dark and lean-necked among the spiky reeds in a
birch-rimmed cove. As the boat slipped near, the loon dived
as if pulled abruptly down by some unseen force. They didn't
see him surface, but later he called on the far side of the lake.
Crazy loon, Norb whispered and grinned so that his yellow
teeth shone in the tan of his bony face.

But it was the fish that made that day memorable. The pike

hit the spinning plug a few yards from the place where they saw the loon. Winston wasn't ready for him. Lulled by the dream-like sense of the day, he had relaxed his grip on his pole, and when that abrupt strike came, he lurched forward to grab the falling pole and almost fell from the boat. *Holy Mike,* Norb shouted behind him, *He's a whopper. Hang on, give him the line!* Winston had stumbled back and braced himself on one knee and let the line whip past his fingers in a blue blur.

Winston fought the fish for more than half an hour, and he knew long before he saw it that it was the biggest fish any of them had ever caught. At last Norb put up the oars and kneeled in the bottom of the boat, the net ready, and when the great sharp-nosed pike came surfacing along side the drifting boat, Norb leaned far over and scooped him up. The great fish lay then, heaving and writhing in silver agony, against the wet, stained boards of the old boat, the hook drawing a thick thread of bright blood from the gaping mouth. With amazement and pity they stared at him, and then Winston struck the life from him with one clean blow.

Back at camp Ozzie and Norb traced the shape of the fish on the wall over the blackened fireplace. *That bruiser,* Ozzie declared, *deserves to be stuffed. Leastways we got to have a picture.* But no one had a camera and they had packed the fish in ice, and later at home they took the picture, Norb standing over the little box, tipping his head to squint into the small round window in the back. Ellen stood beside Winston, her short-skirted dress blowing against her knees, and he himself, full of his own unquestioned power, held her close in one arm, held aloft in his free hand the dead, heavy, beautiful fish, and laughed in the camera's eye.

Now that singular remembered time seemed to Winston more absolute, more commanding than the moment in which he presently stood, an old man in a time he did not like. That past was strongly holding him, locking him into something terrifying in its brightness and lostness. Though he tried to move away from vivid hypnotic past, from that beautiful dead time, to this other place where what he now was would take command, he could not get free. The faces, the voices of old friends were looking out at him from the far side of time, calling out to him in young voices—Ozzie, Norb, Pete and Al and Ellen and even that arching leaping magnificent fish and the sunlight of that Sunday dusk when the camera's eye reached through the moment to an emptier future he had not foreseen.

And so caught on a hook of memory, he heard the boy's voice with uncertainty. Was it Teddy? His grandson? Shouting, "Look, Grandpa, look! The bird, Grandpa, look out!"

Winston stared into the blazing western sky, a coppery cauldron, through which a bird rowed, swift and awesome. Black wide wings beat the molten air, and the stretched long body came fiercely at him, as if he were target. The hard crimson eye burned against his own, the sharp beak glistened. Winston shied, threw his arms over his face, dropped down into an instinctive, astonished crouch. The loon's cry sounded, a breaking lunatic laugh, over his head. The thunderous clap of wingbeats passed close, then became a more and more distant drumming.

Then, only then, did Winston hear, over the fearful beat of blood in his veins, that other far high cry, a human cry, cutting across the dying day. It was a keening wail, a woman's voice— Carrie's—crying a long warning cry. Teddy, Teddy! she called. Winston turned numbly to the terrible sound of it and saw her coming, running as if the earth must fold up beneath her, running with her arms flung open, her face white and wrenched, her mouth wide. He knew from her face something terrible had happened.

"Teddy!" she wailed again in that high alarming voice. "Teddy!" And she came on pounding, terrified legs to the lake shore and onto the pier, and before Winston's dazed and uncomprehending eyes, dived into the water at the pier's end.

She came up gasping, sputtering, the water flying from her mouth and flattened hair. Her face looked wasted and white under its wetness, eyes black. She stared into the green shining shaken depths of the water, gaping and gasping. She dived again and Winston saw her churning about in the water beside the pier. He could not make of her bizarre behavior any sense at all. Then he saw in the water's dim deepness her white arms reach and reach for something dark and shadowy in the water. She came bursting up, something in her arms. It was Teddy.

Only then did Winston understand. He kneeled, helped haul the child up on the pier. He held his grandchild in his arms and stared into the unresponsive face. The child's head fell loosely against his chest. The frail neck would not hold up the head. The mouth was drawn back over the small perfect teeth, and the lips looked dark, tight; the eyes beneath dropped lids bulged as if with horror.

"Teddy, my God. Teddy," Winston whispered. Teddy did not move. Carrie had pulled herself up on the pier. Roughly she took the child from Winston. She laid him on the white peeling boards, stretched him out, and knelt over him, spreading her thighs so she could straddle the thin body. She placed the child's face to one side and began to rock over him, her hands pumping against the cage of his chest. *Oh God,* she muttered on the edge of sobs, *Oh God.* And the boy lay beneath her hands, totally unresisting. His flesh flattened and shrank beneath the pressure of the urgent hands. She turned the boy over again and lifted him so that his shoulders lay over her arm and his dark wet head fell back from the stretched throat. She leaned down to the slack mouth and covered it with her own and blew harshly, hungrily, into it. The amber light touched her face and the child's face, and the water drops falling from their hair and skin were, Winston saw, drops of fire.

Then Carrie stopped, for one moment. She stared up at Winston, her eyes black with hate. "The ambulance," she cried, "damn you, the ambulance." She fell back, weeping, her yearning mouth over the boy's.

Winston tried to turn. He did manage to turn from them and move his feet across the wide obstructing boards of the pier. It seemed he could not run. His feet would not properly lift and come down again. At the bank he stumbled, fell, clawed his way up the slope, and then Ellen was coming. He tried to explain to her, but she looked past him and saw, and she spun away from him and ran to the house. *She* called. It was Ellen who called for help.

Ellen and Carrie both went to the hospital, although they knew by then Teddy would be all right. He was conscious, breathing well. They left Winston behind to watch for the older boys. So he was left alone to recall the event, to recall the hate flaring in Carrie's eyes, to remember his own failures and Ellen's gasped accusations: *Winston, didn't you watch him?*

Later that night, when they brought Teddy home, Winston went to the door of the room and looked in. Teddy was propped up against white pillows, the sheets drawn up to his chin. His eyes were large in the hollows of his eye sockets and shadowed as if with some final discovery. He looked back solemnly, then his mouth moved as if he would smile. Winston stumbled away. Could he bear the child's forgiveness?

The lit bright house, full of the murmurous maternity of the women, seemed a prison. Winston went to the dark porch and looked out at the black slippery water of the lake. Moonlight lay on its scarcely moving surface. Crickets chirred, relentlessly cheerful, in the damp grasses. The air was fresh as Eden. Shame assaulted Winston, and rage.

He got his jacket and his shotgun and walked out into the night. He went along the road, away from the lake, over fields where the corn stood high and blue in the darkness, and into the woods beyond. All night he tramped the dark paths he knew from his lifelong walking there. He considered again and again the extraordinary experience of the early evening. He felt himself standing eternally at the end of the pier, felt himself repeatedly attacked by the great black bird. He listened and listened for the sound of a boy falling into the water. He strained for the note of the boy's cry. Had he not cried out? Searching all night through the sequence of the event, Winston could not find the place where he should have reached out to hold the lad, to save Teddy.

In the chastened quiet before break of day, Winston Berg came to the place where the wood dipped down to the shore of the lake. He found a place on the shore in the shadow of a clump of birch and crouched there. His gun rested ready against his knee.

As the gray mists began to lift from the water's surface and the first burning of yellow edged the sky, he saw what he had come for. The loon moved steadily among the slender reeds. The bright eye roved the morning waters, the neck weaving sinuously in hungry hunting. Cautiously Winston lifted the gun, sighted, pressed the trigger.

In that precise moment a call rose from the bird's throat. The wild warble broke against the sound of the gun. In a sudden churning of water, the loon folded slowly down to ragged stillness. In the widening rings of staining water a few black feathers swirled.

Winston turned away, went with his gun to the edge of the wood. He leaned against a tree, trembling with tiredness. The smell of powder stung his nose, teared his eyes. A pain grew in his chest, and he put his hand against it as if he could soothe it away. Then he heard the child Teddy shouting.

The boy was running toward him in the morning light. His white clothes, pajamas, of course, were rimmed with the gold of the rising sun, and his brown hair was burnished to copper. How beautiful he looked. And he ran so swiftly, so lightly, who could believe he had just returned from death's door?

The boy had stopped before him and looked into his face. He wrapped his arms around Winston's waist and leaned against him. "Grandpa," he asked, "Why did you shoot the loon?"

His Father's Son

Tom Saint Clair's father was a large handsome man, thick of body and luminous of face, who confided to any and all new acquaintances that at sixteen he had been a criminal. He gave this information with a look of vigorous joy, and always ended the account of his youthful failures by saying, "Everything I am I owe to Gladys and to Gladys' father."

His wife Gladys, Tom's mother, was also large, but not handsome. Big-boned, broad of bosom and hip, her face was narrow, long-nosed, and sallow.

Although he wished she were prettier, Tom loved his mother. He loved his father more. He did not understand why his father always wanted to put himself down with that story. He heard Arthur Saint Clair's words with wonder and dismay. "A juvenile crook," he said. "A real criminal. A bum. A young no-good punk." The harshest words he could think of, he applied to the boy he had been.

Tom knew that the fierce condemnation was not entirely deserved. He had heard the tales often enough. His father was from a large family in a bleak mining town in northern Minnesota. His own father, laid off during the Depression, worked little, drank too much, roared around that town in wild rage, creating disorder and resentment and ending up in the town jail. He beat his wife and sons alike when the anger was upon him, and there was never enough money for food and clothing and rent. Whatever had happened to the boy Arthur Saint Clair had been, Tom felt, was accounted for by that bleak, underprivileged life. Hadn't he heard how his father could not stay after school for the season's sport, how he could not belong to the Boy Scout Troop, how he was unable to own skates or hockey stick or baseball glove or bike? And how he had been up at dawn, Arthur Saint Clair at the age of eleven and twelve, delivering papers in the steel-trap cold of Minnesota winters, and after school at Mr. Fergusson's grocery store carrying heavy boxes and crates, stocking the shelves, sweeping, shovelling snow, stoking the furnace—all that needed to be done which old Mr. Fergusson couldn't do. He was paid twenty-five cents an hour. He'd had nothing, that boy Arthur. Only hard work, deprivation, neglect, and even exploitation by his distracted helpless parents. Anyone would excuse, forgive, Tom knew, that wild year in which his father had "gone bad."

"Started to drink," his father said accusingly of the boy he had been and now scorned. "Bad company. Hung around the poolhall, shooting crap, smoking like a chimney, boozing around. Wanted money and didn't want to work. Bummed around with the town's no-goods. Drove my mother wild, I did."

Yes, Tom thought, his mother. His mother, somewhere there in the brittle Minnesota winter nights, weeping over her lot—her unkempt house, her needy kids, her brutal husband, and now this betraying son who in the end stole a car and ended up in reform school. Yes, Tom felt pity for her. But he could not blame the tall thin desperate boy he imagined his father.

No, not "bad." A victim. Helpless, Tom saw him. He saw in his father's past a pain his father seemed to ignore, praising his wife Gladys and his wife's father for saving him, keeping him from his terrible criminal drives.

"Why, Gladys' dad," he would tell the bland-faced curious visitors as they sat in the Phillipine-mahogany-panelled, nylon-carpeted order of their suburban living room, "came to the reform school there in Red Wing, Minnesota, and took me to his farm place and treated me like his own son. First time in my life someone stepped in and wanted to help me be someone respectable and worthwhile! Lectured me, taught me, argued with me. Even gave me a good walloping a time or two when I got out of line. Tamed me down, he did. A fine man, Dad Bower. A great man. It got so I loved him more than Jesus Christ himself. I could have bowed down and worshipped him. That's how much I thought of him. He was a real father to me. A fine man."

And Gladys, Tom's mother, listened to the familiar account soberly, nodding firmly at all Dad Bower had been, a little smile turning up the corners of her thin mouth, pale color creeping into her cheeks as Arthur Saint Clair beamed at her in pride and gratitude, recounting what had been done for him.

"But you worked, Dad, didn't you?" Tom would interrupt, wanting what? Wanting justice for the boy his father would not defend? Wanting less condemnation of someone whose life now reflected upon his own?

"Yes, yes," Gladys Saint Clair would say. "He worked like a trooper on the farm. Dawn to dark, just like Grandpa. He was a good boy, your father was."

"But that's just it," Arthur Saint Clair would protest, thrusting himself out of his chair, striding to the brick hearth where he leaned against the fireplace wall, full of energy, sweeping the air with a broad gold-calloused hand. "They'd keep saying that. *You're a good boy, Art. A fine boy. Just went a little bad, that's all. Got in with bad company, that's what it was.* Always made excuses for me. Always believed in me. *You're a good boy, Art.* Dad Bower said that every day. Every darned day, so full of faith he was. All that faith in a poor dumb no-good kid he took on trust from the reform school."

Sometimes the telling of that tale was directed at him, Tom knew. Not to warn him, but rather to praise him. Commending him for being a better kid that his father had been.

Admiring Tom's wisdom, his reliability, his unspoiled future.

Sometimes the tale was repeated for his mother, Gladys. The telling made some kind of payment for what she had given him. It gave her the credit for everything Arthur Saint Clair had gained—a well-paying job, a nice house, a pleasant neighborhood, the office of elder in the church, presidency of the Parents' Club, membership in the Elks. A man in good with his community. A reliable respected citizen. All because of her.

But perhaps the tale of delinquency, of juvenile crime, was told to all comers, friends and neighbors and new acquaintances, because of something Arthur Saint Clair was doing for himself. Tom didn't see that, didn't discern that there might be in the need to tell another need more profound and more deeply hidden than the others.

But in the end Arthur Saint Clair betrayed them all.

It began when the Gilroy Construction Company won a contract with the State Highway Department for the construction of a cloverleaf overpass outside of Sacramento. The job was big, contracted to be finished within six months. The whole crew would have to live down there. Art Saint Clair, who operated big equipment for Gilroy, told his wife and son that he and the others would have to live wherever they could, in motels and hotels and trailer camps and rented rooms, working around the clock to get the thing done in time.

"I'll be gone most of the summer, Gladys, I guess," Arthur said. In the thin blue of the early July evening, the glumness of his face made him strange to their eyes. "Guess I'll get home some weekends. Not every week, though."

"We'll manage," Gladys said, firm, a good sport. Competence was her prize virtue. "We'll keep busy, Tom and I. Paint the house, maybe. And I'll be having lots of canning to do, too." Gladys was the only woman in the neighborhood who bought crates of strawberries, peaches, pears and grapes and put up the fruit in glass jars for winter use.

"Now don't overdo, Gladys," Art cautioned. "Tom here can do the yardwork. Sixteen now. He's big enough for that. Why don't you join the swim club this summer and have yourself a relaxing time? Get tan. Read. Lie around for a change." It seemed that he wanted them to take in special pleasures to make up for his absence. And he grew more cheerful at the possibility. "I'll miss you both, God knows. I never sleep good away from home. And the food. It'll be terrible. Pre-fab dinners seven nights a week. But maybe you can come down, sometimes, Gladys, share my room weekends." His optimism was back in full, lighting up his face. "You can leave Tom in charge here at home, Glad. He's responsible now."

But Gladys had always been a conscientious mother. Her cheeks drew inward, her lips puckered.

"I don't like to do that, Art," she said. "I wouldn't want to leave him alone."

"I'll be fine, Mom," Tom told her. He felt the weight of his father's confident hand on his shoulder.

But then the fatherless summer weeks began, and they were strangely dull. Sitting face to face with his mother at the supper table, their dinner already dished up and the plates set in the center of green plastic mats, the cutlery and paper napkins beside the plates (now that there were only the two of them, she saw no point in dirtying up the serving dishes, she matter-of-factly said), Tom found nothing to say. The pattern of pleasant comradery to which he aspired eluded him. He made an effort to relate happenings from his mornings in summer school and his afternoons at the park where he had a part-time job with the Recreation Department. But his words came slowly. Gladys met these narratives with slow and somehow effortful responses, as if she too found her head willing but her tongue incapable. It had been his father, Tom perceived, who moved the three of them into open, lively exchange, whose interest and enthusiasm made their lives seem important and unique. A peculiar lethargy closed down around him, closing him into more and more silence. He and his mother lived out the routine holding their lives together, but the central purposefulness was gone. Tom grew moody. In an obscure way it seemed his father's fault that everything had gone empty and boring in the long summer of uneventful days and quiet nights.

The first weekend in August his father came home. He was so deeply browned that his thick gray hair looked nearly white against his lined bony brow. Dirt was grimed into the rims of his nails and into the pores on the backs of his hands and even in the hairy muscled forearms. He was red-eyed with sun and dirt and exhaustion. He kept falling asleep, in the lawn chair, in the leather lounge chair in front of the television set, stretched out on the davenport reading the paper. And he, too, had forgotten how to talk. Talk suddenly seemed for him not a celebration and a sharing but a ritualistic chore which must be gotten through.

Tom hung around the house hoping for something to restore them to what they were used to being. He tried to tell a funny tale about the little fat kid who wanted to be on the ball team but was scared of the ball and too clumsy to run. His father listened, nodded, gave off a limp grin, sank deeper in his chair, closed his eyes, groaned.

Three weeks later he was home again, and he acted the same way—exhausted and vacant. When he left again Tom fell back into larger silence. Perhaps he noticed that his mother too was sunk into excessive, even morbid quietness. Perhaps he saw that she became, by the end of August, strangely slow, physically ponderous in a way that was, despite her size, not like her. She was even incompetent. For one whole week she failed to dust the house. Meals were composed of canned soups and hot dogs and hamburgers. The garden went dry and the soil hardened with neglect. Once she complained, "At least he could call once in a while," her mouth falling into an unclear scallop.

But then suddenly she revived. She became wildly industrious. She canned tomatoes and plums and even figs. She went to Sears & Roebuck and got a supply of rubber-based yellow paint and began to slap the thick gooey yellow over the house's white siding. She worked as if she were furiously changing the face of the whole world. Sometimes she made Tom help her. Mostly she worked alone.

One night Tom wandered into the garage at dusk where she stooped over a gallon bucket washing out her brushes. September had come. Labor Day weekend lay ahead. "When will Dad be home?" Tom asked. She stopped bending the gray bristles back and forth. He saw her body grow rigid. She did not raise her eyes to meet his. "I don't know," she said flatly. "I haven't heard."

School started. To Tom, the frenetic eager September enthusiasms of his peers seemed foolish. School itself seemed pointless, boring. He was inattentive in class. He didn't bother much with his homework. In the first English examination, he got a D; an F in geometry. And then one Friday afternoon he came home to hear his father's voice in the kitchen, emphatic, harsh, angry, and positive.

"I don't know why it happened," he was saying. "I didn't mean for it to happen. I never looked for it to happen. My God, Gladys, you know how loyal I've been. But it has happened. That's all. It has happened."

Tom could see his mother standing by the table, her large paint-stained hands flat and helpless on its surface. Her face, turned partially aside, was yellow and narrow and ugly. The outward curve of her cheek grew silver with the astonishing fall of a heavy tear.

Tom almost fell into the room.

"What is it? What is it, Dad? What's the matter?" he said,

and found that he was choking, already crying himself.

His father pushed back his chair, scraping up from the vinyl flooring an ugly tearing sound.

"Come on," he said, something unyielding or cruel in his voice. "Come on, Tom. We're taking a ride."

Arthur Saint Clair climbed up behind of the wheel of the Pomeroy truck and Tom climbed onto the high seat on the passenger side. His father threw in the gears, let the clutch out with a bang. They spun crazily away from the curb.

They drove down the child-crowded after-school avenues, down pastoral tree-lined Shady Lane to the entrance to Phoenix Lake Park. His father pulled in under the shade of a clump of redwood trees and climbed out. "Come on," he ordered.

"No," Tom wanted to say. He wanted to stay where he was, frozen to the hot leather seat. He wanted to refuse what was coming, to resist complicity in the revelation that lay ahead. But he obeyed. He followed his father over the trail and around the shore of the lake. Low in its rusty-looking banks, the lake was nearly brown. They walked fast, and the dust rose from the path and clogged their nostrils, dried their mouths. The four o'clock sun was fierce, beating the moisture of their bodies to the surface.

At last in the thickness of oak and toyon his father stopped beside a fallen half-decayed tree trunk and motioned for Tom to sit down. Then he lowered himself to sit beside him.

And then slowly, the words seeming to stop up his mouth as he spoke them, Arthur Saint Clair told how it was. He had met someone. Someone he now loved. He was leaving Gladys. To be with this other woman. He looked deeply unhappy saying it. There was nothing of joy in his face. Only a fierce determination, a will that seemed to hint of harsh oppositions still to be met. His big calloused hands clutched his own knees as if they were the enemy.

Tom listened as if to a confusing tv show. Distant from the

situation. Scornful of it. But then realization fell on him like a stone.

"No, you can't," he said. Childlike, he spoke in high broken phrases. "You said. You always said. You can't. You can't."

There had been a contract. The story Arthur Saint Clair had told and retold: it had been a promise. To her. To Tom. To everyone. To himself, even. How could he pretend to forget it now? As if he had never promised, never told it at all? One last protest came from Tom's mouth. It was the truth he had been given.

"You can't go. You can't leave us. You owe it all to her."

His father's head swung toward him as if it had been hit from the other side. The red-rimmed blue eyes stared at him, wild, not believing what he saw. The bones in his cheeks and nose and forehead were white knobs in the darkened flesh. His hand came up, swung, hit Tom hard in the face.

At once his father grabbed him and held him, his breathing sounding like chains going in and out of his broad chest. But Tom felt no comfort in the long remorseful embrace.

Finally he had to meet her, the person his father now loved. He took a bus to Sacramento and his father met him at the depot. They had dinner together in her small neat apartment. She was a small woman and she had shining yellow hair done up in beauty shop curls. The bones in her narrow wrists were as small as chicken bones, and her fingertips were pink ovals which made graceful designs in the air or against the silverware or lying upon the arm of a chair.

But it was not just her prettiness. Her face was full of signs, quick signals, arresting messages. Laughlines marked the corners of her eyes and rimmed her lipsticked mouth. Then at times her eyes were wonderfully sad. She watched Tom's father as if everything he did were of great importance. She seemed to think each word Tom's father spoke had to be memorized. So Tom had to understand, though that did not help him to forgive.

At home, Gladys grew uglier and more awkward, heavy with shame and injured love. "It's no fair," she burst out once, her mouth still half-full of food. "I gave him everything. Everything." She left the table and stumbled toward the rejected bedroom. Again on a night when Tom had spent the evening taking in the strident luminous colors of the tv screen, he heard her in the kitchen. "How can he?" she cried, "after all those years?" Tom pretended he had not heard. She had spoken to no one, after all.

They provided no comfort for one another, Gladys and Tom. They turned away from one another, each finding his personal pain enough. Did they blame one another, too, for not being sufficient to keep with them the one who gave meaning to their lives? And did each see guilt in the other's sullen face, restrained body?

Gladys no longer urged Tom to do his homework. He quit the football team. He gave up his Saturday job with the Recreation Department. She seemed not to notice. Tom had the car whenever he wanted. She, after all, had no use for it, had no place to go. She gave him what money he asked for. Arthur Saint Clair, always well-paid, provided quite enough.

One night when Tom was driving home from aimless cruising up and down San Rafael's main street, he saw a garage door standing open and the lit interior unoccupied. Something made him pull slowly to the curb. A large piece of raw plywood was mounted on two sawhorses. An electric saw lay upon the wood's surface. Tom sat quietly for a while staring at that bright empty place. Whoever was inside the dimly lit house seemed to have forgotten the project begun there in the garage. Perhaps for ten minutes, perhaps for fifteen, Tom waited for someone to come out, for something to happen in the saw-dust littered, tool-cluttered interior.

At last he quietly opened the car door. He slipped out and, keeping to the tree-shadowed grass, went slowly toward the garage. He stopped a moment just at the edge of the driveway outside the wide doorway. No one came. Nothing stirred. Only the dim sound of a distant television came into the damp, cool darkness surrounding him.

He took three steps into the white light of the exposed garage, lifted the saw into his arms, bent to pull the electric cord from its plug, and stepped back into the dark outside. He walked quickly back to the car. He slid into the front seat, dumped the saw to the cushion beside him, put in the clutch and let the car roll quietly down the gently sloping avenue. At the corner he let out the clutch. The motor caught. He drove quickly the remaining mile home. In his ears his heart sounded like jungle drums. His cheeks felt touched by flames.

Nothing came of the incident. He kept the saw behind the sacks of compost in the shed his father had built behind the back yard fence. One day he sold it to a classmate for ten dollars. He said he had no use for it now that his father had gone. Nearly a month later he stole again—a bicycle left leaning in the falling dusk against a bank by an open field. He neither wanted nor needed it, however, and he threw it out of the trunk a few miles from where he had picked it up. A week after that, when he observed a house standing in darkness between its lighted neighbors, he tried another garage. He found two good hand saws, an electric drill, and an edging plane.

Theft was a simple thing, he learned. People rarely locked their garages. Women were always leaving their houses and running to their cars to go off and get their kids at school or to buy some forgotten thing at Safeway. All it took was alertness and a certain cool.

One time after he saw a woman leave her house, he walked in, and sauntering into the bedroom wing, came upon an old, nearly bald woman, a grandmother, sitting on the pot, peeing. She looked at him with vacant shocked eyes, and for a moment as startled as she, he froze. But then he simply turned back and walked out and ran across the back yard and down the block. In a few minutes he walked back around the block and down the other side to his car and drove away. No doubt the old woman called the police, but he was not caught.

He began to lift radios, televisions, stereo sets. He had no interest in what he stole and no use for the things. He sold one or two things to kids at school, but he knew he couldn't do much of that without getting caught.

Sometimes he left the stolen things in ditches or by country roadsides. Sometimes he smashed the things with his tire iron and, disgusted and contemptuous flung the remains on the broad shoulders of the highway. He was never caught.

And then one March afternoon when a high wind roamed a suddenly blue sky, and their small house seemed large with its own insignificance, the doorbell chimed. Two police officers stood on the step. One took Tom's arm in a tight hand and spoke his name.

"Yes," Tom said. "That's right."

In the living room his mother called out, "What? What is it, Tom? Tom?"

"You Mrs. Saint Clair?" the policeman asked into her wooden yellow face. "Don't want to alarm you, mam. Not unnecessarily, that is. But your son here, Tom's been involved in a bit of trouble, I'm afraid. A bit of thievery, that is. That right, son?" he asked like a cruel lover, leaning close to Tom's quiet face.

"That's right," Tom said.

They took him away. His mother was left weeping into her cupped palms, her thin mouth split into a wide grimace of wonder, disbelief, and despair.

They called his father from Sacramento, and Tom was led into a small, sparsely furnished room to face him where he stood waiting, big, confused, and guilty in a way Tom had never seen before.

"Why?" his father said after long, stony silence. "Tom, why?"

But no one needed to answer that. Tom knew his father knew what he was only beginning to understand: the powers of love and need and the circumlocutions of the obligated blood.

Plastic Edge to Plastic Edge

On this burnished Sunday morning in May, Dan and Valerie are driving north from San Rafael to the Sonoma wine country where their old friend Murray is marryng a woman approximately half his age. The day is particularly bright, the highway shimmers like a polished stove top, and the surrounding hills are rich enameled greens.

Valerie, leaning her arm on the doorframe and her dark head on her fist, is merely dryly resigned. Marriages, divorces. Marriages, divorces. It all used to mean something. Years back when someone she was fond of married, she felt true delight, celebrated with extravagant gifts. And those first divorces. How she had shared grief, frustration. Now weddings seem to be only first motions toward certain separations. For every friend's wedding promises, there is news of someone else unraveling the marriage vows.

Dan, however, is obviously happy—to be out in the glorious weather, to be going to the celebration. Always a participator, whatever the occasion, he moves in close to the event, does not get caught, as Valerie does, in the distances of irony. But it seems to Valerie that sometimes he shows little discrimination, and she feels now an old irritation at his failure to judge. He seems more flexible than she, but perhaps he is simply indifferent to Murray's choices, to the sadness of the ravaging break in his long marriage.

How different Dan was when he was young. Then he saw in black and white, judged quickly and positively. Valerie sometimes thinks that it is being a doctor that has changed him; caring for patients, witnessing their foibles and their tragedies, has made him see every human event with equable acceptance. She looks at him now, driving competently, the creases of pleasure in his face not hiding the fine lines showing wear, showing weariness.

"I keeping thinking of Lila, don't you?" she asks, and studies his expression for signs. Is she watching for betrayal? Does she want, really, out of oblique resentment, to shadow his lightheartedness, to punish him for his blithe acceptance of Murray's inconstancy?

Dan frowns. "Lila's a strong woman," he says, "and still very attractive. She'll be all right."

Yes, that's probably true. Lila is self-reliant, resilient. She'll be all right. Valerie saw her, just the past week, in Franchini's market, among the broccoli and cauliflower. Tall and vivid, very composed. Lila commented on the coming marriage. She and Murray had grown too far apart; they were no longer interested in the same things. Valerie believes that despite the perfect equanimity Lila affected, a note of compensatory bravery sounded in her words. It was Murray, after all, who had decided upon the divorce.

Rounding a curve in the rolling land, they come to a wooden road sign inscribed: Murray Warren. They turn left, bump down a length of unpaved roadway and arrive at a cattle gate, stop in a small flume of dust. A young boy stands near the open gate, waving his thin arms in broad dramatic gestures. He shouts in a high authoritative voice, "Park there!" and pumps his arm wildly. He is so pompous and so small that he is comic. As Dan eases the car onto the grassy field, the boy leaps in front of them and officiously guides them. Possessed as he is by excitement, the boy is catalyst, augury.

Valerie glances at Dan, catches the delighted gleam in his

amber eyes. Yes, he is in tune, as usual. Married so long, Valerie thinks, like Siamese twins they infect each other's feelings, know each other's thoughts. Without words, as if traveling on connected bloodstreams, these cycles of emotion occur, the linked changes of mood. Sometimes that seems marvelous, and sometimes very comfortable, and sometimes . . .Well, marriage! Two human beings give up their differences to become one, overcome their separateness, diminish their loneliness, but also lose their individuality. How often she feels like Dan's shadow. How often her identity seems to be only mother of *his* children, partner in *his* various projects, *his* social secretary, *his* wife. Does anyone know her just as herself—Valerie, separate person?

Dan is reaching into the back seat for his blue jacket. Valerie reaches for her wide-brimmed straw hat. They step from the car into the clear light.

They have heard reports about Murray's vineyard, the antique barn, the Victorian house. But the reports have not prepared them for what they see. "Good lord," Dan exclaims. "Look at that."

Some distance away, the house—narrow-windowed, two-storied, square, porched and pillared—stands on a plateau of level ground. It looks over a rush-rimmed, man-made lake that shimmers darkly under the high sun, and beyond that to the orderly, patterned fields, the rows of vines, newly greened, acres and acres of them, stopping only at the tree-hidden river.

"Grant Wood," Valerie murmurs, at once perversely sardonic. "Andrew Wyeth . . . !" Yes, Murray must have such images in his head. He has shaped this place to fit a dream, has created a mythic setting, an Eden, for his new woman, his new life, himself. While Dan admires, appreciates, Valerie is stiffly indignant. "It's pretentious, it's not real," she asserts. "The place needs actors, film scripts, cameras!"

But of course the actors are present, at least a hundred of

them, Dan and herself included. South of the house is an
ancient white oak. Under its immense branches a table is set
up, covered with trays of plastic glasses and crates of red
apples. On sawhorses behind the table a large oak barrel rests.
From it a young man in overalls is decanting wine into
carafes. A young woman in calico blouse and skirt is pouring
from the carafes into the waiting plastic glasses. Around the
table, in the dapple of lemon sun and blue shade, is gathered
a crowd of summery people. Middle-aged women wearing
long, lacy dresses; middle-aged men in pastel slacks and bou-
clé shirts or dark trousers and linen jackets; young women
wearing bare-backed prints; young men in jeans and casual
shirts.

Some guests are lounging in the grass beside the lake.
Others stroll about, their hats and jackets swinging in dreamy
arms.

No, Valerie corrects, walking with Dan into the oak tree's
shade, not Andrew Wyeth. Vuillard! The unburdened, drifting pastel look of the people, the patterned blue and brown
and green landscape, the wine shimmering in carafes, in
glasses. Yes, Murray's arrangement is perfect, his romantic
fantasy achieved.

Dan moves toward the table. Valerie stops where Emmy
Callam greets her. Emmy passes a plump hand through the
benevolent air, queries on a lift of brow, "How do you like
the spread, Val?"

Valerie slips her arm around Emmy's waist, gives a quick
companionable hug. "I'm positively covetous," she replies.
The edge of mockery in her words serves to hide, even from
herself, the element of true confession.

Dan brings wine in two squat glasses, gives one to Valerie,
lifts his own to Emmy's. "Zinfandel, Murray's first crush,"
he informs them. He sniffs the wine's bouquet, sips thought-

fully, pronounces it quite good, though green.

At that moment some woman sings out, "Look, there they come!" A carriage is moving slowly along the macadam road. Two chestnut horses with tossing heads and prancing steps draw an antique black surrey. The driver on the high box seat holds the reins at ceremonial height. Behind him Murray and his bride ride in charming splendor. Following the carriage, walking in pairs, in matched strides, are eight black-gowned, white-collared hatless men. Each holds his clasped holy hands against his sternum.

"Eight priests?" Valerie disbelievingly questions.

"Brothers," Emmy informs. "From the retreat." She watches, frowning icily. "Isn't that terribly romantic?" She folds her arms high up under her bosom, sniffs imperiously.

"Say, you two biddies," Dan rebukes them, grinning for lightness. "It's a wedding, remember?"

Valerie and Emmy feel sheepish, offended. They slide quick defensive looks toward each other and watch, after that, in silence. The guests, startled into gaiety by the coming parade, gather along the earthen roadway, laughing, cheering, for all the world as if they were flung back into childhood and a circus was coming.

The gleaming horses, bridled with bells, garlanded with flowers and blue ribbons, draw up smartly to the house. They throw their heads in conscious disdain. Dust lifts from the stopped wheels, rises in a thin cloud that spins golden in the sun, and from that shimmering aura Murray beams out. His grin is wide as a pumpkin's, his gloved wave as regal as Henry the Eighth's. He is wearing kilts, and the brass-buttoned jacket is taut over his proud chest.

The bride, however, neither smiles nor waves. She holds her head high for inspection. In her auburn hair, white flowers are woven, and a blue ribbon adorns the curls massed thickly at the crown. On the steps of the house, a bagpiper has taken his place. He lifts from his pompous instrument loud, wheedling, arrogant tunes.

Oh, they are a royal pair, this bride and groom, the laird of the manor and his maid. Valerie sips her tart wine and watches the crowd cooperate in illusion, taking up their supportive, admiring roles.

Murray is standing in the surrey. His smile persists like a toothache. He puts his hand out to his bride. She rises to his command, and the close-fitting Victorian gown emphasizes her willowiness. Murray leaps from the high step. The kilt flashes over bulging thighs, gray knee socks curve over muscular calves. His bride gathers her skirts and lightly leaps to his side.

Ah, the city people, Valerie observes, Murray's old friends, middle-aged, office-bound doctors and lawyers and brokers, invited to witness Murray's successes, aren't they pale and deprived beside him? Envy shows on their faces. If they could choose, surely they would choose a life like this. Murray knows they would. He beams on them all, beneficent.

Valerie notes how Murray's blooming energy sparks the men's eyes, draws reluctant smiles. Yes, if Murray is cause for envy, he is also reason for hope. *So this is fifty,* their eyes are saying.

Well, fifty is quite young, after all. Fifty looks good, full of possibility, full of romance. Dan, too, Valerie judges, seeing how he stands, his red head thrown back, brown eyes merry, mouth sweet with wine, is perhaps taking some new perspective on his own life from viewing Murray's. "But he must love her," a woman Valerie does not know whispers to her sagging-throated friend, as if some debate were going on.

The women eye the bride with doubt, as if learning the configurations of threat. They have to believe in love, assert the dominance of the heart, for their own sakes. Only love that endures past corrupted middle-aged bodies, middle-aged losses, can safeguard their precarious peace.

In proof of love and its sanctity, one of the black-garbed men, the one who is the priest, approaches the immaculate shining-windowed house. He climbs the steps and stops where a wide blue ribbon bars entry to the plant-lush porch. He opens his book of prayers and sets his palm against the air for quiet. At his nod, Murray and his bride mount the steps and stand at the priest's left, facing, as royalty must, the attending crowd. The priest intones a blessing of the house, reading the prayers in a sustained tenor tone. His consonants are plucked perfectly from tongue, palate, teeth. The wind lifts the silver strands of hair crossing his bald dome, stirs the folds of black cassock. Murray's kilts move in red ripples, the bride's gown in white waves. The priest's hands turn, light-boned and eloquent, beneath his chanted words. Valerie half expects doves to rise up, signals from heaven.

Emmy fails to murmur along in the Lord's Prayer, though she is truly devout. Instead she studies the statement of vines over the earth, the inscriptions of a hawk on far air.

After the firm *Amen,* the bride is handed a large scissors. She leans toward the satin barrier. She snips, the groom scoops her up in muscular arms, hoists her over the threshold into the virgin holy house.

In the reception line Emmy turns back to whisper, "Good God, Val, she hasn't got a wrinkle!" and goes on to offer Murray a chastened, ambiguous kiss, as does Valerie in her turn. Valerie must kiss the bride too; her pride demands such generosity. The bride's hands, when Valerie grasps them, are hard with calluses.

Afterwards, gathered on the broad porch overlooking the fertile fields, Dan explains. "They say she drives a tractor like a man. She's a real goer, Murray's woman. Quite a gal." His jovial admiration puts him clearly in the enemy's camp. He too, Valerie imagines, would like such a mate. Certainly a young wife demonstrates to the world a man's virility, his worth. Naturally Dan would wonder whether he, too, though the least bit over the hill but still vigorous, obviously successful and certainly attractive to women, could be loved by a spirited handsome young woman like the bride. Aren't all the middle-aged husbands wondering that?

Cross with her own cool perceptions, conscious of her years, Valerie slips away to where Emmy chats with Liz Burnett. Liz is recounting how she ran into Agnes Carson in Long's Drug Store. Liz hadn't seen her in months, and when she said, "How are you, Agnes?" Agnes had burst into tears. Ray, her husband, had fallen in love with a twenty-two-year old law clerk and wanted to marry her; he hoped to father a male child and was demanding a divorce. Agnes, at sixty, loved only him and wanted him back. "She's pathetic," Liz asserts, her mouth wry with distaste. Valerie remembers how Agnes used to look like Queen Wilhelmina, full-bodied and stately. Now the skin under her chin is creped, her upper arms are looped with scallops of puckered flesh, and age does not protect from heartache, from wounded pride, from loss. No, not all.

And just last Monday Valerie had phoned Carol Wilson, whom she has known almost forever. Carol announced that she and Jake were separating. Carol is deeply in love with a professor of political science, a man committed to social change, alive to new ideas, not hung up on business, money, work. So Carol is writing poems to her new love, but Jake, when Valerie called him, was shocked, angry, crushed.

Valerie feels anger toward Carol. Jake Wilson is a fine, generous man. He loves his wife, his children. Is it right to purchase one's happiness at someone else's unwilling expense? And was the exchange worthwhile, in the end? Gained: a sensual, energizing, ego-rewarding new love. Lost: loyalty, faith, the years' investment of shared experience, family.

When Liz strides off, Emmy sighs. "We're the last of the one-marriage breed, Val."

Valerie responds on hard, glittering notes. "We're ridiculous, Emmy, hanging on to outworn convention. One man, one marriage. We're out of fashion."

Emmy gives a brief laugh. "But it's too late, now, Val. Who'd *want* me, except Ed?" and wanders off resignedly to find him.

Valerie stands solitary in the open space, watching the caterers in starched white carry trays to famished guests. Small tender rolls filled with pink beef, rosy ham, creamy turkey; mushroom caps puffed up with melting cheese; rounds of bread heaped with bright shrimp. Valerie refuses all, denies appetite, condescends to a glass from the waiter's tray.

Alone she walks over the dry grass toward the border of the vineyards, feeling her solitariness, her differences. She passes at some distance Al Sparrow lounging on the grass, slim and dandyish in a white nip-waisted suit and ruffled blue shirt. He leans close to a small brunette, babbles away with a pleased rosy expression. What has become of Lorraine, his first wife? Where is Jan, his second? What has happened to all the halves of married pairs she no longer sees?

On the lake the light opens and closes on wind-stirred ripples. The leaves of the far oak shiver, turn bronze. The sky sweeps back to impermeable glazed blue. Valerie holds on to her wobbling hat.

The day Carol told her she was leaving Jake, Valerie stood by the phone making out a grocery list and suddenly began to make a list of broken marriages. In no time at all, she had dashed off twenty-eight names of friends, acquaintances. The end of family. Migrating fathers, rotating mothers. The demise of lasting love.

Full of darkness in the glittering day, Valerie turns and

slowly walks back. She sees Dan on the porch, talking in absorbed intimacy with Liz, his auburn hair like copper, his face shining and warm. He attends Liz as if nothing in the world could distract him. They seem closer, Val thinks, more private together than any husband and wife.

Often before she has seen women in such intimate conversation with Dan. It has to do, perhaps with his being a doctor. Women drawn to doctors turn to them with confessions of their most personal concerns—at parties, at ordinary social dinners. But those dialogues between Dan and some other woman exclude Valerie, make her seem alien, an unwelcome intruder. Sometimes she feels not especially necessary to him; that closeness that ordinarily belongs only to husband and wife Dan seems to share with many other women. She is, Valerie thinks, only more steadily his companion than they, more commonly his company, that's all.

Refusing claim, refusing to impose conjugal restrictions, Valerie now angles away from him. Be a millstone? Play the heavy? Not she, never! In the grassy field to her left Emmy is talking with Nora Barton, who is six feet tall and implacably good-willed. They call to her, and Valerie joins them. She listens as they admire the restored house—its authentic if rather ugly antiques; the sleigh bed with its hand-crocheted antique spread; the bathroom with its huge claw-footed tub and brass fixtures set before a low window viewing lake and vineyards; the kitchen with enormous new ranch stove, two ovens, huge grill. It all suggests a bigger-than-life domestic bliss. The women recall their own beginnings in married life: the shabby apartments, making do with scrounged furniture, dime-store dishes, Goodwill pots. They laugh, remembering babies, diapers, croup, chicken pox, no household help, rare baby-sitters.

Valerie does not laugh. "What's going to become of us all?" she blurts. "What is going to happen?"

Nora gives her hearty hoot of laughter, shrugs, turns the

talk to summer at Tahoe. Valerie understands. No one knows
what it will come to. Hell in a handbasket. End of an age.

On the porch Dan is now listening to the quick chatter of
a gold-haired, green-frocked woman Valerie does not know.
Their shared gaiety deepens Valerie's gloom. Bleakly, she tips
her glass to her lips, toasting Dan's enduring charm. Of
course such women amuse him, intrigue him. Why should
he be different from Murray Warren or Al Sparrow or Ray
Carson? Monogamy is not a natural state, she concedes.

And yes, she has to concede, twenty-four years of marriage
is absurd. It reveals lack of imagination, lack of adventure-
someness. How dull, really, to know exactly how the other
brushes his teeth, the rhythms of his nighttime breathing.
How ridiculous those matched turnings in the routine marriage bed!

Suddenly, Valerie believes she loves no one. She is, abruptly, utterly bored. She would, perhaps, like a lover—someone
young, temperamental, fierce. That one there—his hard
thighs; his tumbled, curly, glossy hair. But, ah, how silly. She
is forty-four.

A stir of changed motion claims Valerie's attention. The
bride and groom are making their way to the lake's edge.
Murry's two grown daughters and several other young people
pull a rowboat from its mooring, draw it up onto the bank.
Murray climbs into the boat, stands wide-legged for balance.
He holds out a gallant hand, the bride lifts high her delicate
skirts, takes his hand and jumps aboard. Murray settles her
on the broad seat in the prow, takes up the oars. The photogra-
pher goes to his knees, recording for history the journey to
the other shore.

The boat is shoved off, the guests cheer and fling rice in
bright arches over the bridal pair. Murray's dipping oars draw
the boat through blue concentric rings. In the dazzing light

they seem to be moving beyond tarnish, beyond the touch of time.

Valerie feels her breath quicken with desire and remorse. To start again, to gather priests to ring one's life with magic and luck. To have no burden of error, no knowledge of compromise, to have only hope circling your new mornings. What profound pleasure in that. What renewal.

She does not hear Dan come up behind her. When his arm circles her waist, she is startled, remote, and almost draws away. Smiling but intent, Dan studies her face and perceives what she is feeling.

"Val," he says, "wish them luck. They'll need it."

She looks long into Dan's calm face. How foolishly she resists change, battles where issues are already decided. An old fault, springing from a childish insistence on permanence. And as she looks at him, she knows she does not need to question. She knows she can trust him. His steadfastness has never failed in the long years of childbearing, child raising. Surely it will hold, despite the time's pressures for variation, despite the vivid and unreliable yearnings of these middle years.

Valerie lifts her glass, Dan lifts his. They touch plastic edge to plastic edge, smile for what they do not need to say. In companionable sympathy, they watch the boat's rocking journey over the small lake, sipping the wine in honor of idyllic, eternal love.

Mountain Man, Mountain Man

They had had too much of people, and too much of city hubbub, and even too much at last of the books and papers and the pursuit of ideas which made up their usual lives. Now in the high country of pine and mountain by the North Fork of the San Joaquin River, they revelled in simplicities.

Laurie, in particular, went there hypnotized by differences. In spite of Allen's descriptions, she was not prepared for what she found. She was awed by the craggy perfection of rock upon rock, mounting in dazzling angles and planes of its own building. She marvelled at the hard cirque of peaks rearing and knifing upward into the great magnanimous sky. She stood dazed under the intensity of light that raked that stretching sky, moving with the earth's turning from silvered white mornings to brassy noons and on into the incomparable purple nights.

A city person, not used to space and solitudes, Laurie found no words for what the place did to her, for the way in which it changed her. She only stood and looked at the remote, pure world about her and murmured, "It's beautiful, Allen. It's simply beautiful," and that did not say anything of what she felt.

But Allen was at home here. He was changed, but he was at home. The wild place seemed to awaken a wildness in him. As if he were a creature native to mountain country, he drew the energy of the place into himself. Already, in the tremulous light of beginning day, he had sprung from sleep. Snuggled in the burrow of her sleeping bag upon the hillock of pine needles, Laurie heard him blow on his fingers and stamp his feet against the cold. She listened to him shake his way into his rough mountain clothing and then clatter about gathering kindling and logs. After a while she peered sleepily out at him.

He stood back a little from the fire which leaped up in its ring of stones, snapping at the frosty air. Allen held both hands toward the pale orange flames, and his face was ruddy from sunburn and the fire's burning. For a few moments he stood so, a broad, fair young man full of eager energy, his wide unsecret face showing his delight in the well-built, dancing fire. Then he turned, swooped up the two plastic buckets from the rough log table, and ran toward the tumbling stream.

Laurie turned over on the piney bed, groaned. All day before she had followed Allen over the rocky banks beside the river while he fished. It was a hunting, moving, pursuing kind of fishing. If he did not get a strike after the first several casts of his fly, Allen moved on to another spot where the green water broke white over submerged rock and the elusive trout might lie hidden in the deep stillnesses below. All day he roamed, flicking his flies at the river's wild surface, and by the time he turned back to camp even he was limply weary. Sun and exhaustion had burned red in his face and, as for Laurie, she had trailed in his wake like a half-dead cat, tired, sore, exasperated with weariness. And after the long night's sleep, she ached with stiffness. She turned over to sleep again.

But in no time at all Allen came to the woods-shadowed edge of the pine grove where she lay. He knelt beside her, holding a plastic mug near her face so that the fragrant steam of coffee rose up about her. "Why do you get up so early?" Laurie murmured and smiled.

"Early?" Allen shouted as if she were twenty feet away. "Early? Why, it's day, Laurie. Look at that, the sun's already up." He swept one arm in a wide arc, spreading out the golden world for her view. "We have to start, Laurie."

"Start where?" Laurie asked. She gulped at the coffee. Steam flowered and faded before her breath.

"We're going to the East Fork, today, Laurie. It's gorgeous up there. From the ridge over the river you can see the Minarets."

Laurie looked at him cautiously. She boosted herself up in the sleeping bag. She felt every muscle in its move. "What are the Minarets?" she asked. "How far is the East Fork? Oh Lord, I'm stiff."

Allen laughed. "They're mountains. Six or seven miles, probably. Maybe eight. You'll limber up." His face was careless of her, full of anticipation and that self-absorbed energy that had burned in him steadily all the days they had been there.

"You go," Laurie said quietly. "I'll stay here and read and sleep."

He looked at her sharply, and then, as if he had been released, he said, "All right," breathed deeply of the sharp air, pulled his arms back like hinges, stretched, grinned. "I'll be back early," he said, and packed up his gear and a lunch, strode off over the ridges of rock. Like a lad in a fairy tale, Laurie thought, eagerly seeking his destiny.

And she did not mind. Half-waking, half-sleeping, she lay under the arch of pine and waited for the sun's light to touch the morning air with warmth. She listened to the stream tumbling within its rock walls, to the stirrings and twitterings of the small, dun-colored birds that invaded the camp clearing, to the unidentified and seemingly sourceless whispers and snappings of wood-sounds that came from within the grove of pines beyond her.

After a while she got up, dressed, and had breakfast. As the sun rose higher she wandered along the stream's banks, taking in the vast and changeless landscape ringing the small place where they stayed. When she looked at her watch and saw that it was only a little after ten, a deepness grew within her. Inside it the steady beat of her heart seemed slow and hollow and large. She returned to the camp and got a book. She went to the stream's edge and sat down upon a large, smooth ledge, resting her back against a great rock.

She could not read. She grew greatly conscious of her loneliness and greatly conscious of ancient dominance of the place in which she silently sat. She felt quite lost, lost from the sense of herself, as if in the presence of such largeness there was neither possibility of, nor need for, human significance.

Once she saw a hawk swing on the high air as if upon a spiraling string, and then he slipped off the sky and she felt bereaved, as if a human love had been lost. She thought of Allen and how he had gone from her as if he, too, were pulled by an invisible line. And she then considered carefully what she now perceived—that he had been separate from her all the time they had been up here. She knew then how places took from their inhabitants and how they gave to them, too. Where one place freed one, another imprisoned one. And one could not be the same person in one place as in another, and the mysteries of such enchantments were not altogether knowable.

Laurie shivered a little, scanned the blazing sky for motion, saw nothing at all. Even the small birds that chittered in the pines near the camp were still. There was no sound but that of the rushing river, no motion but that of water that poured through its rock bed in such furious purity that its own motion obscured the crevices it covered.

The sun poured down upon her. Its vertical heat struck through her entirely. The unread book fell from her hand. She slept. When she awoke in the early afternoon the sense of lostness was gone. The aloneness had become nothing, and she knew neither impatience nor boredom nor fear. She was hot, and strangely light-headed, so she got up and went to the place where the high splashing of the stream left a deposit of quiet water in a smooth basin.

She stripped off her sweatshirt, her jean shorts, her underthings. She dipped her foot into the convenient pool, shivered delightedly, slid down under the clear undistorting water. She sat leaning her head against the wall of rock behind her. The sun touched her face and neck and shoulders and breasts. Water covered belly and thighs and shins and toes. She sat as if she were a child, unhurried, untroubled, unaware of time, in her stony tub.

But all at once, abruptly, as if she had heard someone call, she knew someone was near. As if she had even heard the sound of that imagined call, she turned her head slowly, immediately, accurately, in the direction where he was.

The strange man stood directly across the stream from her. A tall man. Extraordinarily tall. Narrow, knife-sharp face. Skin as dark as bark, sun-browned. Red beard. A crooked straw hat on his head. His long, ropey arms were stretched over the stream to the leaning of his pole. A creel over his shoulder. A fisherman. And he stood right across the chasm of water, not more than twenty feet away. Twenty feet from where Laurie sat alone in her rocky tub. She closed her eyes.

Where had he come from? How had he got there? They had been there four days. They had seen no one else. Not a sign of anyone else. And Allen. Allen had said he had never seen anyone else up there. He had promised her privacy, hadn't he? And now she sat naked in the exposed rock under the eyes of a total stranger. Allen, she muttered, locked into the heavy breathing within her breast. She knew he would not come, would not help. She felt betrayed.

Her eyes slid helplessly open. The man was still there. He was indeed grotesquely there. Laurie stared across the green and white rushing water at the bearded stranger, and he did not look at her. But suddenly he lifted his pole from the stream, swung it up over his shoulder, turned away. He stood quiet, lankly idle, and it seemed to Laurie that he offered her privacy for dressing.

She grabbed her sweatshirt. Still half-submerged, she pulled it on. She huddled down in her tub, stared at the straw-hatted man who did not move under her gaze. He stood like a pole beside the stream on the other side.

Laurie climbed out of her bath. She jerked furiously back into her clothes. Hooks would not catch. The jeans zipper caught. The bottom of her sweatshirt dripped wet over her jeans. At last she stood on the shelf of rock, dressed, ready to leap down, to run. There were places to hide, somewhere in the rocks. Or in the little wood.

But she saw that the man had not even looked back at her. In the moment she stood poised to run, she saw his pole flash in the sun. The silver line spun out over the stream's green. The fly dropped to the tumbling river surface, and the stretch of line shone under the sun's light like a silver thread. That thread stretched almost invisible on the stream's length, and Laurie saw the stranger spin the little wheel under his big brown hand, and the silver line shortened, thickened. The long, straw-hatted, bearded man swayed and leaned attentively to the tight, shiny, metallic string, and then once more the pole rose, limber and flashing in his hands, and he rolled the line in toward the pole's tip.

Quick as a flash of lightning, again the pole flickered over his knobby shoulder, cutting across the mountain's light. It unleashed the silver length of its thread to the water's turmoil. The light line glistened, stretched, moved far with the water's swirling. The fisherman studied its going, watchful as a lover. Then after a few moments the reel spun in the stranger's hand. The line tightened, drew slowly in, snapped back at last, a silver band, to the lifted tip of the rod.

A third time the fisherman's rod snapped through the blue air. A third time the swift line fled beneath the gilding sun, met the foam and curl of the stream, rode downward on the water's journey.

Then, abruptly, the rod stiffened, quivered, bowed. The stranger reached far out over the stream, yielding to the rod. Then he shifted himself into firm opposition and took up the line in slow, hard turnings. The rod bowed, and leaned in his hand.

The bright fish vaulted from the water, arced and shimmered on air, writhed in flashing agony, shook off shiny wetness. The fisherman drew him deftly in, lifted him at last on the limb of his pole, grasped him in one large, outstretched hand, and securely held him.

And only then did the stranger look across the leaping waters at Laurie. From beneath the brim of his straw hat his eyes flashed darkly out at her. His smile struck abruptly, a dazzling whiteness in the bark-darkness of his face. The narrow, sharp-boned face rimmed in the coppery beard lit up with absolute joy, and the fisherman lifted his arm and held the fish aloft for Laurie to see, as if she were a partner, a participant in the game. Gravely, Laurie nodded.

Then he slipped the creel from his shoulder, folded the great lean length of himself down to ground, knelt, pulled the still arcing fish from his hook. He lay the fish in the depths of his wicker creel and carefully placed the creel in the blue shadow of a thrusting rock.

Then once more the tall, bearded man stood on the rock ledge above the stream. He worked at the fly on the end of his line. He lifted his rod, glanced once at Laurie as if to instruct her, whipped his line across the churning water. Laurie sat herself down on the rocky platform and solemnly watched him. She had forgot about running, did not think now of fear.

Twice more the slender rod bent in a loop with a hooked fish. Twice more a fish stretched curved and silver on the afternoon air and came in whipping resistance into the stranger's hand. And when the third fish was nested in the basket of the creel, the strange man put up his line and reel. He bent down like a cricket and lifted the creel to his shoulder. He looked across the stream, swung his arm like a semaphore, pointed downstream. He nodded vigorously, and the white smile cut like a blade across his face. He shouted, joyously, something Laurie could not hear, but she understood that he would cross the stream. The fisherman was coming over to her side.

Laurie watched the stranger stride downstream, taking rock and gully in great stretches of long leg. Her cheeks were taken by a sudden burning, and in her breast her heart seemed to flash like a struggling fish. She ought to go, she thought. She ought to disappear. But escape did not seem possible. She felt bound to the rock on which she sat, and where in all that openness of land could she find one safe spot in which to hide? Laurie glanced over her shoulder in the direction Allen had left so long ago that morning and then turned back to the stranger's words.

"Howdy," he said. "Jim Carson's the name." He stood just below her. He set down his pole and swept his hat from his head. He bowed a little, shoved the hat back on, held out one hand. The dark face was wreathed with the lines of his smile, and in the chequered shade of the shabby straw hat, his eyes were like twin flames in dark water. "A fine day, isn't it?" he said, and laughed, and the bright eyes took her in, her brown hair loose about shoulders and back, her own brown eyes and tanned face, her sweatshirt, jeans, and bare feet. "Where are your folks?" he asked.

His dark eyes swept the nearby emptiness of their camp. Laurie looked where he looked. On the quiet air the last of the fire's heat shimmered upward. Dust rode on slanting blades of sun, touching upon the table where tins and boxes of food, inverted bowls and pots stood in casual order, upon the little bench Allen had set against two jack pines, and upon the singularly revealing pair of sleeping bags lying at the wood's edge.

"My husband," Laurie said, and could not keep the quaver from her throat. "My husband is upstream fishing."

"What's your name?" the stranger asked.

"Laurie," she said, wary and shy. "Laurie Green."

"Well, Laurie," he gravely said, "do you know what kind of bird that is?" Jim Carson nodded toward a small bird that hopped in the bare earth of the camp clearing, poking at invisible crumbs, as imperturbably busy as if he had no notion but that the place was entirely his. It gave off little chirps of sound, regular as a heartbeat on the silent air. Laurie shook her head.

"It's a nuthatch, a piney nuthatch. They chirp like that the livelong day," he said, and grinned. "Like they got some kind of timer inside them." He looked at Laurie with a clear, direct gaze. "Any coffee there in that pot, Laurie?" he asked. "It'd taste mighty good along about now."

As if he were host and she the guest, he led her into the camp clearing. He set his creel in the leafy shade, leaned his rod against a tree trunk, and found up-ended upon the table the two plastic mugs. He took the aluminum pot from its place upon the stone rim of the fire pit without even a flinch at the hot metal handle. He poured the thick, sticky looking brew half and half into the two cups and handed one to Laurie. He sat down on Allen's log bench and sipped noisily the bitter liquid. He swallowed, sighed, grinned at Laurie.

"A fine spot, this camp right here. I always did like it," he said.

"Oh," Laurie said, surprised, offended. It was Allen's private place. "Have you camped here?"

"Oh, many a time," Jim Carson said. "In fact I planned to stay here this trip. But you folks were already set up."

"Oh," Laurie said again, and frowned down at her coffee

cup because he sat there, an interloper, sipping their coffee, unbidden, unwelcome, proprietary.

"Now don't you mind, Laurie," Jim Carson said as if he saw all the things she thought. "I've got my own place downstream. You're no bother to me and I'm no bother to you. Been up here before?" he asked.

Laurie told how Allen had come in those past times, and that he had wanted to show this place to her, so they had planned this vacation for more than two years and now at last had taken the time from their studies and work to pack in for ten days. Jim Carson listened and nodded his head, apparently pleased.

"Never was much for studying myself," he said. He lifted his mug to his wide mouth, drained it, smacked his lips and looked sorrowfully at Laurie. "Been part of this country all my life," he told her. "My father before me and my grandpa before that. Carsons don't fit into city life. Not at all. We're mountain folk, and this is where we belong." He looked at the grove and the river and the ringing peaks with a peculiar mournful expression.

"But do you live in the mountains all year round?" Laurie wonderingly asked.

"Winter and summer," the big man replied. "Come winter I join up with some logging crew and make out that way, and then in the summer I just take off. Spend all my time in high country. Time was," Jim Carson said, and his eyes were cold as ice, "when I never saw a soul the whole long way. I'd tramp the ridges all summer long and the only things I saw was birds and rabbits and weasels and goats. That's the only living things I saw. And fish." He sighed, then, deeply, as for those times.

"But don't you get lonely?" Laurie cried as if she would save him from some threat he did not see.

For a moment he looked at her with veiled eyes. In the cast of shade his face was like stone. "Yes," he said, "it's a lonely life."

He sat very quietly then, leaning back against the tree, his long legs stretched before him. His lids closed down over his dark, shining eyes, and the black of his lashes touched the lined cheeks. His great hands lay still on the lean thighs. He sat as if sleeping, the bony face remote as if with pain, and Laurie pitied him because she had never known anyone as solitary as he.

Then, suddenly he shuddered a little, sighed, opened his eyes. His legs jackknifed, cranked him upward. "Well," he said, settling the straw hat further down on his forehead, "I'd better get going."

"No," Laurie suddenly said. "Stay and have supper with us." Her face turned a betraying red.

Jim Carson looked at her carefully. He said that he guessed he could get back to his camp by sundown even if he did stay and have supper there. Then he got his creel, sat down again on the bench, and arranged the flies in his case. He showed Laurie the intricate feathered things, brightly-colored as jewels and as light as dandelion fluff, which he himself had devised and tied. He told her which flies were best for which fish, and Laurie nodded as if she would fish herself and needed to know how.

The sun grew hot in the clearing, and Jim Carson led her into shady woods. There in the glade the light was cool and green as water, and the dark, high pines seemed like a cavern's walls. Jim Carson named each tree, pointed out the mountain sorrel's flat heart-leaves, the scratchy tongues of cinque-foil, mountain-heather, sierra stonecrop. He knew the name of every bird and identified twitter and song. And when they had enough of that they sat on a log by a small space at the edge of the wood. Jim Carson reached in his deep shirt pocket and brought out a cloth envelope. He took from the envelope a slim silver tube. He put the flute to his lips, and his long fingers flew over the stops. Clear and high notes came as his fingers moved. The high, bright sounds seemed particularly proper to the mountain place, and Laurie listened, fascinated, delighted. The melodies were of an old kind, a skipping and lilting of melodic line, like old madrigal songs of medieval days.

As the strange mountain man leaned to his playing his face was sharp with pleasure. What Laurie had felt of pity passed into something she could not name. A shiver flew over her spine. She suddenly envied him. She thought he could teach her something he had not revealed.

And then he stopped playing and laughed on a deep breath, his eyes on Laurie, secret and dark. When he lifted the flute again to his lips, he nodded at her. Laurie knew the tune from some forgotten past, and she got up from her place beneath the great pine and began to dance to the light trills of the minuet. She gave herself joyously to the spins and turns the rhythms demanded, and she grew breathless, and very warm. When the music stopped, she wheeled dizzily in her place, laughing with her pleasure and exertion.

She turned toward the mountain man, stumbled a little, and fell into his reaching arms. She lay like a trembling bird against the rough wool of his shirt. Through the heavy cloth she heard the beat of his heart like thunder. He led her to a soft and mossy place and gently laid her down, holding her fluttering heart against his. His eyes were deep and dark as mountain nights, his mouth like a mountain river, and about the shady quiet, air ran in green hungry waves, over them entirely, over them both.

The sun stood like brass in the western sky when Allen came. His coming startled Laurie as if she had thought he would never return. He stood before her, hot, red-faced, his red shirt stained dark over his shoulders and collar, his trousers and boots gray with dust. "Why Allen," Laurie cried, her breath shaking like turning leaves. Behind her the mountain man hummed a small tune on his flute. "Whatever are you doing here?'' she asked. She shook back her hair, folded her arms about her waist, blushed, frowned.

Allen stared at the red-bearded stranger, and then at Laurie. His blue eyes flickered. His mouth shuttled helplessly between droops and smiles. How silly he looks, Laurie suddenly thought, like a foolish baboon. And her giggle came quick as a hiccup.

"Allen," she said, "this is Jim Carson," and she waved an airy hand at the distance between them. Allen almost bowed. But Jim Carson stretched up from his place on the log, strode over the pine-needled floor, and towering high over the awkward younger man, he held out his big, long-fingered hand.

"Glad to meet you," he heartily boomed. "Welcome to these parts. Glad to have you here."

"Well," Allen said, and coldly shook hands. He scowled and looked at Laurie, demanding explanation.

"He came by," Laurie thinly said, as if it were an unfair obligation. "Mr. Carson came by, fishing. I was reading down by the stream. He camps here a lot."

"That's right," Jim Carson boomed. "This camp spot is one of my favorites. Always did like the place." He looked at Allen as if judging an opponent, and his smile, Laurie thought, was just short of scornful.

And at Jim Carson's words and the smile, Allen's posture stiffened. His blue eyes narrowed, turned light and icy. He turned away from the green-gold glade. He walked out of the woods to the open camp. Laurie followed him, and following them came Jim Carson.

Allen placed his creel on the table top, his rod beside it. His head dropped tiredly forward. The leaning sun touched his head, and his blond hair and fair skin seemed to give off light, and even the short fair hair on his neck took up the shining like stiff threads of gold. In her breast, Laurie felt a hard, dull ache, a gray film came over her eyes. "Allen," she said, but behind her the mountain man moved brusquely and startled her thoughts away.

"Well," he said loudly. "I guess it's time to go. It's time I got started back to my own place." He glanced at Laurie coldly, sadly, and took two long strides to the tree where his own rod leaned.

"Why no," Laurie quavered. She had to stop him from going. "Supper. You said you'd stay for supper, Jim." But Allen turned and looked at her.

"I didn't get enough fish," he said. "I caught only three. And they're small. Not enough for all of us."

"Three fish?" Laurie cried. "Only three fish? You were gone all day, Allen. Is that all you caught?" And how silly, she crossly thought. How silly he looks, so solemn, so stubborn, with only three fish.

"Well, I have some nice big ones myself," Jim Carson said. "Enough for us all." He pulled open the lid of his wicker creel, dipped swiftly into it and held up on the palms of his hands the three large trout in a cluster of green-tongued fern.

Allen looked studiously at the blue-gray fish. He turned away and began to unpack his own canvas creel.

"Sorry," Allen said, "you're not welcome here."

And that is all he is going to say, Laurie thought. Allen stood with his back toward them, stiff as a tree. And Jim Carson's face emptied of all fire and light. Before Laurie's eyes it thinned down, narrowed. The mouth, curved all day to smiling, crossed his face like a scar. With a dark, bitter look he stared at Allen.

"Well, you impudent little pup," he drawled. "Why, if I meant any harm, I would have done it then, back when I came and found her sitting in the river with nothing on. Naked as a jaybird, she was. Isn't that right, Laurie?"

Laurie faltered, blushed, caught between betrayal and loyalty, and chose. In a moment as quick as the beat of a bird's wing, she knew her position and swiftly chose. She laughed. The clear, careless drop of her laughter fell over them all like dropping snow. And when she heard it, she gasped herself.

Allen slowly turned about. He stared at the lanky mountain man. Slowly his fair head thrust forward on his straining neck. His shoulders humped like a bull's.

"Allen," Laurie cried. "Allen, don't."

But it was not Allen she was protecting.

Jim Carson snorted, swooped up his things. He shrugged, laughed aloud, and strode swiftly off, taking the ground in immense, long strides. He stopped near the edge of the crying stream.

"City folks," he called back in a voice like a trumpet. "City folks should stay where they belong. In city places."

And Allen turned away from the sight of him clambering away over the looming rocks. He turned and looked at Laurie, a long somber, regretful gaze.

"We have to leave," he said at last. "First thing in the morning we have to leave."

"Leave? Leave? But Allen, why? We waited so long to come. We planned it for years." But Laurie understood that her protests were useless. She saw that Allen stood near the rough log table, and in his hand, gripped so hard that his knuckles shone like white stones, was his hunting knife. It's not my fault, she said to herself. It's not, it's not. It's his fault. That's what it is.

But suddenly through the still evening air, distinctly and distantly, she heard the clear, high warblings of a flute. The sounds came gaily in mocking brightness over the air, and slowly Laurie's face grew brilliant with wonder and with shame.

Oatmeal

Every morning for fourteen years, Lottie Wellman had gotten up early enough to make oatmeal for her husband George. George's mother, a gaunt, positive woman, had said that's what George always wanted for breakfast. Lottie took her statement as command and never once failed to have the two bowlfuls of steaming, gray, glutinous cereal on the table when George came from the bedroom, his long fingers still knotting his tie, his coat slung over his shoulder.

But one morning George looked up from his newspaper folded into a column at his elbows and said, "Wish you'd serve something other than oatmeal, Lottie. Never did like it much."

He went back to reading his newspaper as if nothing out of the ordinary had occurred. But Lottie felt the world suddenly spin. Had she heard correctly? She stared at George. His long face was calm, composed as always. His hand was steady on the methodical spoon. He read the paper with objective attention. She saw no visible change.

But when George had left and Lottie stood at the sink, her hands plunged deep in soapy water, she burst into tears. If George could dislike oatmeal for fourteen years and say nothing about it, and if she could not discern in all that time that he did not like oatmeal (brown-sugared and covered with cream) then nothing was certain.

She had thought him an easy-to-please, quiet, contented person, at peace in his orderly home and happy with her, Lottie, his wife. But if she did not know what George thought about oatmeal, then she probably did not know what he thought about anything at all. Whatever she knew of George's mind or heart was nothing but a kind of shell, like the shell of an egg, only a covering for what was important that lay inside it. The idea of that was a bolt of thunder in her head. It exploded there and left her shaking. It was as if the flower-covered earth of her back yard garden had split open to uncover a cave of great depths she had not known existed.

Caves frightened Lottie out of her wits.

At four o'clock that afternoon, Lottie took the chicken from the refrigerator. It lay cold and ugly in her hands: bumpy skin, bluish bones. Who would want to eat that? She felt sure George wouldn't like chicken at all.

She put the chicken down on the counter and went into the living room. She stared out at the garden. The gentians wagged in a negative wind. The rosebush trembled.

George arrived at home at five thirty-six, his usual time. He looked at the bare counter, the cold stove. "Dinner's not ready?" he said. And Lottie saw his face change. The mouth that held carefully onto itself sealed close. The blue triangular eyes turned sharp.

"I didn't know if you liked fricassee," Lottie said.

"Not like fricassee? Since when have I not liked fricassee, for God's sake?"

His words were like bits of cold wind, and for a minute Lottie thought he seemed like a real enemy.

After that Lottie thought up a new breakfast each day. Pancakes: the edges burned. Scrambled eggs: leathery. Fried eggs: dark at the rim, runny at the center. She was not used to exotic breakfasts. George did not complain. Neither did he praise. He ate what she put before him and read the morning allotments of disaster. Secretly Lottie studied his face: the reading objective eyes, the wide cautious mouth. She learned nothing.

After a while George's face came to seem strange from so much studying. She could no longer remember what he looked like before the oatmeal. She asked him each day what he wanted for dinner. "Anything you like," he said. She asked how he liked whatever she fixed: breaded porkchops, Italian spaghetti, sweet and sour ribs. "Fine," he said, or "It's all right," or "Not my favorite." But Lottie felt that what he meant he would not say, and there was no way of knowing what lay under the words he gave.

One day she sat with Marjorie Little on the brick patio in the back yard drinking freeze-dried coffee from yellow pottery cups.

"Something's very peculiar, Marj," Lottie said. "Something's funny about George."

Marj curled her little finger over the chocolate fudge brownie. "Yeah?" she said, "what's funny about George?"

Lottie told about the oatmeal. She told how she could not tell what George liked or didn't like, or what he thought at all.

"Yeah, men are mysteries, all right," Marj said, and reached for another fudge brownie. "I read this letter," she said, glancing once at Lottie, "in 'Dear Abby.' The woman wrote that she had been married to this man for twelve years. They had three girls and a boy. She thought they were happy together, the six of them, and then she found out her husband had another wife in another town and two kids there. She wrote that she loved the jerk and what should she do?"

Lottie listened as if to an oracle.

But if George were hiding something he didn't want anyone to find out, he would have a different look, one that was sly and full of smiles.

"Uh-uh, Marj," she said at last. "I don't think George is up to that." Marj frowned and nibbled at her fudge bar. The shadows of the maple tree flickered over her face. Her red hair went dark, then bright, then dark again.

"Did you read that other thing in the Sunday paper?" she asked. "Fellow in the city. Funny name. Owali or Malamy or something. They found his wife in bed. Dead as stone. Hit over the head with a hammer till they hardly knew her face." Marj swallowed the last of the cookie. "They asked him why he did it," she gloomed. "He said she was stupid. She bored him. So he killed her." Marj lapsed into silence, considering blood and boredom and all looming terror.

After that Lottie had her hair blonded. She bought two new shifts and bright orange sandals. George did not notice. He came home at five thirty-six, changed clothes, ate his dinner, sat before the television, and watched whatever came on till ten thirty. Then he went to bed. His narrow face was always composed, his flat voice quiet, his blue eyes empty of signs.

One afternoon the August temperature soared to one hundred and three. Lottie went around the garden and watered the roots of the tender plants. Then she went indoors and drew a tub of cool water. She sat in the tub a long time. When she got out she lifted the pink towel to drape herself and caught the unsuspecting woman in the mirror. The round sober face. The round blue eyes. And in those eyes Lottie saw what existed: knowledge of doom. Full of stunned astonishment, she stared.

George did not love her. George was bored with her. In the dark cave of George's mind loomed desires for women as exotic and lean, or as rosy and taut, as those in *Vogue* or in *Movie World*. Lottie read the reflected eyes and knew she had to leave.

She hurried to her bedroom and hauled her suitcase down from the high closet shelf. She packed what she thought she would need. She carried the suitcase out into the unbearable day and walked to the bank. She bought one thousand dollars worth of traveler's checks. Then she lugged her suitcase down the avenue to all the supermarkets in which she had identity cards. In each she cashed a personal check. At three o'clock she boarded a bus for downtown. She had $1473.00.

At Seventh and Nicollet, Lottie got off the bus. She went into Dayton's, carried her suitcase to the elevators, and rode up to the fifth floor and went into the women's Rest Room. She dropped her suitcase to the floor and sank into one of the deep plastic chairs and kicked off her shoes.

Where to go, that was the question. Her mind was a blank. Chicago she knew but didn't like. New York terrified her and it was too far. Money also had to be considered. In the little towns she knew—Chicago City, Twin Forks, Long Lake—hiding would not be possible.

On the seat next to her lay a battered morning paper. Lottie picked it up and turned to the want-ad section. She found the column headed Rooms to Rent. She came at last to a small ad which sounded promising. *Wtd: Widow. Share home with older lady. Priv. rm. Ckg., ldry., liv. rm. guest priv. Ph. 732-1417.* She went to the phone and in a quavering voice arranged to see the room.

The house was in an old neighborhood in northeast Minneapolis. Mrs. Nystrom was a tall stooped woman with a face like a peeled potato and a shell-like hearing aid at her ear. She tipped her head and frowned exactingly at the woman standing hot and worried on the shade of her front steps. "Mrs. Timmer," Lottie told her, using her maiden name.

"You a widow?" Mrs. Nystrom shouted. Confused and tired, Lottie took the opportunity. She nodded.

"He leave you much?" Mrs. Nystrom called out.

"I have fourteen hundred dollars to my name." Lottie said.

"Well, come see the room," Mrs. Nystrom bellowed.

It was an upstairs front bedroom, small, papered in clouds of violets. Crisp white curtains crossed the windows. A white chenille spread covered a narrow bed. A wicker desk. A small rocker. Lottie grew weak with desire. "How much is it?" she asked.

"For you a widow, fifteen dollars the month. I need someone in the house." And it was all settled.

There in that quiet house in a neighborhood dark with old trees and narrow streets, Lottie felt far from the small house at the other end of the city where George lived. Mrs. Nystrom had an arthritic back. She was taken up with pain and cures and did not bother Lottie with curiosity. The very first day Lottie went back downtown and cashed all the travelers checks in the stores. Then she rushed back to the house and stayed there most of the time.

At first she worried that George would come. But he never did. Little by little Lottie took on more and more of the household chores. She and Mrs. Nystrom began to take their meals together. Lottie did the cooking. In time she grew braver and began to go out to the neighborhood shopping district to do the shopping, too. Summer ended. The cold and rain of autumn came.

On one day of particularly heavy rain Lottie bundled up in her raincoat and an old dark hat. She went, nervous and bitter as a thief, on the long bus ride back to the neighborhood where she had lived with George Wellman for fourteen years. She held her black umbrella close to her head and hurried through walls of water to the house and let herself in. Drenched with sweat and rain, she pulled another suitcase from the shelf and packed it with her winter clothes. Then she fled out into the weather and hurried back to her new home. Exhausted, she dreamed that night of George chasing her.

But in the following weeks, no one came for her: not George, nor the police, nor any detective she could spy out. Her narrow life with Mrs. Nystrom began to seem safe, and in time even complete and whole, all there had ever been.

One day near Christmas she saw a small sign in the neighborhood Woolworth's. Salesgirl needed. She went in right then. The manager, thin and wry, said she was just what he wanted. A nice, honest, well-mannered, neighborhood lady.

He put her behind the ribbons-and-notions counter. She worried about sending for her social security card until she realized she had not used it since her unmarried days as a secretary. The card came, numbered and impressive, marked with her maiden name. No FBI man came to seek her out.

Lottie liked life in the dime store. Pattie, the blonde girl at the lingerie counter, had husband trouble. He cheated on her and went on drunks and sometimes beat her up. She poured out her troubles to Lottie and said over and over again that she would never leave her man because she loved him too much. Lottie shook her head, worried for her. "You might get killed one of these days," she warned. But Pattie shivered and said, "Maybe so. Could be. But I'm stuck with him. He's my man."

Ethyl Mae, a black woman, worked in housewares. She was big-voiced and given to laughter and had lots of family. Every weekend there was a family wedding or birthday or funeral or christening, and Ethyl Mae came to the Monday-quiet store full of tales of the family doings.

The customers who came in showed Lottie their patterns and materials and asked for advice about ribbons or lace or buttons or zippers. Some of the ladies came in again and again, and Lottie came to know their faces and their tastes and sometimes even their names. In time they came to seem like good friends.

Occasionally Lottie thought about her past life with George, but usually only after she had that troubling dream. In the dream she saw clearly his almost forgotten long pale face. He loomed up tall and bony in the hazy landscape, his long nose blue. He would chase her then, in lengthy stumbling chases. Just as he lunged for her, she woke up, breathing hard in the safe violet-flowered darkness. But she would lie in bed, fearful of sleep, waiting for morning which would allow her to put the nightmare back into its dark place.

While doing the laundry one Sunday morning in Mrs.

Nystrom's basement, Lottie came upon a rusty old hatchet. It must have belonged to the long-absent Mr. Nystrom. She carried it upstairs and put it under her bed. The hatchet seemed to help exorcise the dream. After she hid it there, the dream came less often.

More than a year after Lottie had fled from George, she went downtown to shop for sheets for her bed and a steam iron to replace the heavy old-fashioned iron Mrs. Nystrom owned. In Dayton's downstairs housewares department she examined the light bright-colored irons. She heard a voice that turned her to a block of ice.

George, It was George's voice. Talking to someone.

In a minute she realized that the woman he spoke with seemed to know him well. She sidled to the end of the aisle and peered in the direction of George's voice. There he was. George! With a woman! Examining blenders. "My wife," George was saying to the waiting clerk, "wants a General Electric. Nothing else."

His wife! Lottie stared at the woman. A big-bosomed, broom-haired blonde. Neither fashionable nor young. An ordinary woman. Lottie watched them leave, walking away down the aisle arm in arm. She fell into speechlessness. For days she was quiet and half sick.

And then she felt deeply that she had to do something. That woman did not know. The poor woman whom George had called his wife: it must be that she had no idea of George's true nature. If she knew she would fly away from him.

One day after nights of worry, Lottie picked up the phone and dialed the number. The woman answered.

"Mrs. Wellman?" Lottie whispered. "You have to leave him. You are in danger. Leave him right away!"

For a moment no one answered.

Then the woman called out, "Who is this? Who is this?"

Lottie hung up.

But her worries would not let her go. Ten days later on

her lunch hour she left Ethyl Mae in the middle of a story and went out to the corner to the pay phone and called again. The same voice answered. "Leave him," Lottie whispered urgently. "Run away from him. You have to hurry. Your life is in danger."

Two days later, a Sunday, Mrs. Nystrom napped. Lottie called again. George answered. Lottie held the black instrument as if it were frozen to her palm. That terrifying voice shouted, "Who's there, who's there?" Lottie almost swooned. Then at last the buzzing came along the wire, and she was able to put the phone down on its cradle.

And still she worried. She could not stop from worrying. George chased her through the nights. Every night he threw himself at her and almost caught her. She felt stretched to a thread; tense, fearful, alarmed, certain of dooms.

One last time she called. She stayed home from work, headachey, burdened with her mission, determined to talk the broom-haired lady into saving herself. She tried twice. Both times the foolish woman would only cry out, "Who is this? Who are you?" and paid no mind to what Lottie tried to tell her. Lottie knew what would come.

That week she got the flu. She was home in bed Tuesday and Wednesday. Thursday she felt better but did not go to work in the dimestore. Mrs. Nystrom went to the doctor's. Lottie sat upstairs in her rocker, reading, alone in the house.

She heard the car stop at the curb. She looked out and there was George, unwinding himself, climbing out of the driver's seat.

She did not answer the doorbell. It rang many times. Then what she dreaded most occurred. The knob of the unlocked door turned. The door opened. First his voice, calling *Lottie? Lottie?* And then he began to climb the steps, slowly, calling as he came, "Lottie? Lottie! I know you are there! I know you're there!"

He had seen her in the window then! Sitting there by the window for all the world to see.

It was like the dream. But it was not like the dream since there was nowhere to run. At last she moved herself, scrambled from the rocker to the bed. She reached far under the bed and found the hard handle. She pulled out the heavy weapon.

"I know you're there Lottie," she heard him call on the landing. "Lottie? Lottie!"

And she cowered behind the door, strong with terror, the rusted hatchet lifted high over head, ready for the moment he came into her room.

Learning the Truth of Things

At fourteen, Patsy Winthrop was confident that she understood people and knew about life. Though thin and
brown-haired and only ordinarily pretty, she was precocious
and energetic, and rather bored with her studies at the Frank-
lin Delano Roosevelt High School, a two-story, red-brick
building on 32nd Avenue in south Minneapolis.

Then she met Deacon Pryor, a black boy. He was lean but
well-muscled, and a smile trembled perpetually on his
gray-rose mouth. His body held a kind of tension that made
the air around him seem to snap and turn blue, as if electricity
came off his black skin and hair. He wore clothes that made
you look at him and made you smile: orange or blue sweat
shirts without sleeves, purple or flowered vests over long, gray
underwear shirts, tight bright trousers, velvet capes and torn
army jackets, sandals or pointed black shoes on his long quick
feet.

When she saw him sitting in the top row of the bleachers
in her new 9th grade homeroom, which was really the girls'
gym, Patsy liked him right away. "Who's he? Who's that
black boy?" she whispered to Marlene Phillips and Andrea
Thompson and Kathy Upton, all of whom looked at him
from the edges of the bright hair half-hiding their faces.
They did not know. Patsy leaned to the row behind her, to
Chris Holmes, the mean-mouthed, red-haired terror from
8th grade, whose teeth angled out like an inverted fork and
whose eyes were always narrow with knowing. "Oh, *him!*"
Chris called out loudly, showing off. *"That's* Deacon Pryor.

Deacon Pryor, that's who *he* is!'' And her back arched and her throat stretched to her laughing, looking at the black boy, who turned to the sound of his name.

His eyes were glinting and his teeth were wet and white like stones under water. Chris's face flashed red under the thick spatter of her freckles, and she thrust her tongue out past her slanting teeth, like a huge, pickled red strawberry. Watching, Patsy felt something hit her stomach like a club.

As if it were an element like fire, love took her. She was inside it, held in it, composed of it, being it.

Because the fire was its own force and she its vehicle, she did those things. There was no planning of how to do things, no decisions as to what to do. She was like a tireless robot responding to the tapes someone was running through her head.

At propitious moments every day all over the school, when Deacon Pryor stopped at a water fountain, Patsy was there. After Deacon got elected homeroom vice president, Patsy got herself elected homeroom secretary. She dropped her French class and signed up for Spanish, the same class Deacon Pryor took. She got his phone number and called him at home. She found him in the bleachers at the football games and sat down beside him. Finally, in November, grinning and almost dancing on the dull, tan tiles in the corridor outside the girls' gym, he asked her to the Homecoming Dance.

But her mother said, No, she couldn't go. "No dates until you're sixteen, Patsy," her mother said. "That's the rule. You've known that for a long time. Absolutely not. You can't go."

Patsy argued, pled, wept, got nowhere. Then Patsy wouldn't eat. She wouldn't talk. Four days: not a bite, not a syllable. It was not choice, exactly. She could not have eaten had she wanted to. Nothing would go past the closed place in her throat. Sound itself could not go past. After Patsy saw her mother's strength she went to her room and went to bed, not eating, not talking, sick. Her mother lost her temper, shouted at her, slapped her. After two days she was really worried. Patsy's father, a neat, controlled man who was an internist with quietly elegant offices in the downtown Medical Arts Building and who consoled and counselled eminent people, came into her room and sat on her bed and took her hand.

He put his long, thin, firm, gentle fingers on her cheek, his thumb beneath her chin. He turned her head on the pillow, away from facing the wall to facing him. "Open your eyes, Patsy," he said.

It was his kind, reasonable father voice. She cautiously unscrewed her eyes and peeked out.

"Now you know, Patsy," he said, his face pink as a rose, "we only have your own good. . . ."

But at the end of six words her eyes banged shut. Her head flung itself out of his fingers and twisted away to the wall.

They decided to let her go to the dance. Tired and worried and finally loving, together they came into her room and told her. She could go then, once. But she was not to think that dating was to be a regular thing. Not at fourteen.

When Deacon Pryor roared up to the curb in his revved-up '71 Ford, its rear end high like a motorized grasshopper, and he came dancing on his shining pointed shoes to the door, both her father and mother went pale. Patsy saw in their faces the abrupt starkness. Cold, cold with disapproval, with alarm. At first Patsy thought it was his clothes. He wore a skin-tight shirt, flag-striped and spangled with stars, and blue-and-white striped trousers, tight over a flat belly and round haunches. On his head he had a black flopping hat he didn't take off when he stepped inside.

Patsy introduced them and Deacon was glistening with smiles, but her parents were jerky like puppets.

And when she went for her coat, Patsy's mother followed. "You didn't tell us," she whispered, her fingers spread wide on her chest. "You didn't tell us he was a Negro. Why didn't you tell us?"

When she got home at twelve o'clock, her father opened the front door before the car was stopped at the curb, and from that minute till the minute she ran away, there was no peace.

Her mother, who was conscientious and kindly, who cared for friends and neighbors and even far-away strangers, who taught the children in the Methodist Church School to love their neighbors as Jesus loved His, and her father, who was a sober physician, who was devoted to goodness and discipline, and who was a member of the Methodist Church's governing board, tried to reason with her.

"You mustn't get involved in something you can't handle," her mother said, the dark, slim brows rising slantwise on the smooth white forehead. "Patsy, you're only fourteen. You're playing with fire," she said, her small mouth thickened and unhappy. "At fourteen we mistake the responses of our bodies for real love. You're too young, Patsy. You're not wise enough for race and all that. You're just too young."

"Patsy," her father said, "trust me. This thing with this Pryor boy just isn't right for you. It's a bad thing, all the way around."

"What does his father do?" they asked her. "Where does he live?" Well, if he doesn't have a father, what does his mother do? Do any of your friends *know* him, really? Does he have a job? Is he going to college? Etcetera. Etcetera. Etcetera. Listen, Patsy, I have some experience in life. Interracial relationships usually end up in unhappiness for everyone involved. Patsy, you are being foolish. Patsy, you're stubborn. This is foolishness. Teenage giddiness. Etcetera. Etcetera.

It was all because Deacon Pryor was black. Also because he was from a poor family and lived over a store on 38th Street. And because he had no father. Because he wore those clothes. Because of the way he danced and grinned. All they

said, whatever her parents said, was only a flimsy coverup for
their prejudice. But they did not even know that. Patsy saw
that they were hopelessly stupid about the whole thing. But
they loved her. They kept saying how much they loved her
and it was true. Their anxious faces, their silences told her
that. She knew that they loved her, all right.

"For your own good," her father said, weeks later. "It is
for your own good. You must not see him anymore. I want
your word of honor. You won't date him anymore nor will
you go out of your way to talk to him at school. I forbid you.
As long as you're fed and clothed and provided for, you have
to obey. So end it, now. That's an order. I want your word
of honor."

But Patsy Winthrop could not give her word, could not
promise. It was like being asked to stop breathing.

Her father had never before lost control. He had never
before been unjust or unfair or unloving to her. He had never
even shouted at her. But now he was furious and inflexible.He
took away all her privileges. No more nights out. No more
allowance. No participation in after-school activities. No
phone calls. He enlisted the principal and her teachers. He
himself drove her to school in the mornings. He had her
mother pick her up after school, every day, at three-thirty.
The house was grim with contest. Her mother was jittery and
pale. Her father was stony. Bobby and Joey, her small brothers, went quiet and big-eyed as lizards around the house.
They did not ask her to play. Patsy felt outcast and dispos-
sessed. At school, she felt the shame of her public disenfran-
chisement. At home, loneliness.

The deepening winter outside was a vivid image of Patsy's
life. But in the cold and isolation her feeling for Deacon
Pryor burned, unchanged.

Patsy endured until December. The six weeks from the
perfect night of the homecoming dance seemed a time without limit. If she had ever been happy, that happiness had

belonged to some other creature whose face and body and mind only remotely resembled hers and who was unrelated to what she now was. She lived in silence like a cell.

Then one day during Christmas vacation, her parents gave her permission to go downtown one day with Andrea Thompson and Robin McDuff to do her Christmas shopping, providing she went with the other girls and came promptly home.

It was a low, gray day, dampness in the air. Occasionally, snow came in quick flurries, melting on street and walk as soon as it fell. In the wide front windows of the neighborhood homes the Christmas trees stood elegantly decorated. Down in the little commercial district where the girls waited for the bus, the shops were strung with lights, tinsel bells, green plastic wreaths.

"Just a minute," Patsy suddenly said. She went into the drug store and called Deacon Pryor. By what wonder was it that he was home?

"I have to work," he told her. "I have to be there at two." He was selling Christmas trees in a gas station lot.

But he agreed to meet her at Penney's main entrance at eleven o'clock.

At ten-thirty the girls were in Dayton's trying on sweaters and skirts. Patsy clutched at her stomach, announced she was sick. She had to go home, she told them. Too sick to stay. She ran the whole three blocks to Penney's, slipping and sliding on the snowflakes falling quickly now upon the wet side walks. Then she was there, standing at the entrance. Her breath wrenched in and out of her chest. She felt worry and joy flinging her about like a snowflake.

Would he come? Why was he not there? She had to lean against the window to keep herself steady.

And then he came, his eyelids narrowed down on the light in his eyes, his mouth wide with smiling. From the top of his blue-black head where a red stocking cap perched to the sharp pointed tips of his cowboy boots, he gave sparks to the Christmas air.

Oh, she loved him. She loved him more than anyone or anything in the whole world.

But suddenly she felt her face breaking into pieces like ice crumbling under sudden spring sun, and she stood facing him with tears leaping and jumping down her face.

"Oh, Deacon," she gasped. "Oh Deacon!" And she laid her face against his sheepskin jacket.

"Hey, Baby," he said. Surprise sent his voice up to a little song. "Hey, Patsy Baby-honey, whatsa matter, Baby?"

His hand took her chin and turned it up, and with all the hurrying bundled-up shoppers throwing quick harsh looks at them, he leaned down and put his soft mouth to hers. His fingers went like little light, cold butterflies against her cheeks, brushing at the flood of tears. Deacon Pryor holding her and kissing her was so strange and so lovely that she had to laugh.

"Hey, that's better, Baby. No more of that crying stuff, now, huh, Baby?" He stood holding her, and she wiped her face with a Kleenex pulled from the purse hanging on a strap from her shoulder and felt the crazy happiness coming all over her body.

Hand in hand, they started to walk, up and down the hymn-filled avenues. For safety's sake they wandered away from the big stores, down Fourth Street, down Hennepin, in and out of the small, dingy stores where Catholic statues and German leather goods and used books were dustily offered. Giddy as if she had a fever, Patsy babbled and laughed, fell deeply silent, felt herself floating as if there were no ground under her feet. She spun sometimes in a sudden circle, flung herself back close to Deacon, clung to his arm, held his hand in both hers.

"Wow, you're really something," Deacon whispered.

But then suddenly she saw a street clock. It was a quarter

to three. The day was pushing them, driving at them, meaning to separate them.

"Oh, Deacon," Patsy said. "What are we going to do?"

The question stopped them both in the middle of the walk. They stood in the falling snow and stared into each other's eyes. They both looked at the closing hands of the clock.

"Come on," Deacon said. "Let's get my car."

At first they were simply driving, driving south as if there were no alternative, down the traffic-slow Nicollet Avenue out of the Loop to the part of the city where they lived. But instead of turning off at 48th Street, Deacon kept driving. His wide eyes were solemn on the road, his arm was over Patsy's shoulders where she sat close against him, quiet with terrible sadness. The radio played "White Christmas."

They drove out past the airport and out on a country road. The snowflakes on the windshield gathered in little wet ridges against the shuddering wipers. The fields around them were growing dim, gray under the moving wall of whiteness. Trees and buildings were vague in outline, misted by snow into a world without harsh form, without clear order, without reality.

"Deacon," Patsy said. "Let's not go back."

The words astonished them both. Deacon's foot came off the gas pedal. The car swerved on the lean country road. Patsy herself stiffened, sat upright.

"What you mean, Patsy?" Deacon whispered. His mouth swelled up as if it had been stung.

She did not say, oh, she was fooling. She did not laugh to take away what she had said. She folded her hands together on her knees and looked straight ahead at the turning snow and said the words again, taking them this time as the truth of what she wanted to do.

Deacon swung the car over to the road's shoulder, stopped, turned off the motor. He looked at her once, a quick look sharper than any she had seen in his eyes. Then he stared

straight ahead at the twisting snow. His wide lips drew together. At last a sound blew from them, a long low whistle.

"You mean it, Patsy?" he said. His eyes, were on her face.
"You mean we should just keep on driving? Never go back?"

"We can go to California," Patsy said. The plans were
springing up in her head, possible, plausible, marvelously
whole. "In California they don't care about race like they do
in Minneapolis. We can go to the Haight Ashbury and find
a place and we can both get jobs and we could live there,
Deacon. Nobody could find us, even. It's a big city. We can
just hide, and we can be together then."

For a long time he was quiet. His hands lay on the steering
wheel like two resting pigeons, big and quiet and blue brown.
Then he said as if to the indifferent snow, "But you're only
fifteen, Patsy. Only fifteen."

Fourteen, her mind corrected. But she did not say.

"I don't care," she cried, and flung herself against him,
pushing her face into the wool collar of his jacket. "I'm old
enough. I won't go home again. I love you, Deacon. I've got
forty-three dollars."

He only said, "Oh wow, Baby."

But he suddenly almost leaped away from the steering
wheel and pushed her back against the passenger seat and he
came against her. He kissed her then all over her face and
closed eyes and throat and mouth, his tongue lean and hunting, his wide mouth soft. She could not catch her breath.

But alarms went chasing along her muscles and she stopped
him.

He humped over the steering wheel, both arms resting
there. His face was so still he hardly looked like himself.
After a long time he spoke. "Well, what do you want?" he
said. "What do you want, white girl?"

Like a courtroom or a church, that's how quiet it was.
Patsy watched one snow flake drift sideways and off into
oblique space. From the time it left the cloud to the time it

finally touched the earth, how long would that be?

"I can't go home, Deacon," she said out of her old knowledge. "I want to go away somewhere. With you, Deacon. I love you."

He started the car again. At first he drove slowly, not looking at her, not touching her. He seemed all alone in thoughts that were larger than the passing countryside. She too was alone. Lonely with decisions and endings. But then the aloneness grew too large. The inside of the car with its faint hums of music and disembodied voices seemed as limitless as space, and she slid over, sitting close to the silent boy guiding the car into the logics of the snowy road. After a time his arm lifted and went around her shoulders, held her there. After that, his foot was firmer on the gas pedal, and they wheeled on through the snowy, darkening evening as swiftly as the south-pushing road would take them.

In Albert Lea they stopped at a Conoco station, filled the tank, and got a map. Patsy spread the map on her knees, and into the long night they drove. Once in another small town they pulled to the curb outside a paint-peeled building marked with a Coca Cola sign which also said Groceries. Patsy went in and bought bread and peanut butter, milk and Snickers. They drove on, eating. The road pulled them farther and farther into strange country. Always Patsy chose back roads which in that flat country went in orderly angles paralleling the main highways. Her folks would be looking for her. "They'll call the police," Deacon muttered, his brow ridged, his rose mouth drooping.

"Maybe," Patsy said. "But they'll ask everyone first. They'll call your house and then they'll know you're gone, too. Then maybe they will."

Anxious, she sat close to him, her body tense with her will to make the car speed safely away. They grew sleepy. Somewhere in the early hours past midnight, Deacon pulled into the back yard of a tiny, darkened gas station at the edge of country fields. He eased his car in among a cluster of used, battered cars, old trucks, useless-looking farm machinery. In the barrel-, tire-, and crate-littered yard, the snow drifted down in lacy airiness. When the headlights went off, and then the motor, silence came around them as encircling and as embracing as the continual snow.

"Why have you stopped?" Patsy whispered. "What are you going to do?"

"Sleep, Baby. We're going in that little station and get us some sleep. You watch now."

He left her huddled into her own arms in the front seat and went to the car's trunk. He rattled among his tools, then he slipped through the circles of white snow toward the station and off around the side. She heard the wrenching of wood, a shrieking of stubborn metal. She turned stiff with alarm. But no car came through the still countryside. There was, apparently, no one anywhere out-of-doors to hear. The lovely snow, the pure quiet, held them marvelously safe!

Deacon came back and pulled open her door.

"All set, Baby," he whispered, exuberant. "Nothing to it."

He threw into the back seat his tire jack and wrench, pulled out the Indian blanket he kept there. He took Patsy's hand and led her through the wheeling snow to the small building where the window was hoisted open. He boosted her up. She teetered a moment on the sill, managed to swing her leg over, fell into the oil-and-metal-smelling room. The snow outside made a small lightness inside. She could see enough, after a moment, to move.

"You all right?" Deacon hissed, and lunged into the open window after her. He hung there a minute, like a clown bursting through a paper ring.

Patsy giggled.

Deacon angled in, legs, elbows, finally all of him. He pulled the window shut behind him. He pulled matches from his pocket, struck one against the flint. The quick, small tongue of the light licked at the blue darkness. The room's shapes and angles became indentifiable objects. The shelves shone with cans of oil, stacks of batteries. There was the glint and shine of a candy machine, a huge, cluttered, scarred wooden desk, a rack of flashlights. Deacon grinned, took a flashlight, played its small beam at a low angle about the room. In the corner was the square metal box.

"That's it, " Deacon chortled. He danced to the metal box and found the thermostat. He pushed the gold marker up and up until it touched 80. At once, like a pleased cat, the heater burst into a deep thrumming. A warm wind, conforting as summer, came from its low mouth. The flame in its belly made a pink glowing. Deacon snapped off the flashlight.

"In a minute we'll be snug as two bugs in a' rug. This is home sweet home, baby, home away from home."

He moved all around the room, lifting the things on the desk, putting them down, opening drawers, opening another door upon a toilet and a grimed washbowl.

"Wow, Baby," he said. "All the comforts of home. Even a john."

After he spread the Indian blanket on the floor, Deacon pulled his jacket off and rolled it into a pillow and dropped himself down, sprawling like an exhausted dog. His eyes closed. The smudge of his lashes showed against his cheek.

"Geez, Patsy, Baby," he muttered. "That's a lot of driving. I'm all worn out."

Tired too, Patsy lay down beside him, her jacket rolled like his into a pillow for her head. The dry warmth pouring into the room pushed her like hands toward sleep.

For a long while they slept, nested together like children fallen asleep in the middle of play. Then Patsy woke to Deacon's hands coming under her sweater, moving slowly against her skin. All her body became a still waiting. Wariness spun coldly in her head. When his hand touched her breast, a gasp shook through her.

But she had already acknowledged, had already accepted this as part of what was to come. I love him, she admonished the protest that was pushing her throat for sound. I love him. She let him undo the snaps and zippers of her clothes, and put aside the protecting garments. His mouth was all over her, and his hands. And then there was the hard renting of her secret body, and he was into her. And then it had been done and was all done. A searing seal had been put upon them and upon their love, which no one in the world could undo. "Jesus, Patsy," Deacon said in his throat. "Jesus." Then he slept. Patsy lay close to him in the large-seeming darkness and thought of forever.

But she was troubled and disappointed. So long imagined, so long composed of terror and mystery and dark longing, the act had been insignificant, fretfully simple. While Deacon lay riding the deep breathings of his sleep, Patsy cried. Eventually she slept a while, then awoke again. "Deacon," she whispered, pushing at his shoulder, his arm, his hip. "Deacon, would you do that again?" she urged.

Deacon woke her at dawn. When she came out of the stinking lavatory, she saw Deacon struggling with a locked, green metal box on top of the desk.

"What are you doing, Deacon?" she whispered.

"Honey," Deacon grunted, the weight of one hand on the screw driver wedged into the fine seam of the box's meeting edges, the other hand leaning on the box to keep it steady. "We get to California, we get ourselves good jobs and pay the man back. We can't make it to California, Baby, otherwise."

They spun out into the white dawn, along the empty roads, wary as rabbits. There was no sign of life. Thin streams of smoke rose from the scattered farmhouses, signaling the wakefulness of unseen people. Once they saw a man bundled into a heavy jacket, stocking cap, and boots, stomping through the broad snow toward his barn. No one else was visible for miles and miles and miles. Patsy began to feel easier, trembled less under the closely held Indian blanket. Still she felt the presence of that green money in Deacon's pocket as if it were the actual eye of some pursuer watching over their long journey. She sat separate from him, wide awake with knowledge of complication.

The sun came to the horizon, red and swollen. Long stains of red fell over the blue stretches of snowy fields, and the clusters of poplar trees, barren and stark around the farmhouses, were like high stands of barbed wire. A wind came, scudding along the earth, lifting clouds of snow before it, which twisted like harried spirits over the land.

"They'll see our tracks," Patsy said, twisting to look at the road thinning away behind them. "They can follow our tracks, Deacon. We have to get out on the highway. Then they can't tell which tracks are ours."

For a while then they drove down the wide main highway. Already the great yellow plows were wheeling along, flinging the fallen snow to the road's edge. They stopped for breakfast at a truckers' diner. Deacon pulled several dollars from his pocket and paid the gloomy-faced waitress. Patsy noted exactly how much it cost.

Back in the car again she got the money from him and counted it. Altogether, counting the $2.45 for breakfast, it came to $68.78. Patsy got her pen and wrote the amount in the back of her small blue address book.

"What was the name of that station, Deacon?" she asked.

"Jeez, Baby," he said. "Don't know its name. Didn't ever see its name at all."

"What was the town, Deacon?" Patsy asked.

"The town. Let's see, now. Don't know the name of that town, Patsy Honey."

That night in a medium-sized town in Ohio, Deacon stopped along a side street near a roller skating rink. He rummaged in the back seat, reaching under the cushion. Then he took off, leaving Patsy alone in the parked car. Darkness

was heavy, the place terribly quiet. He was gone what seemed
a long time, and when he climbed back in behind the wheel,
he was jerky with hurry. They sped out of town and down
the country road carelessly, taking the curves too fast, hitting
patches of ice in sudden lunges.

"Deacon," Patsy said at last, putting her hand on his arm,
cautioning. "What did you do back there?"

"Just sold a couple of joints, Baby, that's all. Boy, they were
real eager. Got us thirty bucks, Baby. Now we got enough
bread to get us there."

Two days later, suddenly behind them there was a spinning
red light and then the high wail of a siren. Two cops, one
red-faced and old, the other lean and bold, with a nose like
a butcher's thumb, came toward them, their hands resting on
their guns.

"Your driver's license," the young one said. His legs were
spread wide, his lower lip like a mug's rim. "Uh huh," he
said. "Yep, you're the one. Deacon Pryor, huh?" Was the
look in his eyes really happiness? "O.K., Mister Pryor, you're
under arrest, my young friend." He had his gun in his hand,
the other cop offered handcuffs. "Step outside here, Pryor.
You too, Miss."

They stood on the edge of the highway, giving one frail
wrist each to the wedding handcuffs. The cop slapped at
Deacon's body, shoulders to ankles. Then he passed his hands
all over Patsy's body, too. The older cop watched. He gave
them a push toward the police car, where the red light
wheeled. Deacon looked at no one. His feet slid heavily along
the snowy ground. Patsy suddenly stopped. She wheeled to
face the cops.

"Where're you taking us?" she cried out. "Why are you
arresting us? What right you got, stopping us?"

They laughed. The fat one pushed her. She kicked at them,
full of hate.

After all that, the house on 42nd Street was a tomb. In her

upstairs bedroom, Mrs. Winthrop lay under percale sheets and wept for the death of respectability and hope. Dr. Winthrop fed his wife Stelazine and held himself in silence. How remote, how frigid, how unapproachable he had become! He had buried then, in the four days she had been gone, whatever love he had had for his daughter Patsy. All he had left for her was iron tolerence and determined responsibility.

Patsy was on probation, a ward of the juvenile court. Every Tuesday night, the probation officer came to their house and held conferences with the family on how to communicate and how to establish trust. Her father was furious and silent. Her mother wept. Her small brothers were sullen. How could she have run away from them like that?

But Deacon, who was black and whose father was not around, was seventeen, more than two years older than she. He was charged with robbery and statutory rape and possession of marijuana. But because Deacon had no record, and the reform schools were pitifully overcroweded, and Deacon promised to pay back the stolen money, and the judge was a maternal woman, he got a suspended sentence and four years' probation. He would have to transfer to Vocational High at semester's end.

Patsy and Deacon were not to talk to one another, never see one another, never even speak on the phone, not ever.

Still, in English class Patsy told Mr. Serranto, her teacher, a parse-lipped man, that she had gotten the curse and had to go to the restroom. Instead, she went to the library where Deacon Pryor had his study hour. She walked to where he sat, his head down on crossed arms, and dropped a pellet of paper on his notebook. She went out and waited in the hall. In a few minutes he came, his eyes moving from side to side to watch the empty corridor. Patsy took hold of his arm.

"Oh, Deacon," she said. "Deacon, I love you."

She felt how woodenly he stood and how empty looking his eyes remained. "Deacon, you love me don't you?"

He shook away from her as if she carried disease.

"You keep away from me, Patsy," he whispered. "You keep away or I'm likely to end up in Stillwater."

Patsy fled to the restroom and wept so hard that she had to go home. If love could die like that, so fast and so soon, in Deacon's heart, nothing in the world held any good.

In January, Deacon transferred to Vocational High. Patsy's parents put her in the Christian Hope Academy. It was a very Jesus-oriented place. There was chapel every day. Prayer groups met before school. Some of the girls there really loved Jesus and went about with faces pink with God-happiness. Some of the teachers, too. Even some of the boys.

But Patsy's heart was sick with knowledge of the mortality of love and the commonness of cruel betrayals. Her grief kept her from making friends and kept her, too, from finding Jesus. She felt quite sure that, like all the rest of the people she knew, God Himself was against her.

The Peculiar Vision Of Mrs. Winkler

In the white-walled, vaulted room the two black-robed men sat, rigid and circumspect, one at the golden-oak table, the other in the elevated golden-oak box. Before them Mrs. Winkler, wearing a rosy-red Davidow suit and clever matching shoes, looked like a bright exclamation point.

"Mrs. Winkler," said the judge loftily—a gaunt man, he had a bulging forehead, sharp blue eyes, a nose like a delicate scythe— "you were strolling down Fifth Avenue in San Rafael on Saturday, April fifth, 1969, totally, as the report asserts, *nude?*"

"Yes, Your Honor," Mrs Winkler said meekly. An expensively dressed, conservatively groomed, shapely young matron of thirty, she clutched her turtle bag in both gloved hands.

"Suppose," said the judge, his mouth gone tender, ironic, "suppose you tell me, Mrs. Winkler, the way it came to happen. The simple bare facts." He lifted a languid hand. The long forefinger and the long thumb twanged at the bridge of his nose.

"Well, it *is* really very simple, Your Honor," Mrs. Winkler said. Her dark, curly head tipped a little to one side. "It happened first on a Monday morning. I was dressing for my garden club meeting. Every other Monday we meet at the Art and Garden Center in Ross." She looked at the judge as if asking his approval.

"Yes," he said, his voice dry as paper, the large head nodding, "my wife goes to her garden club on alternate

Mondays, too. As did my mother. And as did my grandmother. In fact, both grandmothers." He dropped his narrow hand over the gust of a conservative yawn and, patient as a turtle, looked down on Mrs. Winkler.

"Well, I had just put on my little yellow flannel skirt, Your Honor," Mrs. Winkler said studiously, "and the orange-and-yellow-and-white knitted top and my navy pumps. I was just slipping into a navy sweater— the Evan-Picone cable stitch—when all of a sudden these words came . . . ."

They had come like a holy shout, like some magnificently proclaimed edict, the words shaping themselves, brilliantly golden-red, high in the air of the spacious green-and-white bedroom, amid the dissipating fumes of Mrs. Winkler's sprayed Fabergé. Mrs. Winkler stood absolutely arrested, one arm thrust halfway through a sweater sleeve. She attended the vivid, dazzling proclamation. WAR, announced the marvelous words, IS NOT NECESSARY. Cymbals seemed to be clanging around them, and a strange, exotic, amplified humming that in its closely woven, unearthly harmonies seemed to bring into the room a wild, spinning magnitude of space. "Oh, my," breathed Mrs. Winkler, looking acutely at the message.

Had she possibly read those words in the morning *Chronicle?* She cast back over the recalled news: A new ambassador to the United Nations had been appointed (Aaron Lester? Loren Astor? Somebody); there had been a skirmish at Hoa Bihn (or was it Ninh Hoa? Somewhere); a minor temblor had knocked cups from kitchen cupboards in Santa Rosa (or Santa Clara?); the students at Columbia University (or perhaps Harvard?) had ended their strike. Weather. Herb Caen, Dear Abby. Horoscope. No, Mrs. Winkler decided, studying the compelling, dominant words, she had not read them in the paper.

But there they triumphantly were! Emblazoned on the air, deafening in their assertion. WAR IS NOT NECESSARY. Where had they come from? Why were they there? What was all the careening, ethereal music? Anxiously, resolutely, Mrs. Winkler turned her back on the phenomenon. It was all a delusion, she told herself. She jerked on the sweater, plucked up her purse. She hurried away, down the hall to the white-tiled front entry; picked up the yellow workbasket with its metal frogs, green tapes, shears, florists' clay and the blue-glazed flower container; went out the front door into the fresh California morning air.

She opened the garage door, climbed into her sky-blue Buick convertible, backed out. She got out, closed the garage door, backed deftly out of the long driveway and drove the curving road downhill. She whizzed down the green expanse of the maple-arched Bolinas Avenue to Sir Francis Drake Boulevard.

But at the intersection there, instead of turning right toward the Art and Garden Center, she turned left and went into the village. She tooled along the narrow, car-congested Main Street to The Village Card and Stationary Shop. She parked at the green-painted curb, got out, pushed open the shop's bright-red door and walked in. She stood for a moment enclosed in the bright yellows, scarlets, blues, greens, and purples of cards and papers and ribbons—a baroque rainbow.

"Oh, yes," she said at last to the yellow-haired, pink-cheeked clerk, "some poster paint. And a large piece of composition board. Red paint. Yellow board."

She then went to the Village Hardware Store and bought a yellow yard-stick and red thumbtacks. She climbed back into the blue convertible, placed the yellow composition board carefully on the sleek blue-and-white-plastic-covered passenger seat and began to paint: WAR IS NOT NECES-SARY. "Lovely," she said aloud, and suddenly exceedingly happy, as if surrounded by exalting chorales, she drove several blocks to the Safeway store and parked in the lavender shade of a blooming hawthorne tree. She climbed out from behind the wheel, went around to the other side of the car, and removed the yellow yardstick and the large red-and-yellow sign. She tacked board to stick, lifted the sign to her shoulder, and began to pace back and forth in front of the pink-brick store.

Down the blossomy spring avenue (maples yellow-green, Ceanothus deeply blue, cherries airy pink, acacias strident yellow) came old Mr. Cowperthwaite. His white hair ruffled in the breeze; his ebony walking cane swung jauntily. "Lovely," he called out, gallant and deaf. "You look absolutely lovely, Mrs. Winkler, my dear. The very breath of spring!" he cried, and swung himself along on his exuberant cane.

Ardina Isherwood darted from her car to the Safeway door. "Darling," she called, "where's that thing playing? When's opening night? Darling, I'll talk to you at bridge! Terrible rush!" And her orange dress flashed through the swinging glass door.

All morning and most of the afternoon Mrs. Winkler walked back and forth in front of the store. The balls of her feet burned from the concrete sidewalk. The tender flesh of her shoulder grew chafed under the weight of the sign. Rushing pedestrians and harried shoppers passed her all day long with not so much as a backward glance at the magnificent, gaudy sign. No one heeded the bright, important words. No one cares, Mrs. Winkler thought. No one cares at all. She went home weary, full of sighs, oppressed by a vast and inexpressible sadness.

On Tuesday morning she was accosted again. When the alarm zinged at her ear, Mrs. Winkler popped out of bed. She went to the sea-green bathroom, used the sea-green toilet, entered the lighted sea-green shower and stood beneath the warm, steady spray. Then she reached for her deep-napped, forest-green bath towel and wrapped herself in it. She patted her face with pink moisturizing lotion, stroked a bright-coral lipstick across her lips, pulled a gold-backed brush through her hair. She donned her poppy-patterned morning coat and went down the long hall to the kitchen. She filled the copper teakettle, set it on the stove, and folded the crisp white paper into the white cone of the coffee maker. It seemed an ordinary day.

She set blue-and-white plates on yellow-plastic mats, shook up the frozen orange juice in the yellow-plastic shaker. Then she went back down the hall and awakened her son Whitfield, her daughter Sally, and her husband Whitfield Winkler, Sr. When they were fed and gone, Mrs. Winkler put the orange-and-blue cereal boxes in the varnished cupboards, the blue-and-yellow milk and butter cartons back in the blue refrigerator. She rinsed the dishes under the faucet, arranged them neatly on the plastic shelf of the blue-doored dishwasher, poured the pink soap granules into the little black soap cups, shut the door and pushed the starter. Then she went to the bedroom to dress. It still seemed quite an ordinary Tuesday.

Tuesday was Mrs. Winkler's day for golf. Every fair Tuesday she joined her friends at the Meadow Club for Ladies' Day. She would never be much of a golfer, Mrs. Winkler acknowledged that. But she liked walking over the course set high in the pastoral hills, and she enjoyed the girls' chatty company, the marvelous crab salad lunch (and a glass of sherry or two?), and after lunch the bridge game. She was better at bridge than at golf. So Tuesdays were marvelous days, all in all.

Mrs. Winkler leaned toward the mirror in the green-and-white bedroom. She spread the light-amber tint of make-up over her face, arched her eyebrows with the little red-handled pencil, redid her lipstick with the fine golden brush. She pulled on her short golf skirt (a bright navy-and

white plaid), a white knitted Arnold Palmer shirt, a cardi-
nal-red cardigan sweater. She slipped a red bandeau into her
hair. She was ready to go.

She reached into her glove drawer for her sunglasses, and
at that moment, as though she had been struck by a sudden
spotlight, she stood transfixed at the blaze of words flaring
across the light morning air. WAR IS NOT NECESSARY,
they proclaimed in vibrating, blinding flashes, and around
them the dissonant, symphonic sounds rocketed. "Oh heavens," Mrs. Winkler breathed, and clutched the edge of her
cherrywood chest. "Oh, please," she murmured, "not today,
It's my day for golf. Won't you please go away."

But the words quivered there, implacable as fire. Like fire
they burned away all other thoughts. Without further protest
Mrs. Winkler took up her shoulder bag, went to the garage,
took out the blue convertible, drove down the curving hillside avenue and turned left into the village. She stopped on
the corner of Pine and Main, slid out and entered the yellow
door of the Village Paint and Varnish Store.

"One small can of red enamel," she said absently to the
lanky green-smocked clerk, "Also one small can of orange
enamel and a one-inch paintbrush," she said.

She took up the little, red-and-white-striped bag of paint
supplies and returned to her car. She drove out to Highway
101 and turned north. At the indicated turnoff she spun off
the highway onto the tree-lined approach to the Civic Center. She parked in one of the numerous white-defined parking spaces, took her parcel and her bag and hurried into the
long, concrete building. She entered the elevator, rode with
the music to the top floor, emerged, went out the door that
led to the narrow decking that flanked the windows of the
top story. She opened the little striped bag, set the little
yellow cans on the floor before her, the paintbrush beside
them. She removed her bright sweater, folded it neatly, and
placed it at one side, pried open the cans with her car key,

dipped the silky brush into the glistening paint and began painting the slogan on the wonderfully long expanse of wall.

When at last she finished, she thought it very effective. The orange-and-red striped letters stood out in strong contrast to the pale-salmon color of the building. Surely, she thought, the marvelous words would be stunningly visible from the grounds below, from the highway beyond, where the unending stream of cars traversed the California countryside, and even from all the homes dotting the high, ringing hills.

She closed the paint cans, put brush and cans back into the little paper bag, returned to the elevator, descended, and went out of the building. She stood in the shimmering California day in the middle of the vast, tarred parking area and gazed up at what she had accomplished. WAR IS NOT NECESSARY, the red-and-orange letters cried out to all the world. Happiness came to Mrs. Winkler in floods of complicated harmonies, and she almost heard a distant voice sonorously murmur, *"Well done, my dear; well done."* Contented then, at peace, she got into her blue convertible and drove to the Meadow Club for a hand or two of bridge.

Before returning home that evening Mrs. Winkler drove back to the highway and north to the great Civic Center. It was just four o'clock. The county employees were streaming out of the building on the face of which shimmered the resplendent slogan. Mrs. Winkler watched the tired and energetic clerks, secretaries, bureaucrats, and officials scurry and scramble their way across the acres of tar to their green and yellow and white and red and black cars scattered across the black field.

None of them saw. Not one, that she could determine, turned to see. They did not even glance upon the words that cried out so eloquently from the long concrete building looming behind them.

"Why, no one notices," she said aloud, and in bewilderment sat watching from her open blue convertible until the last of them had wheeled away from the lot and she sat alone with a fleet of empty orange school buses.

At home she quickly scanned the *Independent Journal* the conservative little local newspaper. It carried only its usual modicum of trivial local news: bridge luncheons, traffic citations, school district tax appeals, committee meetings on teen-age morals, on alcholism, and on marriage, announcements of church bazaars and charity fairs. There was nothing at all about the project on which Mrs. Winkler had spent most of her golfing Tuesday. (Well, she thought, wait till they discover it!)

The next morning, Wednesday, Mrs. Winkler did her midweek cleanup. She pushed the beige vacuum cleaner over all the moss-green carpets, dusted the waxed walnut console, the teak tables, the ebony piano. At noon she showered in the green-tiled bath, brightened her face with the beige and coral of make-up and lipstick, slipped into her pink girdle and bra, her pink half-slip, her nylons. Then she donned a starched pink-and-white striped uniform, a stiff pink apron, a high little crown of pink hat. It was her afternoon to be a Pink Lady in Ward 7 of the County Hospital. She started off dutifully in the blue convertible, but when she came to the boulevard she turned off toward the highway and the Civic Center.

Once more she sat in the large, black, white-lined parking lot. She observed all the people coming and going in and out of the building. Hurrying, abstracted, no one in all the crowd noticed. Not one lifted his head to the brightly painted letters that called out for attention. WAR IS NOT NECESSARY, they proclaimed, but no one listened at all. Solemnly, slowly, Mrs. Winkler drove away.

Thursday Mrs. Winkler pulled on her green slacks and yellow sweat shirt. It was her day for the garden. She fed the blue phlox, pinched the tips of the crimson fuchsias, sprayed the yellow roses. She drove to the nursery for annuals and went out to the Civic Center and gazed sorrowfully at the neglected slogan. That night she found an item in the *Independent Journal*. It took one inch of space. It was on page twenty-eight. "It was discovered today," the tiny, ineffectual print read, "that an unidentified vandal defaced a wall of the Civic Center. The work was apparently that of a member of a subversive political group. County officials have had the offense removed."

Mrs. Winkler read the little article twice. She pulled several soft yellow tissues from her pocket and wept a moment. "I tried," she explained sadly to whatever obligation it was that demanded apology. "I did what I could," she said, and went to the blue-and-white kitchen to comfort herself with a cup of tea.

Friday morning at eight thirty Mrs. Winkler went to the bus stop to pick up her cleaning girl, Beatrice, took her to the house, and left for her appointment at the beauty salon. She had her hair and nails done, returned home, donned her red Davidow suit, met her friends at the Art and Garden Center, and went with them to the afternoon symphony in San Francisco. The day was full. She did not think of her peace project.

On Saturday mornings Mrs. Winkler customarily went out to do her weekend shopping. Since on this April Saturday, Whitfield, Jr., and Mr. Winkler were playing in a father-son golf tournament at the Meadow Club and Sally had to practice for the June Aquacade, Mrs. Winkler decided she would also go into San Rafael to Macy's to pick up some of the milled oatmeal soap she particularly liked. She had showered and toweled dry and stood ready to slide the pale-yellow Lycra girdle over her thighs when the vision took hold.

She gasped. She stretched herself upright, gazed at her body in the mirror. Her eyes widened. Her mouth opened to a helpless O. She saw the shimmering letters, heard the seductive, spiraling music. "No!" she exclaimed at last, and vigorously shook her head. "I couldn't do that. Of course I can't do a thing like that." But her own gray eyes stared back her, hypnotic and chastising; the rounded mouth became firm in an imperative pout. The music wound itself deafeningly, wildly about her, and she leaned over the drawer and rummaged furiously for a crimson lipstick. Carefully she drew the indicated words: WAR on the rounding wall of one breast; IS on the balancing curve of the other; NOT centered on the curve of abdomen just above the navel; NECESSARY spaced carefully down one thigh and then repeated down the other thigh. She gazed at herself once more in the mirror, shook her head slowly and nodded. She brushed her hair, rouged her mouth, went to her closet, pulled on her Kelly green raincoat and a pair of sandals. She got into her car and drove to San Rafael.

When she got to Fifth Avenue, as if intended by her fates, a parking space emptied for her right in front of Macy's. She parked, got out of the car, put a dime in the parking meter, took off her coat, and began to stroll down the avenue.

She walked slowly, her head held high, her eyes on the vision that had come to her in the sea-green privacy of her bath. The high sun fell like balm on her body. She heard a strange, distant music. And she went as she was bidden, dignified and proper, the slogan presented to all the world.

And everyone noticed. Pedestrians stopped and stared. Shoppers poured out of the stores and stood crowded in doorways and beside buildings to see her. Cars stopped in the streets, and even on rooftops the gasping public appeared. Mrs. Winkler was astonished. The reception was greater than she had imagined. She nodded happily at her audience. Her face seemed to hold a beatific light.

I got all the way up one side of Fifth Avenue—from Leuten's Place to D Street—and halfway down the other. Then the officer arrested me," Mrs. Winkler told the judge modestly. "And then there were those pictures in the paper."

"I saw those," the judge said in his papery voice. His blue eyes searched Mrs. Winkler's face sharply. The long finger and thumb played at the bridge of his nose. Then the long hands rested fingertips to fingertips in a high angle against the black expanse of his chest. His mouth pulled to a thoughtful pursing. Below him the placid clerk waited, stopped with his airy scribbling.

"Have you ever had visions before, Mrs. Winkler?" the judge inquired at last.

"No, Your Honor," Mrs. Winkler answered. She stood before him in the rosy-red Davidow suit, her cheeks brightened to almost the same color. Her slim hands trembled a little over the turtle bag. "I'm really a very ordinary person," she said, her words falling softly as rose petals. "I don't know where the vision came from. But I couldn't refuse to do what I should, Your Honor. I did what I was told to do. One has to do the right things in this world, Your Honor," Mrs. Winkler whispered, and blushed. "War is not necessary, sir," she said.

Up in his high golden box the judge sat in silence. Behind him the great white wall lifted like the wing of a temple. Below the clerk's pen scratched away.

"We all want peace, Mrs. Winkler," the judge intoned. He was leaning toward her, looking at her with mercy and with kindness. His sweetly boned hands lay at rest on the edge of his shining box. "But there are ways to perpetrate peace that fall within the requirement of law and order, Mrs. Winkler. We cannot allow private visions to lead us into bizarre, unorthodox and indeed illegal behavior."

Mrs. Winkler was gazing fixedly at him where he leaned splendidly black against the great expanse of pure white wall, and slowly her face grew full of light, transfused with hope. Her mouth bloomed with a glorious smile. Her eyes were lighted heavens.

"Oh, Judge, Your Honor," she breathed. "Oh, Judge, look."

His blue eyes met hers, sharpened into incredulity, into skepticism, into perception. Slowly he turned and gazed at the wall that stretched wide and high behind him. His face took on a look of bewilderment and one of intent listening, and then one of mystery and of exaltation. Mrs. Winkler knew that the judge, black-robed, silver-haired, hawk-nosed, heard as she heard that astonishing, compelling music, that his blue eyes took in the same flaming vision she saw, that he felt himself lifted on great, wheeling wings of sound.

"Well, Mrs. Winkler," the judge muttered when he at last turned back to face her. "I pronounce you guilty." He rapped his gavel smartly, nodded sagely at the clerk, levied the fine.

Then together they went, grave as two children, the judge in his black robes, Mrs. Winkler in her rosy-red suit, out along the avenue to the nearest art store. There they bought two cans of rosy, antique-gilt paint, some stencil patterns in large Gothic letters, and two sable-haired brushes, and returned once more to the chamber where the white wall waited.

October

I

Michael is gone. Is gone. Again.

Everytime he disappears we think the worst.

Oh, has he gone again? My wife says, coming from sleep. Her face is pale. She smiles, as if it is only a nuisance. Naughty.

The dawn came. The whole world coming into light as if under strange seas. Already then, he was gone. The empty bed. Empty bathroom. Empty kitchen. Michael's gone, we said. He's gone again. The clock objectively coolly starkly: six-ten.

The attic? she says. Michael likes high places. We pretend. It is a game. We go up the stairs in the angled darkness, call Michael, Michael? Down to the cellar Michael never likes. Musty with shades, cobwebbed furnace. He is not there.

Empty porch. Empty garage.

The street? she says. The street. Is empty.

Down the avenue the maples hold the dark night in leafiness, keeping the shape of themselves away from analytic light. In the gutters the shadows run darkly. A late cat slithers on his own black image from darkness to darkness across the glittering cobalt paving.

Of course, we say together. The tree. A high place. Out again into the dew-tangled grass, crossing the beaded blades on careless eager feet, we come to the tree. A high oak. Older than old surrounding houses. Spreads heavy rough-hided limbs high over yard and high house. Three sparrows scatter skyward toward breaking blue.

Michael, Michael. The whole leafy landscape of tunnels and caves holds nothing but its own green leafings, blue spiderwebs, abandoned nests.

Once when Michael was gone. A long time, only two then, how long we cried and peered! Wandered calling his name. Our hearts like livers in our chests. He was on the high ridge of roof. Three stories high. Sitting there grinning. Thinking what? That we were foolish hunting him? He was smarter, hiding there? But how did he get there? she cried, anger, relief. Up the tree, probably, out on the stretching limb, across to the treacherous shingled edge. Sitting comfy on the high peak above the crying hunting neighborhood. Michael!

And now the clock spreads its baffled hands. Nine-fifteen. The word is out. The neighbors come. Exhilarated!

Gone again? That little fellow gone again? Mr. Hardie: broad red sour face. Likes U.S. flags. On his front door, back door. In his car windows. Leaning smartly redwhite&blue from the front of his hardware store! Because Commies are destroying the world. If they can. Put up your flags or we will all fall down. Dominoes in a black militant row. Mr. Hardie studies the victories of Commies, the plots of UNICEF. Saturdays he washes and waxes his black Buick. Every Saturday Michael watches him. Sunday Mr. Hardie drives the black Buick to church. Slowly. Three blocks. Mrs. Hardie sits in the passenger seat. He pink-edged eyes on the disciplined road. He noise pointing. Properly. Michael sits on the curb. Waves to them, his friends.

Gone again, that little devil! How long's he been gone this time? Checked with the police? Heartiness comes over Hardie. The red sourness dims. Plotting bright in his squinty eyes. Have you tried the closets?

The closets, she says. Yes, the closets. Third time. I go with her knowing the emptiness of dark long closets. Thick with dusty clothes, with old winters. Not there. The dryer? she says. Her eyes to my eyes sneaky with doubt. No Michael.

Not in the dryer. Not in the hamper. Not in the yellow plastic rag basket. Where?

The clock, wrist wall and mantle. Ten-thirty-four.

I'll check the neighborhood, Mr. Hardie rumbles. Belly forward, off he goes.

One after another they come: neighbors. Helpful, eager.

Oh that poor child. How he does torment us. Mrs. Christiansen: seventy-four. Her hands cling together, the veins blue over the ridging handbones. Skin like egg-membrane.

Oh he is all right, we say. Once he was gone six hours. Once five.

The clocks. Ticking. Coming to eleven. Hurrying the morning. Already four and one half hours.

Down the avenue the children cry, Michael! Their shouts bright triangles hung out for carnival. A game. A game. It is. Only a game. Michael is king who holds the kingdom of secrets. Shivering secrets. Hidden! To be sought for, discovered, secret! Michael, they cry, running like tossed beads into the growing day. The sun scatters yellow on the blue-green street, on the cool grass. Michael! He is the maker of games. The hider they seek, the secreter who hides! Down the yellow-slivered lanes, the wide fields. Mi-chael!

> Once when he was gone. A far hunting. Up and down avenues. In and out houses. Stores. Fields. Library. Trees. Over the day a church bell clanged. Tongues of jangled tempers. Bell-falls of broken day. And afterward in the church. The priest with Michael. Found. In the belfry. Swinging on bell ropes. The black priest: scholarly glasses glinting. The small boy: laughing. Pulling smiles from pale Father's face. Laughing. While mothers fathers playmates friends and cops worried.

Now we have walked, walked. Called and called. Our eyes like cross winds in winter. Will not share. Fear to share.

Coffee. Here now. Have some coffee. Mrs. Capello, mother of eight, brings us a cup. Hands like asbestos. Face like an old purse. Sandwich beside the cup. It's a worry, a child like that.

I'd give him a beating once he gets home. Her eyes like old shirts. Tongue flannel with slow doubt. Eight of her own. None lost.

Bread in our mouths. Locks on our throats.

He'll come home. When he wants to. He'll come back. The girl: long hair closes over round dreams in her face. Her child on her hip. Her light hand filters afternoon air. Kids like that. They always come back. She understands. Blows away crisis like dandelion seed. Dreams are true, her vague eyes say. In the garage behind the Capello house she nurtures dreams. With candles and slow smoke. Michael will come. Incantations. Oms.

Yes we say. Yes of course.

And the policeman comes. All step back for him. Space. Gruff as a billy goat. Sure as a club. Questions like ordered bricks. Eyes: blue triangles. We'll find him. Have him home soon.

Yes. Yes. Yes. Yes. We know. We know. Her mouth like a leaf. Her eyes turn for a safe place.

How many places. How many trees. How many stores. How many ditches. Like a vacuum cleaner bag the long day tears. Dusk falling. Shredding to darkness, droppings of night. Eyes full of trees, head full of tunnels. Feet going, going. Throat scraped for last sounds. Michael? Is gone.
Michael?
Michael?
How dark?

II

Chief Buchanigni. Metal star on blue-black chest. Eyes blue-black. Opaque for safety. Bulletin: all points. His hands like good baskets. Outside the night. Uniform darkness. The stars. All points. Are they holes? Michael asked. Holes in the darkness. All points.

Search party. Hills. Canyons. Arroyos. Woods. Hedges.

The long uneven slopes of grasses. Bloodhounds. Nose to earth down the long gray dawns. Nose to earth. Nose knows. Nothing. Nothing knows. Michael is gone. Dog search man search heart search.

Reservoirs.

> *Morning. Blades of silver dropping through black trees. Sky like a great fish back: scaled with cloud. The wind in trees. Sun, fishing soft shadows. Pittosporum, laurel; daisies, marigold; juniper, redwood—dew-strung, web-strung.*

No word. No word.

The phone is a black hole.

In her eyes I see my eyes. Like blown eggs. Hollow shells of no seeing. Why do we not hear? she whispers. Words like the phone's dead wire. No answer. No connection. A thin buzzing on the wires of hearing. Wait. Only Michael must come. Must.

I keep seeing his feet, she says. His little feet. Those small bones. Tiny bending bones. The footprints. Wet from the bath. Prints. All over I see them. Footprints. His perfect little footprints.

Yes, I say.

> *Perfect prints. Prince prints. How beautiful his feet. How beautiful upon the bathroom floor the small feet.*

They will bring news, I say, good news.

His feet, she says. His little feet.

All over the land: all points.

Her eyes: walls against walls.

Her body: grave.

Michael, waiting we die.

III

October. Over the long land fires burn. Smoke billows over the Sierra spine.

Ants crawl. Invade us. Cover the cupboard counters, fill the sink with crawling. The yellow jackets swing in the air, trailing long dry concerts. Flies blue the air.

Rain. Oh, we need rain.

In the bed. Her body is cold. Back to back, two icicles in the hot October darkness.

The Hartwells are getting a divorce, Mrs. Christiansen reports, her hands wringing. At night we hear them. Shouting. The bangs of things thrown.

The Forrester boy lies in the hospital. Thieving. Shot.

Mrs. Capello's hippie girl renter is in jail. On a drug charge. A social worker came, took the wailing child.

War in the Far East.

War in the Near East.

Murders in Petaluma.

Gang rape in Mendocino.

It is Halloween. Smoky avenue. Stained skies. Dim windows, candles gutter. At the door they come, ghosts of children, spooks and goblins and monsters and crooks. Their wrenched plastic faces. Their greedy hands. She will not come down. She cannot see them. I put in their fingers the sweets, buying peace.

He is gone.

Is.

Gone.

Michael?

The Secret

Ella and Rudolph had a secret. It occupied the apartment like the summer air, so close and stifling that it seemed hard for Ruth to breathe, and hard to think clearly. Ruth saw the secret in the looks slanting from Ella's eyes to Rudolph's and back again, and in the loose thin smiles that hid their teeth. Even after Rudolph left for work the secret would be there, lurking in the shadows under the curved and fluted furniture, filling the dark triangles behind the black paneled doors.

Now Rudolph stood in the kitchen doorway. The sun from the hallway window touched the front of his blue uniform. The brass buttons gleamed against the cloth. His hat hung far back on his head, and his high forehead shone in the sunlight. He lifted one long, loose-knuckled hand and waved. The fingers flapped like knotted strings.

"Bye-bye, Ruthie." His laughter huffed through his long nose. No sound came out of his wide grinning mouth. He looked past Ruth at Ella, who stood behind her, soft and puffy in her flower-spattered robe. One of his heavy eyelids slid down over the glinting eye, and sent the secret to Ella to keep till he got home again.

Then he went, shutting out the hall's sunlight as he closed the door. Ella got up and drew the kitchen shades all the way down to keep out the day's heat. Ruth could feel the room closing around them. She wanted to go home.

Last Sunday they had sat under the branches of the willow tree in the back yard at home, sipping iced tea from her mother's high narrow glasses. Then they had seemed jolly and kind. Rudolph had smiled and smiled under the wash of green light. He listened to everything her father said as though he were hearing a funny story, and sometimes he winked at Ruth as though she surely knew what amused him. When her mother said, Oh, have one more, Ella laughed and lifted another of the walnut bars from the cut-glass plate. Her fingers curled like a doll's. She opened her pouty mouth and took such dainty bites that her lips never touched the cookie's edge. Behind her, the peonies leaned their weighty heads as though to watch.

Ruth sat on the cushiony grass at their feet and looked at them, not hearing their words, but only the party noises falling on Sunday air.

Ella looked down at her, tossed her head like an actress.

"Rudy," she cried, "look at Ruthie! Look at her, Rudy. Have you ever seen such eyes? Isn't she a darling, Rudy?"

And Ruth smiled back at them, loving their gay mysterious ways. Then Ella leaned out from her chair. Her flowered dress fell away from the deep white place of her bosom. Her smile lit her rosy face.

"Wouldn't sweet Ruthie like to come and stay with poor lonesome Ella?"she cried. Her question sounded like a song, and she seemed very sad. "Poor Ella and Rudolph haven't got a little girl, at all," she said.

Behind her Rudolph bobbed his head and grinned sorrowfully. It had seemed, almost, that they were gay and needy children. Ruth had felt grown up and kindly and had consented to come.

But she hadn't known. She hadn't guessed. At first, when Rudolph had bent his long frame down to her and crouched beside her like a great grasshopper, she had thought he had something special to tell her. But whatever he said to her in his sleek whisper, it was never what Ruth expected to hear. He seemed to laugh at her then for what she didn't know, and what he wouldn't tell.

She hated the secret now. Could she tell Ella that she wanted to go home?

The breakfast dishes were cleared away. Ella was bustling through the dining room, running a gray rag over the curves and knobs of the furniture. The dust-rag smelled of naptha. Could Ruth tell her? Could she say it right out loud in this dusky room where the secret climbed the air like honeysuckle? Or would she sound frightened, baby-like, rude?

A little sound flew from Ella's lips. She rubbed the animal feel of the high-backed chairs. It seemed impossible to say anything at all into that humming, and Ruth watched Ella finish the chairs and go on down the hall to her bedroom.

Ruth went into the living room and sat down on the davenport. She picked up the newspaper from the glass-topped coffee table and looked at it. Around her the room was dim and quiet. It was different from any place she had been. The furniture gave off what light there was. The tables and chests shone in the corners and against the walls. The silky covers on the chairs gleamed softly. Ruth felt as though she were in a deep upholstered cave. On top of the high, curved chest stood the china hen and the gilt clock. The clock tocked busily. It dropped its hours with a tinkle like falling glass, and whenever Ruth looked at it, it seemed to lie about the time. It was always later than she had thought, or much, much earlier. In the curved mirror over the chest, Ruth saw an image of herself, a stranger, tiny, tiny with a head too big for the squashed and crippled body, the watching eyes swollen and dark. The mirror tipped, turned. The clock sang.

Ruth jumped up and pushed through the pressing air out to the front porch. Summer bugs bumped against the screens. The day's light poured into her face like wind. She leaned her forehead against the screen and breathed of the green air. She looked down on the plots of grass in front of the high houses that lined the street. The grass patches were like

squares on a game board. The houses, giant blocks. A pair of
yellow moths wavered through the sunlight below.

Ruth knew they wanted to please her. Ella bought her
marshmallow cookies and gum and always asked what Ruth
liked best to eat. One night Rudolph had brought her a
coloring book and the next a long wandering airy balloon.
And there was the little doll. Ella had bought it in the dime
store and Ruth liked the doll, it was so plump and seri-
ous-looking.

If she did not have to play Rudolph's chicken game it
would probably be all right. At home she earned her allowance by taking out the garbage and by picking up her room.
Here, each morning, she had to carry the stool over to the
high chest, climb up on it and find the pennies lying beside
the china hen. Rudolph and Ella watched while she got
them, looked at each other with sliding eyes, laughed. Ruth
thought chickens and eggs simple enough, and their laughter
made her feel awkward and embarrassed. What it meant to
them, she did not know. It was part of their secret.

The porch door swished open. Ella came carrying the little
doll and her big sewing satchel. "What's Ruthie doing out
here all alone?" she cried. She let her feet go out from under
her and thumped down into the wicker rocker. She sighed.
"Today we must sew a dress for Ruthie's dolly. The fat dolly
has to have some clothes, yes, she does!"

Ella's smile wound into her cheeks. Her eyes flicked like
fish to the corners to look at Ruth.

Ruth felt the color rising into her face. She bowed her
head and studied the black pyramided pattern of the straw
rug.

Ella saw that she blushed. She tossed her head back. Her
bosom trembled with laughter. Ruth's face grew hotter. Her
mouth plumped itself into a pout. Ella stopped laughing.

"Oh, my." She blinked her wet eyes and rummaged in the
satchel. "Let's see, we have to find dolly a pretty piece of
goods."

She held out a red polka dot and a blue dimity and Ruth chose the blue. Ella folded the cloth and snipped out the shape of a dress. She slipped a length of thread through her needle, started a seam. Her needle flew in and out of the cloth. Small straight stitches followed after. She finished one seam and gave the dress to Ruth, showing her where to sew. Ruth worked cautiously. She put the needle down on one side of the cloth and pushed it up through the other. Each stitch was a different size. They staggered crookedly along the edge of the cloth.

Ella was sewing a bonnet. Her curly head tipped from side to side like a bobbing marigold. A wind moved and stirred the poplars that grew near the edge of the porch. The green light coming through the wall of leaves wavered across Ruth's sewing. The leaves whispered, Ruth grew contented and sleepy.

Suddenly the poking needle struck Ruth's finger. She jumped, dropped her sewing. Her eyes stung. On the tip of the pricked finger, a small globe of bright blood rose, swelled, broke. A wavering trail of red dropped down the length of her finger.

Ella jumped up and nestled the finger in both hands.

"Oh, the poor little girl! She hurt her finger! Oh poor Ruthie, such a bad hurt!"

Ruth pulled the finger from Ella's hands and sucked on it. Ella tumbled all the scraps from her satchel onto the chair. She tore a strip from the length of white cloth. Ruth held out the finger and Ella wound a bandage thickly over the tip and down the whole finger in close spirals. She crossed the ends of the strip over the back of Ruth's hand and tied them in a small neat bow at the wrist.

"There. That's better," she said and sighed. Her bosom rose and fell. She gave Ruth the rocker. She sat in one of the straight chairs and began to sew again. As she sewed she sang comfortingly.

Ruth pushed herself in the rocker. She held the swathed

hand nested in her lap. The fingertip seemed to have a small heart of its own. Its sturdy beat demanded Ruth's attention and she was glad that Ella's crooning covered the silence of the apartment.

At five o'clock, when Rudolph's high, thin whistle wound up the back stairs ahead of him, Ella was cooking dinner.

"Hello," he said as he came in, his wide saucer-shaped smile lifting his cheeks and squeezing at his watching eyes, and at that the sleeping secret wakened.

He went to Ella where she tended the porkchops frying on the stove. He stood behind her and wrapped his arms around her. He buried his nose and chin in the folds of her pink neck. Ella giggled. Then she looked sideways at Ruth, abruptly poked her elbow into Rudolph's chest, giggled again.

Ruth went into the living room. She looked at the morning paper. After a while Rudolph followed. He paused by the lamp table to pick up the unfinished cigar that had lain in the ash tray all day. He sucked at it, lighting it, his eyes almost shut. He looked past the sprays of smoke at Ruth, grinning to himself. Then he saw the bandage.

"Well," he whispered, bending close to her. The smell of his cigar stung Ruth's nose. "What happened to our little girl?"

Ruth looked down at the big bandage.

"I stuck my needle in it."

Rudolph unhinged himself upward. His laugh chuffed through his nose.

"Stuck your needle in it? Why, that's no way to treat my little girl!" He slapped his knee. His laughter hissed through clouds of smoke.

Then Ella came. Her face was like a strawberry from being over the stove.

"The fat dolly has a dress now, Rudy," she said. Their eyes rolled like marbles toward one another and their smiles were alike. "Show Rudolph the dolly, Ruthie."

Ruth went out to the porch and picked up the little doll. She turned it in her hands. The round face was framed by the bonnet and the long blue dress covered all the hard small body except for the curved arms. Ruth tiptoed to the couch at the end of the porch and tucked the doll under the pile of pillows.

"Ruthie!" Ella called.

Ruth did not move. The leaves of the poplars beside the porch turned from green to silver.

"Ruthie, come to dinner. Dinner's ready, Ruthie."

Ruth turned, went back into the still apartment, and her arms hung stiff with guilt at her sides.

When supper was done they sat again on the porch. The poplars grew bluer and bluer in the rosy evening light. Rudolph read the paper, Ella embroidered red flowers on a yellow apron, and Ruth lay on the straw rug and played solitaire with cards slicker and stiffer than any she got to play with at home. She felt very lonesome. Ella hummed, the newspaper crackled, the poplar murmured. Ruth did not tell them that she wanted to go home. Cigar smoke twined whitely on darkening air. The first stars came out and Ella and Rudolph put aside their amusements. They sighed toward one another, smiled softly at Ruth, got up to go in.

When Ruth lay on the davenport, alone at last in the dark of the living room, tucked into the folded sheet like a pencil in a narrow envelope, tears slid from the sides of her eyes into the hard pillow under her head. She had meant to tell them how she wanted to go home.

She awakened because she was frightened but she didn't know why. She thought perhaps it was what she had dreamed, but then she felt it was something else. The strange room in which she lay was not altogether dark, and it was not light, either. She knew that the clock had just chimed, and now its beat sounded knowing and pleased. She felt that she was not alone in the room. Something was watching her. Something seemed to breathe the air she breathed, to look out from the dark secret places she dared not look into. She could not move and could not close her eyes. Her heart thumped and gave her away. Her knees were locked and aching.

Who was there?

Rudolph? Was he there, watching? Why did he watch her so?

The secret. Because of the secret. If she lay very still nothing would notice her, nothing would happen. But the thumping in her chest was loud. In her ears little words were saying, I want to go home, I want to go home.

Suddenly the clocked bleated. Rudolph's alarm blazed through the rooms. Ruth jumped, sat upright. She saw, then, the whole apartment had grown quite light, that everything in the room—the furniture, the drapes, the lamps, vases and figurines—stood in their usual places and were harmless. Nothing else was there.

Then she heard the sounds of Rudolph's slippers on the thick carpet of the hall. Quickly, Ruth lay down and turned toward the back of the davenport as though she were asleep.

He went slowly and slyly across the room to the high chest and back again to the archway.

"I wonder," he cried in a loud high voice, "if the chickie brought any pennies for our little girl last night? Maybe she was a naughty girl yesterday and the chickie said no pennies for that little girl." He paused, called in a louder and higher voice. "Do you suppose that happened, Ella?"

It was the signal. She would have to play the game. In brief despair Ruth wondered how a voice that came so far out of a man could be so high. She got up. She got the round plump footstool and carried it over to the chest. The clock tocked coolly above her. Her legs felt uncertain. She climbed up on the stool and picked up the two pennies lying against their

reflections beside the fat china hen. Behind her Rudolph
laughed softly. The chuffs in his nose were like a distant train.

"Ella, come and see what the chickie brought our little
girl!"

Ella came through the hall door, her eyes still squeezing
themselves together with sleep. She clucked foggily as she
fumbled to tie the belt of her robe.

"Well, well. What a lucky little girl!" She yawned.

But Ruth had made a discovery. She had the pennies out
on her flat, opened hand and she looked down at the finger
and its bandage.

"It hurts," she wailed. "I want to go home."

Rudolph was bent over her, his face wrinkled with surprise.

"What? What's this?"

"Oh, the poor little thing," Ella answered, wide-eyed and
tender.

Ruth stood before them, quivering and snuffling until
Rudolph lifted her up into his arms and carried her to the
kitchen and set her on the high stool.

"We'd better take that bandage off and see what's going
on."

His long twiggy fingers undid the bow and wound away
the strip of cloth. The finger came out with pink marks
spiraling over the skin. Rudolph looked at it soberly. Then
quick glances flew between Rudolph and Ella. A shadow fell
between them. A sign of cold understanding went from eye
to eye.

"I think my stomach hurts," Ruth said then, and gulped
helplessly, caught in her apprehension and her lies.

"There, there, little girl," Rudolph crooned in a high,
false voice. "It's going to be all right, you'll see. We'll be all
fixed up in no time."

He filled the teakettle with water and set it on the stove.
He rummaged in the cupboard and took out a blue-speckled
bowl and poured baking soda into it.

They wrapped Ruth in a blanket with a warm rubber bottle against her stomach, set her in the rocker. She soaked her finger in the blue bowl set on the stool beside her.

Then Rudolph was late for work and hurried out the door with a piece of toast in his hand for his breakfast.

Ruth sat in the rocker wrapped in the cocoon of the blanket and ate the breakfast Ella brought her on a tray. All morning she soaked her finger in bowlfuls of warm water while Ella did the chores. She thought peacefully of her mother and father and the plain wonders of the home she could now return to.

They had lunch of soup and little triangular sandwiches, and after that Ella went into a dark closet behind one of the high black doors in the living room. She came out blowing dust from a strangely-shaped wooden box. Ruth saw that there were strings stretched across the top of the box past a small hole in the middle, and there was a panel of buttons that looked like several rows of doorbells. Ella sat down on the davenport beside Ruth and placed the box on her knees.

"What is it?" Ruth asked.

"It's an autoharp. Listen." Ella ran her fingers over the strings. A sound thin and light as the first fall of rain spilled into the room. Ella stopped and ran the bottom of her apron over the keys. She looked into Ruth's face.

"It's beautiful," Ruth whispered.

Ella smiled and tipped her curly head to one side. Her fingers moved quickly from button to button on the white panel. Ruth listened to the melody fall in small bell tones.

"Put your finger here, Ruthie." Ella pointed to one of the pearly buttons. Her pink hand closed over Ruth's, moved it. A small clear note rocked from the string. "Now here, and here, and now here," and the bright chimes stumbled out into the room.

When Rudolph's whistle sounded in the back hall, Ruth

looked up from the autoharp on the table before her, surprised
that he was already home. He came in, his hat far back on
his head and a napkin-wrapped ice cream cone in his hand.

"How's our little girl? Well enough to eat a little ice
cream?" His smile was soft, solemn. Melting ice cream ran
over the napkin and fell in fat circles on the floor.

Rudolph asked her courteously how her finger felt, whether she had had a nice day, whether she enjoyed the autoharp,
and was packed and ready to go home. He seemed sad and
formal in his attentiveness. Ella told him she could play
Twinkle Little Star. He was astonished at her precociousness.
She had to perform for him. She went stumblingly through
the little song. He marveled generously.

Then without warning, just now when she had almost
forgotten to be wary, the bargain came.

Rudolph leaned across the table. His eyes were dark and
cold. They were like water under ice. They held Ruth's so
that she could look nowhere but into their darkness.

"Now that Ruthie is well again wouldn't she like to stay
a little longer?" The murmur was soft and unrelenting.
Around them the air was still and waiting.

It did not seem possible, it did not seem enough, to say No.
It seemed that something would happen to her if she refused.
The waiting, looming silence would burst into accusations
and pointing fingers and she would surely be punished and
denied escape. In the shadowy apartment Ruth felt lost.
There was no one there to help her.

She knew that if she said Yes, she would stay, they would
suddenly break into their jolly banter and rollicking laughter,
and the secret-filled activity would sweep around her once
more, circling her like perfumed vines.

She drew a long quavering breath. She took her eyes from
Rudolph's and looked down at her hands clinging to one
another in her lap. She so longed for her mother that she felt
compressed into the shape of one mute and crippled word.

"I want to go home," she said, despairing and exhausted, unable to yield to them, unable to submit.

And it was that simply finished. They turned from her as though it mattered not at all. Their faces became smooth and remote. Rudolph called her father and told him that Ruth wanted to go home then rather than on Sunday. During supper Rudolph and Ella chattered together as though Ruth were not there. They offered her portions of food with cool politeness and did not notice her lack of appetite.

After supper Ruth stood on the porch in the hot golden evening and watched for her father's car. She felt tired, as though she had spent the day on a hot beach. When her parents came, looking strangely new and familiar, Ruth felt herself filled with a tide of love and gratitude.

But when her father came up the stairs and greeted Ella and Rudolph, he looked at her as he did when she had been a bit rude. His smile was a little distant. There was a chastising reserve in his eyes. That need for him pouring from Ruth was stopped midway, checked by his unexpected disapproval. She looked at her mother, uncertain, confused.

Her mother bent over her, kissed her, put her curved palm against Ruth's forehead.

"Well, Ruth Ann," she murmured in the remembered comforting croon, "are you feeling better, dear?"

Then she rose, turned to Ella, laughed lightly.

"It's hard," she said lightly, as though Ella must share her amusement, "the first time away from home."

Ruth felt betrayed. She looked into her mother's face trying to understand. Why didn't they see? Didn't they know how it had been there?

Her father was jerking his chin positively, puffing intently on his pipe as he argued with the blandly smiling Rudolph, and her mother and Ella were chattering vividly together and paying no attention to the men.

"Well, it was as fine a string of fish as I've ever caught," her father was saying. His chin lifted and he tapped his pipe on the frail glass ashtray.

"But you really ought to take a couple of days and get up to Grand Marais." Rudolph nodded authoritatively, smiling and smiling. "That's real fishing, up there."

"But don't add the sugar till the eggs are very light," her mother admonished Ella.

"Oh, but they'll never be as good as yours!" Ella shook her head in joy and dismay.

Then all at once Ruth knew, astonished, that her own parents knew the secret, that they kept it and guarded it. They seemed then, not her protectors, at all.

Ruth watched and listened. She saw that they were all playing a kind of game, a game she didn't know. She couldn't tell what their goals were, or what their maneuvers meant. She thought of the game children played—the game in which they followed and taunted the chosen witch—followed with a gay and nonchalant bravery, full of both joy and anxiety, uncertain sometimes as to which was real, the fun or the fear.

Ruth held her plastic covered suitcase on her knees and the doll under her elbow, hanging on to them as if their hard surfaces could help. When the coffee and cookies and visiting were finished and her parents ready to go, her father lifted her in his arms and started down the steps. He held her close and Ruth felt his forgiveness. But she could not yet forgive them.

Just as her father took the last curved steps, Rudolph, holding Ella close against him, put on his loose grin, winked. He burrowed his chin in Ella's plump neck and in his glinting eye the secret glittered. Ruth knew it would pursue her even when she got home.

Ladybug, Fly Away Home

1

‗‗‗‗‗ CONTEMPLATION. *The ablution has been made,*
‗ ‗ *But not yet the offering.*
‗ ‗ *Full of trust they look up to him.*

—I Ching

2

Such a dream: through the house, looking for Samuel. His red hair. He is not here and has left no message. I am extremely disappointed, but I am not at all sure why. What has he to tell me, anyway? What has he to do with my life?

Through cracks of the floorboards I see a red glowing. Is it fire? Yes, yes. I see small flames, yellow, now, and lapping. Someone must call the fire department. Who will call? Is there no one to help? Will the house burn down? Burn down?

3

There she is, sitting in the back of the classroom, apart from the other students, asserting her difference, her superiority, by the islanding empty desks. Laura, her round face shining, glazed pink. An angelic look, as if she has transcended the earthly. Shawl over her shoulders covering new-sprouted wings. But I know better. Her eyes reveal suffering. She is suffering so that the heartbeats of her pain send rosiness to the skin. Yes, she looks quite beautiful. But that steady gaze is demanding, it is deep with hunger. What does she want of me? What?

Her need, her need.

Haven't I listened enough?

She is twenty-four. *I cannot cope with life,* she tells me. She had a miserable affair with a black man. *Everything that went wrong he blamed on my being white. But I loved him, I loved him.* Crazy then, she wandered. Went home to live with her father, who is, she reports, crazy himself. He tries to fit life to his idea of himself. He is idealistic, but cruel. He will not help her. He does not love her. *Yes,* she says, plucking long threads from the tattered dirty shawl, *he is mad.*

I've taken a job, she told me on Tuesday, *with this lawyer and his wife. I'm supposed to be a sort of companion to the children. Help them with their homework, help them be creative. I thought it would be a good job, I mean, I thought I would be part of the family. But the little boy, he's crazy.*

What do you mean, crazy? I ask. Yes, I try to understand.

I mean he runs around all the time, throws things. He can't sit still. He shouts things, Fuck you, Go to hell, you bitch. *I mean he's really terrible.*

There are three other children, five cats, two dogs, snakes. They make her do dishes, wash clothes. She is only a slave there. They do not pay her.

You must talk to them, Laura.

Yes, she assents, head bowed, fingers working the gray strands.

If they are still unfair, you'll have to find another job.

Yes, she assents. *I thought I'd be part of the family. At Shabbos dinner they didn't ask me to sit down. I had to stay in the kitchen.* She lifts her eyes, stares at me, tears rising.

Does she believe I am wise?

My psychiatrist says I'm paranoid. She watches me, close as conscience.

Are you? I ask.

Maybe. The brown curls fall over a forehead like Athena's. *I have no place else to go.*

So now on Thursday at 11:50 her dark eyes fix on me, full of request. But the other students surround me, make appointments, plead for more time on their papers. And then Laura is gone. I tell myself she should have waited. I would have asked her to lunch.

4

Ardys is sitting at my desk, a thick stack of student papers at her elbow. She lifts the top paper, opens it, looks at the back page, writes on the grade sheet, places the paper to her left. Her face is pale and she looks very tired.

What happened? I ask.

They moved him to Sonoma County Jail. For his own good, they say. To keep him away from that prisoner who got him into the brawl. Now it will take hours to go visit. Her lips lift on one side, making her face twist.

She keeps lifting papers, making immaculate marks on the squared sheet. *He complains: "Why did this happen to me?" It's the third time. Drunk driving. A felony this time, he's eighteen. At least they're having him see a psychiatrist.*

The girl is lying in the hospital. The column of grades lengthens under Ardys' efficient hands.

It is awful, she mutters, *how one's children work against one's happiness. By ourselves Cappy and I are fine. Something like this pulls us apart.*

Suddenly her head drops forward, as if its stalk had snapped. The fingers of both hands grasp the skull, the hair gray and tumbled over the knuckles. She weeps: *What right have children to do such things? What right have they to ruin their parents' lives?*

I put my arm around her narrow shoulders, I go out in the hall and get her a cup of coffee. Outside the dusty March window a scatter of starlings flicker across a pale sky, and by the library steps the crooked old plum tree holds up to the lemon light a great cluster of bloom.

How does one comfort? What is there to do?

5

Because the door is open, I walk into Gerald's office. But Bridget is there. The silence is obvious pause in argument. Bridget looks at me, and I see I am made judge. Tommy had to stay home from school, a fever. The babysitter has another job. Bridget has an appointment with her mother's lawyer. *I can't call him, now,* she insists. *He's a busy man.* She lifts a hand, pushes the red wayward curls from her cheek, pushing away anxiety.

Gerald is ruffled, he feels put upon.

I can't miss the Senate meeting, that whole business of English requirements comes up today.

Bridget believes her business over the estate and her mother's health is more important. Gerald looks at me, martyred. I understand. Ten years in the department, living hand in glove. Bridget will explode into one of her tantrums. Famous. Her absolute lack of restraint, her shouting. One sees it coming, the flush riding up the sides of her neck, the handsome mouth stretching.

Gerald tries bargaining, pink-cheeked, boyish with shame.

Could you stay home till two? I could get home by two.

Bridget sputters: *Gerald, you always expect . . .*

I leave; no arbiter, no judge.

Other boys of ten could be left alone an hour or two. But Tommy on a calm morning in autumn dropped lit matches into the gasoline tanks of two parked cars. Astonished, Gerald and Bridget take on guilt.

What did I do wrong? Bridget plaintively queries, but expects reassurance.

Now Gerald steps into my office. He wants me to go to the Senate meeting, speak for the department. He gives me sheaves of papers. He stands then at the doorway and under the neon light his fine long nose makes a sharp knifelike shadow over his mouth and chin. The look he gives is tentative: should he flee? should he speak?

What can I do about Bridget? he quavers. *What can I do?*

Does he expect an answer? Does he believe I know? They are all seeing a therapist, all three. I look down at the page of poetry where light slides off the words: "Nothing is so beautiful as Spring/When weeds, in wheels, shoot long and lovely and lush;/ . . . What is all this juice and all this joy?/A strain of the earth's sweet being in the beginning/In Eden garden."

Oh, Bridget, I say. *Bridget is all right.*

6

The phone rings. A Mrs. Bradford: high anxious voice. *Can't you change his grade? He's just not a creative person. He's very sweet, but he's just not creative. He can't write essays. I mean, he's really upset about this. He has to pass this course, he's going into forestry. I mean, Randy is very hot tempered. I'm afraid what he'll do, getting an F like that.* Yes. A fierce violent young man. Should I be afraid?

7

a) The Academic Senate accepts the Curriculum Committee's recommendation: all English requirements will be dropped. The vote is 9 to 2.

b) The Academic Senate accepts recommendations of the Sabbatical Leave Committee. Gered Hallowitz is granted sabbatical leave to explore alternative lifestyles. Aileen Weber is refused sabbatical leave for post-graduate studies at Cambridge.

c) Arnold Fell stands up and shouts: "When did balling in communes become more valuable to higher education than academic studies? What the hell is this institution coming to?"

d) Arnold Fell is gaunt. Bags under his eyes. Six months

ago his daughter, fourteen, disappeared hitchhiking home
from the skating rink. Weekends he haunts hippie hangouts,
bars. Puts up posters, advertises. Is she alive? Is she dead?

8

I long to be alone, but there he is, lying on the davenport. The
blue light of the television flickers over the fleshy white face,
the dull eyes, incongruous audacious moustache. *Hello, Steve,*
I give out. How long has he been here? Only two weeks? But
the third time, uninvited. He arrives on the doorstep, all his
belongings in his car. The car breaking down. His ears aching, his throat raw. Hungry. He comes from the east, drives
over plains and Rockies, lands on the doorstep. He needs us,
this classmate of a son not home. Needs our food, our home,
our ears.

He thinks he will work. He has registered at employment
agencies. He waits for the phone, for a job falling into his lap.
He sleeps till eleven, sits like that all day, staring at the
blinking screen. Eats yogurt and milk.

You should go to the firms, I tell him. *Apply at the banks in
person.*

He takes no advice. He wants to not rush, make the right
choice. Something will come along. Something is pending.
He will wait.

He follows me out to the kitchen. I begin to unload the
grocery bags. He watches, doleful, leaning elbows on counter
top.

Did the agency call you about the job? I ask.

His hands droop together, a pair of doves. *It was gone,* he
mutters.

Have you been out today? I query, as if his warden.

Guilty, suffering, he shakes his head. *Nope, been in all day.
My throat's bad again. I think it's my tonsils.*

I give him a chore: out of some convention, not need for
his assistance. He sets the table, goes to the piano. Last au-

tumn, he has informed me, he tried to commit suicide. Camus's Caligula is his hero. I protest, he becomes angry. He used to paint, wild confused canvases. Now he composes, plays hours at a time, dissonant, fortissimo, passionate hymns of himself.

Suffering over student papers, tomorrow's reading assignment, I cover my ears. Sometimes I demand silence. He feels abused.

He has a camera, worth $600, he says. He shows me self-portraits—profiles: solemn stares under thick brows, nude shots: the heavy upper body hairy from head to waist. *I may be an artist, someday,* he says.

Art has no value, he also insists. *Art is not worthwhile.*

He denies a contradiction, prefers absurdity.

Can I not send him away? What is it I owe him?

The piano is silent. The little vegetables are simmering in their pots, the pink steaks ready for the grill. I hear his steps sounding through the dining room, stopping at the kitchen door. I turn, wait.

Can I borrow some more money? he asks.

9

The ring of the phone rides through the steamy kitchen air. It is Laura. Her words choke with weeping.

Can I come to live with you? Just for a while? Three or four weeks?

I hold the phone away from my ear. On the stove the small pots beat their lids. Are they exploding? Is that fire flaring in the oven? The light fixture: sending out small sparks?

Is the house burning? Is the whole bright place closing about me? Who will send help?

The Follower

The house echoed, past the routine, interminable shows on television, to large unequalled silence. Arlene, the last of Maura and Fred Norwoods's children, had left on a September afternoon for the crowded separateness of college life. And then that solitude which Maura had felt encroaching all through the busyness of a blue July and a golden August came and took her prisoner.

She filled her days with activity—with gardening, reading, shopping, mornings of tennis, afternoons of bridge, whole days of volunteer work at the hospital. With all that she evaded the sense of loneliness. Until night came.

Then silence took on presence. It breathed in the long hall's shadows and in those dark unoccupied rooms where the boys had scuffled and tumbled their way toward departure, and huddled in that ruffled room where stiff-faced dolls looked out upon emptiness. The silence and the emptiness seemed to call up happier fuller times, and by contrast Maura's present aloneness grew almost too vivid to bear.

One October night after Maura had carefully eaten the dinner she did not want, she sat in the brightly-lit living room waiting for Fred to call from Bakersfield or Marysville or Sacramento. He would have finished his day also, and he would call because he knew her loneliness and also because he suffered his own kind of loneliness at day's end.

She sat in Fred's old leather chair. Her library books cluttered the polished table beside the chair. The mellow light of the tall brass lamp fell on the page of the Singer story. She pursued the story conscientiously, wanting to be caught up in it, to be completely distracted.

Suddenly she heard a sound. A strange sound, a muffled sort of call, as if a small child stirred and moaned in sleep. The book in Maura's hand dropped to the table. Her head lifted. She pushed herself forward in the leather chair, listening for the source of that sound, but heard nothing. Only a rush of wind at the west corner of the house, the brief rattle of a window pane, a creak of distressed wood.

Slowly she sank back into the deep cushions of the chair. But then it seemed to her that the empty house stretched upward and outward about her and became a vast silent spotlighted prison. To escape she rushed to the closet in the front hall. She took her jacket from its hanger and went out into the night.

A west wind occupied the avenue's high trees. The motion of leaf and limb amplified the wind's passage. Even the empty avenue was full of rushing. Pebble and leaf rustled and scurried with the wind. Maura began to walk. She walked against the wind, her face lifted to its disorder. Her skirt flapped about her knees, and the cool freshness made a burning in her cheeks. She walked swiftly, turning where avenues turned, no matter what direction.

After that the walks became nightly excursions. After dinner and dishes and the evening paper, Maura put on her jacket and set out into the darkness. She walked the winding avenues of the quiet suburban neighborhood, passing the lawn-shielded houses where lit windows informed of busy unknown lives. Hedges, yards, trees, streets were new and strange in the dark. Places passed held an air of mystery. She went along the avenues as a child walks through a carnival's aisles—intrigued, delighted, expectant.

She listened to the fine intrigue of night sounds—the hollowed barkings of distant dogs, the shaking hoot of a hidden owl, the stir of mouse or rat in the gutter's leaves. Once she

came upon a ponderous, unperturbed, waddling raccoon, and
once on a frosty night a sudden leafy stir and an abrupt silence
made her turn to the sight of a deer standing motionless and
watchful at the road's edge.

It was on a night in early November that Maura walked
out into the mists of a departing rain. Air moved against her
face in a sea of freshness. Fallen leaves lay like sleek dark fish
upon wet walks and road. The wetness made the night quiet.
No moth stirred. No cricket sang. She walked slowly along
the avenue and even the sound of her footsteps was subdued
by wetness.

She was at peace and thoughtful, and later she did not
know when she might first have known that someone else was
there. A sudden cold ran in rivers over her flesh and warned
her that someone or something walked behind her. And she
knew it had been there for some time.

Something followed her. It lurked in the fog and darkness,
and followed. It paced as she paced, paused when she paused,
lagged sometimes, then rushed silently and swiftly to catch
up, not overtaking her, not yet, only following, watching.

A dog, she thought, moving her breath past the beat in her
breast. It is a dog. She did not look behind her. She looked
ahead to the place where the curves of the road led to a street
light. But a dog, she thought, would accost, explore, accept
or attack. A dog would not lurk silently behind tree and
shrub. Not stalk. It was not a dog that followed.

She walked stiffly. She moved her legs and feet in uninter-
rupted rhythms as if the appearance of ignorance would
shield her from danger, as if the thing following her in the
dark behind her would not come closer if she gave no sign
of recognition. Did her footsteps falter? She knew she must
not allow them to falter. She went through the fog-hung,
dark sea-air toward the dim yellow eye of the streetlamp, her
thoughts breaking, fighting the grip of terror.

A cat, she told herself. Surely it is a cat. She reminded

herself how cats had followed her in the early dusks of her childhood, stalking in the night's darkness as if in deep jungles, rushing out from a tree's shadow to claw at her legs, then rushing away again into darkness, to hide and stalk and rush once more. A cat, she thought. It is a cat. And she waited for the terrifying, comforting rush of a small animal attacking her feet.

But what followed came no nearer. It hid itself and kept its distance. Human. She knew, finally, that it was human. Still she did not run, did not permit herself to run. She went in controlled even steps the interminable way toward the streetlight's circle of safety.

Slowly that light enlarged, came toward her, took her in. Unharmed, unattacked, she entered the rim of light. She walked into the very center of the golden glow and stood on the pale rag of her shadow, enduring the shaking of heart and bone, and waited for whatever, whoever, came behind her.

She did not know how long she waited. Her body took back possession, her mind clarity. Slowly she turned about in her place within the light and looked back into the place where someone had followed. There was, at first, nothing to be seen. Then, in the dark, something moved. There was a small flash of white, a face, a blur of form. Then the sound of falling footsteps, the sound of running, quickly beating out into nothingness. Maura stood alone in the light looking into the formless dark, and she knew that what had followed her was a child.

A child had cunningly trailed her across the night. A child had instructed her in terror, a child had made her mindless and dumb. It was late. Too late for a child to be out. Who would let a child run in the night? What child would be so unwatched?

With the wane of terror, weariness assaulted Maura. Tired and angry she turned from the place in which she stood and walked back through fog and dark the way she had come. If she caught up with the child, she thought indignantly, she would scold him properly and send him home where he belonged. She did not see him however, and after that night's deep sleep and the following day's routine, Maura quite nearly forgot him.

But the next night when she went to get her jacket from the closet, she hesitated. The fear she had experienced the night before possessed her like the original. She took her hand from the hanger and turned back to the living room. Foolish, she told herself. From beginning to end, simply foolish. To be afraid of the dark. Of a small boy.

She dropped down into the leather chair with a sigh. She read for a while, restlessly, arguing against her timidity. Then she put down the book, went again for her jacket and walked out into a brisk moonless night.

But in spite of her admonishments to herself, she went listening, not to the night's own sounds, but for the sounds of the follower of the night before. She did not hear him, however, or sense him near. After a time, her apprehension left her, and as she walked calmly on, she looked up into the rich starriness of the sky over her. She counted out the constellations she had learned in her childhood, the simple obvious configurations of ancient lights. She saw Orion's sword as bright as she ever had, and the lesser starry markings of the heeling hound. The seven sisters were present in total, and the dipper carried a full cup. The clarity of those old wonders restored old contentments, and she turned back to go home with a sense of peace.

And it was then she felt the child come. In the very instant he approached, she knew he was there. She strode rapidly away from him, and she knew that he ran secretly behind her from tree to tree, from bush to shadowed bush, persistently following. She ignored him. She would not encourage him. If she pretended that he did not bother her, he would get no joy from his pestering. To whom could he belong?

The houses she passed going homeward were entirely darkened, or gave out light from one or two windows. The inhabitants were going to bed as she would when she entered the safety of her own home. Surely this child also belonged inside one of the homes she passed and ought to be tucked into some protected bed.

When Maura reached the narrow walk that passed through the tall laurel hedge which formed the boundary of the yard of her home, she paused. She turned once more, as she had the night before. She wanted very much to see the child. She needed to see him. It seemed that his pursuit had given him an identity for which she needed a known face. The night was clear, but she was far from any light and she could not see. But still the air between them stiffened. For a brief interval she knew he stayed near. Then there was the sound of his running. The fall of those footsteps was quick and light and somehow unusual. There was an irregularity in the rhythm, a syncopation, as if he galloped playfully into the night.

Maura stood looking into the dark after him, and a peculiar wonder erased her irritation. She went slowly up the walk and into the house. She went to bed with the puzzle of the haunting, fleeing child taking all her thoughts.

Then it was Friday night and Fred was home for the weekend. There was no occasion for walking. But on Monday evening Maura found herself looking at the clock with impatience. The puzzle of the child intrigued her. There was something meaningful, she felt, in the odd circumstances of their meeting, something in the tenuous relationship shaped in the darkness of autumn nights that was significant. She felt that the child needed her, for what or why she could not guess. He made some claim on her. She wanted to see the child, to confront him, to ask what it was that he wanted of her. So she started out, waiting for him to come.

He began to follow in the same place. He kept the same

distance from her. Maura walked slowly. From time to time she paused, hoping that he would come to her. He did not. In the nights that followed, it was always the same. He followed when she walked, he stopped when she stopped. Once or twice she turned to the darkness where he was, waited long moments, said Yes? into the place he might be. He would not answer, would not reveal himself, and she then turned back to her walking.

It was on Thursday night that it suddenly made sense to her. As soon as she had made the connection, Maura wondered at her obtuseness. He was from the home, of course. That would account for his fugitiveness, for the fact that he was out so late at night, that he crept behind her so hidden, and yes, she was sure of it, afraid.

An old mansion there in the hills had been made into a home for retarded children. Maura had, she realized, walked near that place every night the child had followed. Somehow, he must have gotten out of his bed. He must have seen her walking past those old grounds. Motherless, Maura imagined that he followed her out of a need he did not himself understand.

Maura became determined to speak to the child. That night there was a tyrannous wind. Trees and shrubs bowed and shook before the wind's passage. Maura's skirt flapped about her knees. Her hair blew in disorder. She went stubbornly on. She would not forsake the child. He would want to speak to her. He would come as he had come before, wanting care or comfort or love. And she longed now to give him what he lacked. Did he not stand for all hurt and loss and those sad needs that call for love?

He did not come. At last, Maura went home, entered the lonely house and fell into bed. She spent her sleep in dreams of search.

On Monday morning she drove to the home. A high hedge of pieris sheltered the place from road and eye. There was, she noted, no fence. She drove into the wide circling drive. A weathered white mansion crowned the flat knoll. On the wide lawns, great evergreens and widely branching maples asserted the traditions of old gardens. In the hydrangea bed flanking the drive a bald-headed man spaded. As Maura drove slowly past, he looked up. He grinned the excessive grin of the simple, nodded, flapped a gloved hand at her. She waved timidly back. She parked, climbed the wide steps, entered a large hall. A small brass plaque beside one of the dark paneled doors said *Office*. She stepped inside. A sunroom. Old wicker furniture painted white. Faded chintz on cushions, at the windows. Great green ferns arched out of a wicker fernery. No one was there.

On the top of a small desk a sign stood beside a small bell: *Please Ring*. Maura tapped the button. The chime startled. There followed immediately the sound of quick footsteps crossing the hall outside the room. A tall woman entered. She offered her hand. The blue eyes, set close to a highbridged nose, were interested, firm. But Maura found she could not state her mission.

"I came," she said uncertainly, "I came to inquire."

"Yes," the woman said, as if she had been told everything.

"And is it the small children or our older children you wish to ask about?"

Maura saw that it was assumed that she had one such child herself. She did not correct. "The small children," she murmured, and the woman nodded.

She took Maura on a tour of the grounds. They went to the low, newer buildings clustered around the high old house. In one, women sat at long tables working at sewing machines. The women looked up from their work, briefly, indifferently. In all their faces, difference stood like a brand. In another building young men and old men struggled with crafts. Their arguments and assertions were only somewhat different from what Maura had heard in her own small sons. The grotesqueness came from disproportion, the bodies large, the disputes small.

Then the matron took Maura into a small white building like a country school. The room was furnished like a kinder-garten room. Low sturdy tables, bright chairs. Safe indestruc-tible toys. Several white-gowned attendants moved among the children. But it was the children Maura eagerly observed. A sturdy brown-haired boy with tilted eyes and stubby hands wooed the attention of ˙a chubby blonde girl. She sat straight-legged in the center of the floor, mute, resistant, ignoring the boy and the gaudy ball he wanted to throw. In the corner another child sat weeping, inarticulate, anguished. Another, a thin little girl flung herself at the matron who stood beside Maura. The child clung fiercely to the woman's legs, would not let go. Maura vividly recalled how she had waited for such a child alone in the dark night. Would she have known how to cope with an assault like this? She watched the matron expertly hold the child until the child's face changed, and docility replaced the fierce demanding hate. Could she have had the firmness? The strength?

Ah, surely she could manage. Even that. She searched among all the difficult children for the one who had followed her. She would know him. She was sure of that. But she did not see him. He was not, after all, there.

"Come," the matron said at last. "You will want to see the main house. The dining room is there and the rooms where the children sleep."

Maura followed the woman across the room and out anoth-er door into a smaller room. And there at a scratched oak table a young woman sat beside still another child. An open book lay on the table before them. The young woman's hand patted the surface of the book.

"Jamie," the teacher said to the child. "Pay attention now. Then you'll get your ice cream."

Maura stopped, arrested. This child was different. The

book, the teacher, indicated that. He was a handsome boy. Eight, or nine. Curls crowned a well-shaped head. He shook his head as the teacher spoke, watching her out of bright dark eyes. Suddenly he flung himself out of his chair and fled to the corner of the room. He crouched there, grinning, his eyes narrowed.

"Come back here, Jamie," his teacher commanded.

The boy laughed. A sudden shout of laughter, excessive, revealing. He jerked upright, stood poised on tiptoe, spread his arms wide to touch the walls behind him.

"Sometimes," the matron said quietly to Maura, "we cannot tell a child's capacities. Jamie may be more disturbed than retarded."

"Come here, Jamie," his teacher repeated.

He watched from beneath level brows. The thick curls fell over his forehead. His mouth curved sensually. Suddenly he looked directly at Maura. A grin sprang across lips and eyes. He gestured, pointing a finger. At her. He nodded sharply, as if a secret stood between them. Then a rioting laugh broke from his lips. He leaped from his corner, darted to the table, sprang from chair to table top. He threw his arms wide like wings and began to whirl in swift circles. But the circles dipped, were elliptical, were crooked. Ah, he was, Maura gasped, crippled. One foot twisted at the ankle. For all his swiftness, his spinning was cleft, syncopated in gait. And then there was no doubt. Would her heart split with pity and with love? Jamie was the follower.

But she held herself stiff for safety's sake. She felt that the matron observed her. She would not betray. Must not.

Afterwards Maura saw where the children slept. The windows were barred. Maura asked whether the children were attended at night. "All night," the matron said, and gestured at chair and desk, "someone is on duty."

Then how did he get out? Distressed, uncertain, Maura did not walk that night. She huddled in Fred's comforting leather chair and pondered what she would do. She counselled herself to tell the matron of the home that Jamie ran about at night, that somehow he escaped the confines of that place and wandered about in the cold autumn weather. But if she did so, she knew she would not be able to see him again. There would be no possibility of knowing what moved him to follow her. She would never know then what he wanted of her. Nor would she be able then, to give him what he needed, what he wanted.

And so she chose. The next night she set out again. The night was calm. A cover of cloud hid the autumn sky. It was not cold. She walked rather slowly, watching all the shadowed places for some sign of human motion. Perhaps he would not come again. She had, perhaps, frightened him, going to the home, finding him out like that.

Then suddenly he was there. He came boldly. She heard the uneven fall of his footsteps. She wanted to stop, to turn and go to him immediately. But she did not want to frighten him away. She walked slowly on. It was better to let him come to her.

But after a while, under the high arching branches of an old oak tree, she stopped. She heard his footsteps stop also. She turned around and quietly waited. Over her head the oak tree stirred, creaked, stilled. The boy did not move. She spoke into the waiting watching darkness. "What is it, my dear? What is it you want?"

The child stepped out from behind the shield of a boulevard tree into the center of the sidewalk. He stood not twenty feet away from her, poised like a wary animal.

Maura did not move, did not speak. She was, for a moment, unable to do either. Then calming herself, able to distinguish him more clearly, she saw that he stood in his place stiffly, like a page in some ancient court, or like a young prince expecting attention. He seemed beautiful. The large dark eyes shone out of a face white as an almond. The curls were a thick bang over the fine eyes. His mouth seemed to tremble.

He stood very still. His head was high. His elbows were close to his sides, and in his hands he held some object—a bowl or a box or a tin.

"Yes," Maura said, as if he had asked something. The oak leaves moved, commenting. A strange remoteness, like drowsiness, moved in a slow tide over Maura. She felt suspended in something not real. Perhaps she only dreamed. But the child's reality confronted her. Slowly she began to move toward him, careful not to frighten him, careful to keep him from fleeing as he always had before.

He waited, his head dropped to his chest. She could see as she came close to him how the luxuriant hair curled over his temples and over the tops of his ears. She wished to touch him. She wanted to hold the crippled child close, to lean her cheek against his shining curls, speak the mothering words he had perhaps never heard.

Then she stood before him. He looked at her without raising his head. She saw the narrowing of his eyes. The can or tin he held carefully in his hands gave off a dim shine. Maura's arms opened.

"Yes. Yes, my little one," she said.

· Then his head snapped back. His laughter pierced the air like fire. He pulled the lid from the tin and swung it in a high arc. Its contents flew over Maura. The collection of excrement flew into her face, over hair and clothes, face and hands. Maura stood gasping, covered with filth, blind. She heard the wild laughter and the elliptical beat of his running.

Maura fled, running the dark winding way home. She burst into the house and stumbled into the shower without even taking her jacket off. She stood gasping and choking beneath the shower's spray. Revulsion rode in her veins—and terror.

She did not walk again. She confessed to no one what she had experienced. The night's events seemed a grotesque fantasy.

More than ever she kept herself busy. She went out eve-
nings as well as days, films, concerts, lectures—whatever
diversion she could find. Each night she went to bed extremely tired. But in her dreams, with terrible repetition, on dark
windy streets a child ran.

One night Maura sat at the dining room table surrounded
by ribbons and wrappings and the presents she had bought for
Arlene's birthday. She was winding loops of purple ribbon
over her fingers to fashion a bow when a soft tapping sounded
against the window. She looked up. She saw a shape of darkness against the glass. The shape of that slim body, the mold
of head with its crown of curls, she could not fail to know.
She dropped her ribbon, the scissors, the package. She rushed
to the French doors and flung them open.

She saw no one. There was no sound of running. She stood
at the open door, the winter air flowing cold over her flesh.

After that she saw him often, a quick white face glimmering out of the garden's darkness, the slim body clear against
the flicker of leaves. She watched for him, not able to believe
that he was there, not able to deny the evidence of her eyes.
Almost nightly he came. Would she never be rid of him?

One Thursday after dinner, Maura saw him in the garden.
The curly head dipped briefly. One hand lifted, beckoning.
Quietly, with great calm, Maura got up from her place. She
went to the closet for her jacket, returned to the French doors,
went out. She walked across the heavily dewed grass toward
the border of laurel. She saw him there in the darkness, saw
him laugh and run ahead of her. She quietly pursued.

Down the walk, out into the avenue where darkness lay
over tree and shrub and house, she went behind him. Under
the barren maples, through the shadows of cypress, beneath
the black clustering of wide oaks, she walked, the child lilting
and tricking before her. Away from places she knew. Along
strange streets she went where he led.

The rind of moon slid across the spaces of darkness. The thin stars slipped, dimmed. The wind grew larger, blew fiercely. In the deep dark of the long hours before reluctant day, to Maura it was no longer clear at all who led, who pursued, or who followed.

Blue Transfer

I come from sleep as if returning from a far country, a stranger to myself, a stranger to my life. Sluggish, blind against the gray morning light, I pull myself from the clinging bed, grope my way to the bathroom. Although I groan with the night-journey's symptoms of encephalia—swollen face, thick-lidded, watery eyes, tepid thought, dulled body—I do not yet perceive my changed condition. I lean over the basin, fling cold water over my face, fumble for toothbrush, scrub old hours from my mouth. I reach for the bottle of gold oil, dab it from fingers to brow. It is then I feel the mark.

Fingers on forehead I discover a strange, raised shape, strange texture, testing, throw wide awake questions to the mind. My eyes probe the startling mirror. A triangle. A blue triangle marks the skin of my forehead. It lies just under the skin. Blue: darker than my eyes. Grape blue. Blue-jeans blue. The triangle inverted. Its point just above the deepest part of the inward curve between nose and forehead. The two equal sides flare up two inches, two and a half, skimming the inner edge of the brows, stopping short of the hairline, the wide third side crossing definitively the naked brow.

A perfect isosceles triangle.

But what is it? How did it come there? What does it mean?

Beyond astonishment I pursue a glimmer of recognition. Familiar, I've seen that mark, it signifies something. It is the mark . . . of what?

I do not know. Whatever suggestive meanings touched the margins of thought fade back. Fear plunges into my mind.

A stain. It must be a stain. I rub a fierce finger over the left point of the triangle. Against the bone the blue line feels ropey, the texture is thick, slightly rough. It does not erase, does not alter under the rubbing fingertip. Is it not, then, a stain?

The lines—welts, really—are an eighth of an inch wide. They have a corded look, like the skin of angle worms. The mark does not seem deep in the flesh like a strawberry mark; it is not smooth like a burn. In God's name, what? It is rather like a scar. Yes, a scar. Have I injured myself? Have I been injured? Have I forgotten the accident?

I push at the triangle with both forefingers, anticipating pain. There is no pain, no smarting, no old soreness. Not even the tightness of healed wounds, of new skin. No surrounding bruises, no spreading of purple or yellow in the flesh, no sign of a blow. No sign of stitches to suggest I've been in a riot, taken to a hospital, mended somewhere.

Then what has happened? Have I not just wakened in my bed after a usual night's sleep? Have I been somewhere I've forgotten, done something I don't remember? Am I suffering amnesia? Delusions? Am I awake?

My head shakes, involuntarily, fiercely. I squeeze shut my eyes, open them, stare again into the astonishing mirror. Central to the space made by forehead-temples-brows–cheekbones stands the mark, the blue triangle, perfectly shaped, perfectly balanced, perfectly strange and terrible.

Terror rides my blood.

I grab the washcloth, rub it harshly in soap, scrub and scrub my face. When I come up and look to the mirror for salvation, the hideous triangle burns brilliantly, deeply blue against the red, burning, abused skin.

Under my shaking finger the little wheel of the difficult dial fails. On the third try, dull ringings sound in my ear.

Myra clips out a hurried Hello. Yes, she is there, real, alive. I feel grateful, safer.

I ask her whether she saw me yesterday. My words are shaking on unreliable breath. Question and tone surprise her. She demands reassurance. Yes, I tell her, it is I, and repeat my need.

The high, hurried sing of her voice drops, goes careful, slow. Cautiously she tells me yes, I was with her, teaching as usual, that we went for a hike in the late sunny afternoon, a perfect autumn day. She reports what I remember. So I am sane, the world is real. I lift my hand, touch my brow, hopeful. The mark is still there. So I pursue mysteries, ask whether anything unusual happened, during the day, on our walk?

Myra clips back she's late, she has to get off, so do I, she instructs me. There's no time to gab, she'll see me at school.

But I am disfigured. Marked. I cannot go out. Report my absence, I say. I put the receiver in its place, find I am shaking. My fingertips have not left the mark. I start for the mirror, the burr of the phone pulls me back. Myra insists loudly that she must know what's wrong. Something must be the matter, what is it? Suddenly I feel threat of exposure, want privacy, no interference. Evasive, I manage to affect some calmness. I report a bump on my forehead. She suggests hives, boils. I should go to the doctor, she advises. I agree and escape.

In the mirror the triangle is clear and remarkable as before. My cheeks also have triangles, red blotches called up by nerves, a clown face, my new mad appearance! The word *lapis* leaps to my mind. The mark is indeed lapis blue, that clear, deep blue just light of navy. With the quality of deeply buried interior light the lapis stone possesses, a gloss deep in the color, shining out through the covering layer of striated skin.

For the first time the possibility comes to me: the mark may not go away. I may be branded forever. Branded! Is the mark a sign? Does it signify some meaning I am going to uncover? Am I set apart, separate, destined for some event I must, whether I want to or not, discover?

———

The doctor leans forward, dabbing the make-up from my forehead with a fumey, alcohol-soaked cotton pad. A frown webs his cool forehead. His distanced, cool eyes, through narrowed, light-lashed lids, fix on the mark. His tan hair is thinning and under the hard light of the overhead neon fixture, his scalp glistens, ivory with an underglaze of blue. He puts aside the stained cotton, his cool fingers come to my brow. I think I can see beyond the small, clearly distinguishable hair follicles the motion of cells in his delicate brain, the flashing circuits, the darting synapses, the small, complex runnings of mazes, pursuits of logic, of cause and effect, zipping furiously from station to station within that intricately equipped dome.

The tissue is firm, he coolly comments. The tips of his fingers, sophisticated, precise, move over the triangular welt. You haven't been injured? he says, not quite making it a question. The third time. The forefinger presses, the thumb also, flanking the ridge, moving in small, repeated explorations along the sides of the mark. His eyes are on the response of skin to that pressure and release. The busy cells under the skull posit theories, consider disease, injuries, allergies, bizarre events, all those considerations secret, all locked behind the objective, clear, illegible eyes. But the mouth has given up its elusive smiling. The lips are pressing in upon each other, the slight pressure paling the surrounding skin. It is not echymotic, he says. It is a free lesion. Not attached to the bone.

But he is baffled, of course. How could one explain such a thing appearing on one's forehead, overnight, without source, without cause, without sensation, without pain? He tells me he wants his colleague, Dr. B., to look at it. He steps out of the examining room, his nurse enters. A clock-faced woman, orderly, severe, accustomed to tidy routines, antiseptic ideas. She arranges an instrument case on the counter, takes from the cupboard and drawers small vials and tubes. Her starched white back intends to keep me from knowing, but my heart deepens its tocking, quickens, loses hold on its routine, forgets control.

The nurse turns, faces me, a trim smile on her pale lips. Her eyes, however, dart to the blue triangle disfiguring my face. I watch her eyelids turn pink, a tinge of salmon rises to the watery white surfaces of her cheeks. Do you mind, she says, as excuse, not as question, and comes close so that the starched lemon smell of her uniform and her lilac cologne lift into the alcoholic air, mix in dizzying confusion.

Abruptly my chin jerks up, my head spins aside. What I read like a printout in her computer eyes, I reject. I am anomaly, I am a freak.

She is still staring when the doctors enter, Tweedledum, Tweedledee. The nurse steps back self-effacingly. The colleague, the doctor I do not know, nods at me, jolly. His hair springs from his head in theatrical black crinkles. His wide smile springs over large dazzling white teeth. But when he leans close, quick and warm as an inpetuous lover, the scholarly distance moves like a cool wind between us. Only his warm fingers, tapping and probing like small ant feet, keep close connection. His eyes burn, icy as Faust's. I am merely specimen.

It is to my doctor he speaks, their cryptic elliptic sharing. No injury? None. Free, though, the lesion. Yes. Nonechymotic. Yes. No swelling in the surrounding tissue. No inflammation. Yes. No. Unusual. Yes. Very unusual. We'll biopsy, of course. Of course.

The colleague leaves, patching my psyche with a wide band-aid smile. Someone calls the nurse from the room, too. In Dr. A's fingers the scalpel glances. The anesthetic, brief bee-sting. The flick of the scalpel, tissue slips from the blue blade into the small vial, floats in the liquid, tinging it rose. He holds a gauze to my wound, asks me to press it in place. He makes coded notation on a slip of paper, rolls it about the ominous vial, slips a rubber band to secure it. Then he turns and peels a band aid and puts it tautly over the nicked place in my mark.

Do you, I finally warble, think it's malignant?

Oh, he is kind, understands anxiety, fends off panic. He assures calmly of routines, very unlikely, no evidence at all. He will call me as soon as they hear, in a few days.

Malignant. Malignant. I had not thought. Cancer. Am I doomed? Will I suffer long, stinking, ugly months of pain?

But it is foolish to weep. Weeping, I'll have an accident, smash up my car, end up a homicide. In jail. Triangle and all.

For two days I have worried the word. Malignant. It grows in my brain, takes up all the space, anastomoses to heart, veins, bone, consuming my life. Uninvited, yesterday Myra came by, offered my textbooks, marguerites in great bunches. My God, she said, you look like you've been branded. Wanting to comfort, she grew awkward. Stumbled over conventions, bumped into the footstool. Left, tongue-tied, worried, distant.

Yes, branded. Branded with disease? Marked for death? The Grim Reaper has a new warning system. In the dead of night, at the witching hour, he comes with glowing red iron, marks the brow of his future victim.

And who, then, corrals us? Who will round us up, herd us through the dark valley. What cowhands will hoist us up onto the ship of Death? I think of the branded braying cattle slung with ropes and pulleys onto the ships off the white shores of Hawaii.

Branded, yes, I become separate. Myra's eyes were evidence. Already I am deeply lonely.

Doctor A. calls. He reports that the tissue is not malignant. I am safe. I feel an immense letting go, float out into exhausted relief. His hearty voice asks whether the mark is changed, whether it is fading, deepening. I tell him I see no difference, no change at all. He advises a dermatologist. If there is no counterindication, plastic surgery. Not paying full attention, thinking only, it is not malignant, not malignant, I agree. He will make the appointment with Dr. Cristo. His nurse will call me. He will be interested to hear. Keep in touch.

Branded. But not with cancer, not for that death.

I have done it all. Seen the fat, grandfatherly Dr. C., ascetic and clinical Dr. Paley. But I do not care for their interest, their curiosity, their benevolence, their bafflement. I seem to have received a message. A voice, sourceless, nameless, is repeating, Not malignant, not even malevolent: beneficent, benevolent. The sign is good, the brand augurs good. When I look at the triangle in the mirror, centered there in my quite nearly too-wide, too-high forehead, balancing the narrowing triangle of my lower face, I feel comforted to see it still there: that deep lapis lazuli blue, an inky blue moved toward purple, the color the sea appears far out on a sunny day. The balanced lines please me, the defined space. The mark belongs to me, I to it. It is mine, my peculiar sign. Blue is the color of truth, of goodness, of faith, of mercy, of abstract thought. Blue is the color of the sea, of the heavens themselves, of the mother of God, the bird of happiness, the forget-me-not. And of all waters, life-giving, life-sustaining, cleansing, baptizing. Yes, all are blue.

The triangle is balance, contains, does not cross, is related to the number three, which is wholeness, holiness, mystery. The point of the triangle touches exactly the place where Indian Buddhists mark the Third Eye.

Triangles, triangles.

On my horoscope there is a Grand Trine. The astrologist tells me I am an old soul.

What am I to learn? What does it signify?

Suddenly I recall the dream. A peculiarly vivid dream, dreamed months ago. I am standing on the deck of my hillside home. Far below in the green treed valley I see movement, figures beginning to mount the steep slope around which the road intricately winds. But the figures follow no road or path. They come straight up the hill, moving swiftly. There are many of them. They are white, covered entirely in white luminous substance. The neighbors are calling to one another, giving warning. Hurry, they cry, evacuate. They know they have no power against these approaching forms. They are frantic with terror, leap to cars to escape. Flee, we must flee!

But I am fascinated: the odd, powerful, graceful figures speed forward, compelling, strange, beautiful. The leading figure seems to be female, and where a face would be there is only light, refracting, as if the westering sun is touching glass or highly polished plastic. How beautiful they are against the green mountain, the deep azure sky.

As they speed closer, I feel their energy pulsating, feel almost visible power rippling toward me, through me, in dense waves. My body begins to quiver, throbs under that energy. I panic, want to run. The radiations are holding me. I cannot move. I open my mouth to cry out. I can make no sound. Their light is blinding. I stare at the hazed forms, expecting what? Annihilation?

I wake, my heart is pounding, sweat films my body. I turn on the bedside lamp to anchor myself in reality. But the last image of the advancing crowd holds itself in my mind. On the helmets of the white-garbed other-worldly beings was inscribed the blue triangle. Lapis blue. I know it was from the triangular sign that the waves of power poured.

Remembering, my fingers lift to touch the blue cording on my brow. I rise and go again to the mirror. I examine carefully the deep color of my mark, the look of light lying locked within the blue. Is it possible? Could I through that triangle draw in or put forth such energy, such power as I felt from the triangles of my dream visitors?

Can it be, is it possible, that I have become one of them? In that dream vision was there some actual power which is proving itself in this strange real present? Am I marked for transfer?

When?

How?

<hr>

The light on my forehead intensifies. It is giving off a steady blue glowing, not unlike a low gas flame seen through frosted glass.

I meditate, wait for visions, for transmitted messages. My mind tunes itself, sends out its receptors, expects connection. Communications from something out there, something beyond. Yes, from them.

<hr>

Myra, Dr. Anderson, his nurse keep phoning. They want progress reports, want me to come see them, to come to work. They mean well, perhaps. But their calls intrude, interrupt my concentration. Sometimes now I do not answer. I draw the shades against distracting light. I bolt the doors, refuse the ringings.

<hr>

A strange phenomenon. The light of the triangle begins to move into my skull. A misty light, a diffused light, like early dawn, seems to enter my head. And illuminates before it a corridor. Yes, I see a long corridor, fading off into a deeper violet light my vision does not yet penetrate. If I move into the corridor, if I choose to explore that inward passage, I will find many rooms opening off each side. In the slant of light into those first rooms I see myself, not pictures of myself, but my real existing self, in the actual flesh. In the first room I am a child, very young, less than a year old. The child lies in a wicker baby buggy beside an open window over which filmy curtains swell and fade in an early summer breeze. The child's mind is my mind, and what perceptions are in that mind are, as I gaze into the dim corridor, my own. The child is watching the leaves stir, light over shadow, green over green, in the oak tree outside the window. The child is accustoming herself to her place, being in this place, and is at the same time, possessed by remembrance, which eludes her, of another place, another light, another time.

And beyond that, in light that is not light, I see two small girls outside a gate. The one is urging the other to enter. It is time to go in. The other remains stubborn, naughtiness and disobedience, darkening her face. She is whispering seductively to the first, persuading her to do what they know they should not do. The sight of them surprises me, shows me facets of myself I do not recall. I was the good one, I am saying in protest to what I see. I was the obedient one, the one who could not find the will to do what I wanted. I was the giver-up, the giver-in, the mild, the open, I believe. Yet there I am, yes, *I,* introducing rebellion, introducing temptation, for it is my sister who will obey our parents' call; it is I who insist upon deception.

I still meditating, do not yet enter the lilac-blue corridor. If I move into the opening space I will, I understand, learn all those shadowed truths about myself. I will find all the hidden betrayals, the forgotten losses. I will come through a review of days, through passages of experience which will turn all my perceptions and judgements from their present errors. I am afraid, and I am compelled. The mysteries I now hold are safer than those I will find. Yet, I cannot turn away. I hover at the threshold, considering risk, gauging loss.

———

For days I have not eaten. My mind, therefore, has a numinous quality. Thought processes have given way to receptiveness. What comes to me does not come from the usual linking of sensation and idea, cause and effect. I suppose I am in a state of mystic revelation. Knowledge is out there, coming into me in dim yet absorbing perceptions. It is necessary that I keep myself in passive harmony. What is promised is possession in great measure.

Yes, I know that when I walk down that corridor, which holds replication of the memories held in the actual cell structure of my brain, I will literally walk through myself, out of my existence. I will return through what I have experienced in the linear motion of time. I will disappear into my own lived sequence, no, not disappear, return through my life on a long and instructive journey. It will not be a painful journey, for this child in the latticed light of the wicker buggy allows me to understand how objectively my pilgrimage will be taken. I will be observer of my past, I will be gathering together significant episodes and thus also gain at last my true self. There will be accumulating perceptions and illuminations. Then at last completed, enlightened, I will pass through the last places of the corridor into open fields where *they* will be gathered, those others who have also come into their reversals and found the balance of their eternal selves. I know all this as I wait for the moment of reentry.

If they do not phone me, if they do not perturb me, if they do not come and arrest my progress, I will be able to move my slow earth-self inward, like a star moving itself back through its own density into the returning, traceless black hole. Of course, I must make the journey. Anyone who has seen the way cannot turn from it.

Yes, I am entering. Yes, I will come.

Places We Lost

That house was more than ordinarily loved. My father had built and sold houses all over the south side of Minneapolis. Almost every year, we had moved into and out of one of them. Move in, fix it up, sell it. That was the pattern. But that house was built just for us. It was a high-gabled, English country-style house, and when we moved in, mother announced that that was it. She had had her fill of moving, and she had things just the way she wanted them there, from the clever limed-oak phone niche in the hall to the breakfast nook with its trestle table and built-in benches.

Four years later, we were in the middle of the Depression. My father no longer built houses. He worked at intervals for a sash-and-door shop. Mostly he was home. In those days, shabby-looking men knocked on our door and asked for food, and abandoned cats howled in the alleys at night.

In spite of that, we children did not understand. Buddy was still a baby, and Jenny and I were fed. We were clothed. We heard the words—Depression, breadlines, WPA, Mecklenburg scrip. They had a grand and mysterious sound, and we did not comprehend them. When father announced, one day, that the sash-and-door shop had closed, it meant less to us than the quick change in weather that was moving March from winter to spring.

Then, on a Friday night in May, an evening warmer than the calendar allowed, Jenny and I grew keenly aware of the change and loss threatening us all. That it came then, on the same night that Jenny came to something else, launching the

the risk and deceit which harmed us all, was not, perhaps, entirely coincidental.

Usually, Jenny and I were among the first to be called home from the evening games. That night, no one called us. We marveled, at first, at our unexpected freedom. We played Kick the Can furiously as the evening turned dusky, crowding the last minutes with the greatest amount of pleasure. Even after most of the children had gone home and we were much too tired, we played on. At last, there were just three of us—Jenny and I and Carrie Bergman, whose parents had gone to church and didn't know she was out.

We huddled by the telephone pole that had been goal and watched the final excessive blooming of stars in the altogether darkened skies. Still no one called. Jenny looked at me, caught between wanting to be called and wanting to stay there in the dew-sharpened, strange night air. The trees were high black shadows against the lighted sky. Beneath them, fireflies scudded over an unseen earth. Down the avenue, the houses in formal rows were large and remote from us. At last, our sense of freedom grew so immense that we were strange in it, unsure of it, and wanted to escape before it swept us toward things we only sensed and did not wish to know.

"Let's go," Jenny whispered. "Let's go," Carrie agreed.

We turned and ran our separate ways. I clutched Jenny's hand and pulled her as fast as I could down the alley, across the grass, up the concrete walk to our back door. The house was still there. The kitchen windows facing the alley were dark, but the double windows of the dining room gave out an old light.

I stopped when we reached the steps. "Jenny, did you hear mother calling us?" I whispered.

"No, she didn't," Jenny warbled. "She never called us."

"Jenny, we're going to get spanked." I was gloomily sure of it.

Jenny stood still, considering. The crickets' warnings riddled the dark. Finally, she tugged like a fish at the hand in which I still held hers. "Come on," she said carelessly. "Let's go in."

"We'll get spanked." I repeated.

Jenny tossed her head. The fair hair moved like wind in the scant light. "Well, I don't care. I'm going in. Come on, Berit. Let's go." She started up the steps; but on the second one, she stopped. Her hand left mine. Her head leaned toward the night. "Shh," she whispered. "Listen."

I stopped, I waited. I heard nothing. "What? What do you hear?"

"Shh," Jenny whispered again.

Then I heard it, the faint, fine tissue of sound, a thin belling of woe, moving without source into and out of the night.

The sound came again, and we both knew it for what it was. Tenderness quavered out of Jenny's throat in a whispered, half-sung cry. "A kitten. It's a kitten." She went blindly from me towards whatever dark place she thought the sound came from, crooning, "Here, kitty, kitty. Here, kitty." I could hear, in the quick, breathless callings, that extravagance of love which was Jenny's gift and liability and which poured from her toward any small furred thing she ever saw.

Plaintive, haunting mews were coming in answer to her calls. Then both murmurs and mewing ceased, and Jenny stood beside me, holding something against her chest. "Look at him, Berit. Oh, look at him, how tiny he is."

I could not see the kitten in the darkness but she couldn't keep him, anyway. She knew that. She was always bringing home hungry cats, and father never let her keep one. "Put him down, Jenny. Come on. We have to go in."

"He's so tiny, Berit. Look. He's lost, Berit, poor little thing."

I heard the small, rich thrum, the purring. I started up the steps saying, "Put him down, Jenny," and she came after me and didn't put the kitten down. I stopped outside the door, the knob cold and damp in my hand.

"I'm going to ask." Jenny said. The dark prevented seeing; but I knew from the sound of her slow, soft words that in her wide eyes there was that look of determination I was never able to defeat. I wiped my palm against my skirt and pulled open the door.

The weathers of my father's nature blew violently from sublimity and joy to outrage and despair. His knobby, sharp-boned face was seamed and creased by his moods, as lands are marked by their climates' demands. To hear my father angry did not astonish. To hear him shouting at mother gave room for apprehension. But she, who usually would not speak to him unless he was calm, was answering his anger with anger equal to his own, her voice raised to a near shout. In bewilderment, we both stopped on the dark side of the dining-room door.

"Don't be so unreasonable, Emma!" he shouted. "It has to be done."

"No. I will not let you."

"We have to live. It's that simple. What do you think we'll eat? Leaves off the trees, perhaps?"

"Not the house," mother cried in a loud sharp voice. "We don't have to sell the house. We're eating. We're not starving. Not the house!" She sat at the table, the light of the dining-room fixture falling on her coppery hair, her face now lowered into her covering hands.

My father paced around her, circling the round oak table, stopping to lean over her bowed body, and shouting into her ears. "Not starving! Not starving, she says!" With each word, he stabbed the air in front of her with a thrust-out forefinger. "Women! Masters of logic! We'll live in a nice house. We'll walk around with empty bellies, and then, when it's too late, we'll lose the house, anyway. We'll see the day the bank forecloses, that's how it will be!"

From the dark kitchen we watched, trying to find meaning in the storm of words. Why would we sell the house? How could you lose a house? Where would we be if we were not there in that house?

My mother dropped her hands from a pale face in which her eyes were two places of darkness. Then she stood up and put that white face close to my father's knotted one and shouted. "No. No. No."

His mouth snapped like a trap. His lids slitted down against his eyes' fury. His brows were one black streak across the blazing forehead. Overhead, the light fixture still trembled with the shouts, which had frozen now into total silence. Under the flickering, fragmented light, they stood dumbly unyielding, unforgiving, sudden hate flung up between them that grew into a wall of silence, from which neither could move and which neither could destroy.

In that cold, walled silence, the breaths I drew shook past a thick tongue and a closed throat. Against my arm, Jenny's arm trembled with dismay, and we stood locked, two small girls caught on the outer edge of their anger.

Then, in Jenny's arms, the kitten stirred; lifted a small, sleepy head; mewed faintly.

Both faces turned toward the door, turned from anger to remembrance and surprise.

"What are you girls doing here?" My father's bellow was a lesser anger. "Why aren't you in bed?" Then his black brows rode up, up on his corrugated forehead. His eyes pulled wide open. "What's that?" he shouted. "Get that cat out of here!"

In spite of all, Jenny's desire gave sufficient courage. "I thought we could keep—," she ventured, on a high, frail note.

"Get that cat out of here!" He plunged around the table toward us.

We stumbled back toward the safe dark behind us.

But mother had already wheeled from her place, and she came to us with her arms spread, like a winged, red-haired angel. She swept both of us away in the white arc of her arms, away from my black-browed, bellowing father, crying over her turned, sharply defying shoulder, "Stop shouting at the children." His huge fist crashed upon the shining table as she herded us through the kitchen to the back door, where Jenny lowered her arms and gave up the tiny kitten to the larger, cold night.

Upstairs in our bed, we lay cradled in each other's comfortless arms. Jenny's tears dampened the pillow beneath my cheek. Her questions—"Berit, where will the kitten go? How will we lose the house, Berit? Berit, do you think the kitten will die?" — went with us unanswered, threatening, even as we moved hopeless, helpless, into the distance of sleep.

I awakened to total quiet. The light of a late-rising moon had taken our room. Black shadows of quivering leaves flickered in changing patterns against the white wall. Even before I reached out, I knew that the place beside me was empty. Jenny was gone. I listened. I felt the empty space. I raised up on one elbow, looked about the room. "Jenny?" I whispered.

No answer. Had she gone for a drink? To the bathroom? I listened for the sound of running water, for the flush. I heard no sound. I shook the sheet from my legs. I got up. Gooseflesh fled along my arms, between my shoulders. I tiptoed around the bed. My shadow grew long and strange upon the white wall and moved before me as I left the room. I went along the hall, down the stairs, stopped at the bottom. From my parents' room, the usual deep drawn breaths issued in forgetful counterpoint.

"Jenny?" The whisper met with consuming silence. I dared once more. "Jenny?"

There was a tick of noise in the kitchen. A door? Opening? Closing? Then I heard the tiny, singing wire of sound. The kitten. I slipped over the smooth, moon-sheathed linoleum floor to the back door.

The moonlight lay like water upon the concrete steps. Its light made a clearness deprived of detail, sharper than reality. Jenny crouched on the step, her long hair fallen past her face so that its ends swept the glittering steps. Her arms were lifted from her sides, and the curve of her hands was shaped to the saucer's circle. The tiny kitten, spraddle-legged and quivering, looked frail and blue in the moon's light, fumbling at the offered milk.

She had not heard me. I looked down on her and the kitten, set there like a carving in the wash of light. I gave up a giggle. "Jenny," I scolded, "what are you doing?"

She turned her face to me, looked at me, not surprised, but with absolute assurance, as though getting up in a deserted, half-finished night to feed a stray kitten she could not keep was an entirely reasonable and expected action. "He's hungry." Her lips fluttered between smiles and woe. As she turned back to the kitten, the silvered sheath of her hair fell again over the curve of her cheek, hiding the look on her face as her whispers of love and comfort fell upon the kitten's peaked, attentive ears. The fear and unhappiness from which we had taken our sleep were gone. Watching her there, sturdy and strange in the moon-whitened gown that covered even her human feet, I took from her the tiny blue kitten, the lapping tides of stirring moon-watered air, forgetfulness and wonder for myself.

But in the day that followed, and in the long, tense days following it, there was little such relief. A great silence stood between my mother and my father, and it was not peace. Whatever occasional dialogue went between them began abruptly, ended impotently.

Each day, father walked the long way to the Loop. Late in the afternoon, he pulled open the back door, shrugged his coat from weary, humped shoulders, and dropped it to the bench in the breakfast nook. Like someone very old, cautious of his aches, he lowered himself down beside it. Mother set a dishpan full of water on the green linoleum floor in front of him. He tugged at stiff shoes, sticky socks. He dropped his hot, abused feet into the water, moved his toes, groaned. He leaned his elbows on the table, his head on his hands, and growled out tales of jobs gone, homes lost, businesses closed. "America, America," he muttered. "Land of broken promise." On the radio, Father Couglin's speeches, dreary stock quotations, glum news reports fed his despair.

And mother turned only silence against his words. Hearing his grim, unpatriotic speeches, she suffered, perhaps, the pain and embarrassment burning in me. When he was away, she attacked her chores as through she were fighting a battle involving dust mops and laundry tubs and vacuum cleaners. She didn't walk; she ran, as if victory depended on vigilance, and I knew the battle she waged somehow involved her differences with my father. Buddy was cutting his molars, and when she sang comforting, foolish rhymes to him, rocking him toward rest he could not find, her own face held weariness and pain.

But that she hid from father. She turned toward him a cool, impersonal mask, and he showed her a constant, impersonal and frowning bitterness. They remained if not enemies, antagonists, keeping mind and flesh and soul to resistance.

Jenny paid no attention to their warfares. The kitten had claimed her, and there was room in her thoughts only for it, how to care for it, how to keep it for her own. The Saturday morning after that moonlit night, she found a cardboard box in the basement. She sneaked rags out of mother's ragbag. She tucked the box with its nest of rags in a green hollow of the wild honeysuckle crowding the corner of the empty lot next door. She smuggled milk out to it.

From then on, each morning when we started down the alley to school, I had to wait on the damp concrete, shivers riding up and down my legs, while she crept through the dew-wet branches to see the kitten and leave it bits of her lunch.

When we got home in the afternoon, she poured herself a glass of milk and went out on the back steps to drink it. In a few minutes, she brought the emptied glass back to the sink, and then she was gone. I knew she was going to the kitten's hiding place with a jar of milk held against her stomach. And the kitten seemed to know. At least, it made that bush its home and did not betray Jenny by following her home, as kittens usually do.

At first, the necessary deception cost Jenny something. There were fever and shyness in her darkened eyes; a deepened color burned her cheeks, and it seemed that the demands of conscience gave off the same signs of danger as disease. Or perhaps the burning of cheek and eye was, even in the beginning, not the mark of guilt, but only a sign of the heart's whole mission. At any rate, she was changed, and I thought someone ought to notice other than me. No one did.

The passions my parents themselves were enduring took them from their ordinary perceptions. Jenny went her dedicated, deceitful way. I warned her, and scolded her, and worried, and Jenny ignored all that.

On the last Sunday in May, I went down the stairs into the kitchen full of morning sun. I felt at once, in spite of that wealth of brilliant light, that the air was drained and empty. My mother stood by the stove as though she leaned on the spoon moving slowly through the pan of oatmeal. In the heaviness of lids lying over her inward-looking eyes, in the droop of her head, there was defeat.

My father leaned over the Sunday paper, spread out upon the trestle table. He looked up; brows lifted; his teeth gleamed in a showy smile. "Well, there's a fine sleepyhead!" His laugh was loud and not free.

I knew the fine show was for mother, and she was getting

no comfort or amusement from it. I could not laugh and only blushed. Father picked up the funnies he never allowed us to see until after we were home from church. He gave them to me, and I held them and looked at the gaudy, foolish colors and didn't feel like reading them.

"When is he coming?" my mother said, her eyes not lifting from the spoon.

I looked up from the funnies and out the window at the quiet yellow morning and saw Jenny wandering down the alley in her red sweater, her head bent toward the kitten in her arms.

"This afternoon," father answered, and he looked out the window and saw Jenny, too. "Whose cat is that?" he shouted, his anger easier and truer than his joy had been.

I jumped, hesitated, and found deception easy enough to practice. "I think it's Carrie Wallstrom's," I murmured, and, suffering, went and took Buddy, where he leaned from mother's hip, drooling on his fresh shirt. "Stop that Buddy," I fussed, and wiped away the bubbles he blew from his wet, laughing mouth.

My father studied the paper again. "Stop acting as though it's my fault!" he suddenly shouted.

My mother's hand dropped the spoon and fell to her side. She stood with her head lowered to her chest and turned away from us. My father stood up, looked at her, and stomped out of the kitchen, down the basement stairs, banging the doors behind him. . . .

It was noon, and we were eating lunch in the breakfast nook when the doorbell rang.

"That will be Johnson," father announced. His brown eye shone at mother.

She did not look up to see it, but the spoonful of custard she was lifting toward Buddy's wide-opened mouth stopped in mid-air. Buddy's mouth stretched a wide and wider O. Suddenly it blared out a great, wounded bellow. Mother jumped. She popped the spoon into Buddy's mouth. The howl split off. Father went from the kitchen, and mother began to shovel the filled spoon at Buddy's mouth faster that he could swallow.

"Hurry, girls," she said. Her red head dipped toward the dining-room door. "Shush, girls."

The voice joining my father's was a high-pitched man's voice, with a singsong motion to it that hid its sense.

But father's bugle-noted words came clear. "The floors," he said. "The floors are of first-grade oak. And the hardware. Throughout the house, the finest. Look at that fireplace. Wisconsin stone. Had the best mason in the business lay that fireplace. See how those edges join? Beautiful. The dining room," he said. "Fourteen by sixteen."

They came into the kitchen, my father walking with arms folded across his chest, the rolled sleeves of his shirt showing the muscle lying smooth and heavy beneath the browned skin, his jaw out, his mouth stern and glad. Beside him was a taller man, thin in the body and loose-looking under the pin-striped cloth of his suit. His long legs lifted and dropped in a slow, light step, like the legs of a water spider. His oiled cap of gray hair lay flat and smooth over a crown that was as oval as an egg.

"Mr. Johnson, my wife." My father's smile was for Johnson, his frown for mother.

"How do you do," my mother answered, and her tone was light and armored. She moved from table to sink like a dancer, with dirty dishes in her hands.

Mr. Johnson looked down from his high place. His face slipped into and out of a quick, promising, unreliable smile. His small, light eyes ran from corner to corner, taking in the whole room.

"Inlaid linoleum," my father said, looking coldly at my mother's straight back.

"Ah, yes." Mr. Johnson paused. "The stove should go with,

of course," he said. "It fits so nicely there."

There was a jerk in the arc of my mother's arm as she lifted plates from the table. "We'll keep the stove," she said.

Johnson looked at my father. His smile, tolerant and fluid, slid over his face.

A band of red flared across my father's high-boned cheeks and took his ears. "There are plenty of cupboards," he said. "Look at this large storage closet."

"That comfy breakfast nook should catch someone's fancy." Johnson's chant was comforting.

They went to tour the bedrooms.

Afterward, my father came back to the kitchen. He sat down on one of the benches by the trestle table in the nook and looked out the white-curtained window at the leaves of the one great oak tree, holding the sun sharply on their scalloped edges. He looked at the leaves as though he needed to study the intricacies of their twined and shadowed shapes. He said nothing at all.

My mother went to the table. She put her hands on the table's edge. Now she looked down on father as though she were a teacher and he a recalcitrant student. "Well, what did he say?"

My father looked not at her, but only into the dense clusters of leaves. "Forty-five hundred. He says forty-five hundred."

My mother's hands dropped from the table's edge, went to her sides, came up again, and sat on her hipbones in the shape of fists. Her lips pouted with contempt. Her chin lifted. She stared down at father. The light in her eyes snapped out at him. Her hair and cheeks looked on fire. She stood there growing straighter and taller and blazing more vividly with each short moment until she burst into rocketing words.

"Forty-five hundred? Forty-five hundred dollars? Why, that's ridiculous! It cost that much to build. That doesn't even allow for labor! What about that? Isn't your labor worth anything? If that Mr. Johnson thinks we're going to sell this house at a price like that, he's mistaken, that's what he is! Why, I'll sit here till doomsday before I let you give away this house for forty-five hundred dollars!"

But her indignation didn't touch father. Neither the day's heat nor the last of her words affected him. He sat on the bench, looking out at leaves, as though some cold winter had frozen him to the spot, and when the flare of mother's words faded, it seemed that gray, dreary smoke drifted down over us all, darkening my mother's face so that what had been marvelously brilliant became paled and drained before our eyes. But father didn't see that, either.

"Axel, you can't sell for forty-five hundred," my mother whispered at last.

"Mortage, twenty-seven hundred." (He was counting only to himself.) "Rent, probably twenty-five a month. That's three hundred. Food, a hundred a month. Fifteen hundred. One year. It'll do for one year. Perhaps stretch it some. By then, maybe—."

And then he turned from the window and looked at mother; but she bent from his haunted, calculating look, down to Buddy squeezing her knees. She lifted him up and went away with him, murmuring. "Don't cry, Buddy. There, now. Don't cry."

Johnson came and went at irregular intervals. He brought one or two prospective buyers, who went through the house in a desultory way and did not return. My father still walked to town each day and returned with hurt feet and a bad temper. Jenny was in the empty lot almost all of the time. She named the kitten Tiger, although he had a gray coat with a white bib. Mother was quiet and remote. The frown between her fair brows seemed permanent.

Then it was late June, and we were out of school. The blue days were long and unseasonably hot. Mornings we played in the shade of the oak in the back yard, and afternoons we retired to the damp coolness of the basement and played there. Mother answered an ad in the paper and began to do piece-work for a knitting mill. She got twenty-five cents for each finished sleeve. It took her six hours to knit one sleeve. Father forecast total disaster. "Democracy," he intoned. "A beautiful intention. Failed!"

We went to Powderhorn Park on the Fourth of July. We sat on high hills ringing the small pond and watched the fireworks spray across the close, dark sky. At the end, a box of fireworks blew up, and the show ended precipitously in a wild spatter of sound and brilliant, confused flares, rockets, Roman candles and fire fountains. "Fourth of July," Father shouted. "Last rites."

In the middle of July, the middle of the day, we were in the basement, canning peaches. Jenny and I had slipped the wet, limp skins from the fruit. Mother had halved them, stoned them, slid the yellow rounds into the green Mason jars that stood in rows on the newspaper-covered table. On the small, two-burner gas stove, sugar syrup simmered over a blue flame. The cool air was heavy with sweetness. Mother lifted the pot of syrup from the stove.

The doorbell rang.

"Shoot. Who can that be?" She set the pot back on the stove, lifted the corner of her wet, stained apron, and wiped the fine beads from her forehead. "Berit, run up and see."

I ran up the stairs, through the shade-drawn rooms to the front door. As I reached the door, the flat, dull buzz repeated. I pushed down the latch; pulled at the heavy door with both hands, and almost fell forward into the blast of white light.

"Well, hello, little girl, is your mother home?"

I recognized that high voice. I peered into the sun and up. Behind Mr. Johnson I saw another form, a large bulk of darkness, someone strange, a woman. A buyer. Important.

I banged the door shut and ran back through the dim rooms

and down the stairs, shouting, "Mother, it's Mr. Johnson. And someone else."

Upstairs, the doorbell buzzed. Mother dropped her hot pad and towel, ran ahead of me up the stairs, through the house to the front door. "Excuse me," she said, when I pulled the door open again. "Please come in."

Mr. Johnson looked at my mother as though he towed behind him a cargo of untold value. His face was several shades brighter than usual, his grin wider and looser. "This is Mrs. Faulk." He flapped his hand like a flag.

She had a forward-thrusting, presumptuous bosom, a chin tucked forbiddingly back toward a stiff neck. Her black eyes looked all around coldly, possessively, taking everything in and giving nothing out. She swayed into the living room behind the shelf of her bosom like a captain looking over a ship's bridge. "The shades," she commanded.

Mr. Johnson rushed to a window and jerked at the hoop on the string of the shade.

"I'll do that, Mr. Johnson." My mother's voice was new, and I turned and saw that she had learned in one swift lesson the art of condescension. She went from window to window, her back and mouth stiff. The hot sunlight broke into the room's summer shade.

"Wisconsin stone." Mr. Johnson gestured grandly toward the fireplace.

Mrs. Faulk exhaled audibly through her thin nose. She pushed at the carpet with the perforated toe of her black oxford.

Mr. Johnson stooped and flung the carpet back. "Good—excellent condition, the floors," he cried. "Fine housekeeper, fine, fine."

Red spots marred my mother's cheeks. Her lips closed in upon themselves. "I will leave you, Mr. Johnson. Excuse me." She turned away with her chin high, signaling indifference. She shooed us children down the stairs ahead of her into the basement. She lifted the syrup from the burner and poured it into the jars filled with mounded peaches. White steam rose around her. She blew a long breath up toward her hair, lifted an arm, wiped her forehead.

"Is she going to buy the house, Momma?"Jenny looked toward the stairs, as if she expected to find those cold black eyes staring down at her.

Mother didn't answer.

We were to move to a duplex on Cedar Aveue. It was a high, narrow, scabby-looking building. Its brown paint was flaking.

Black screens on the windows and front porch gave it a sinister aspect. The patch of ground that was its front yard was burned dry, and the bushes flanking the steps were woody and tangled. Traffic was steady down Cedar Avenue. At regular intervals, streetcars roared through its steady hum.

"It's temporary," father repeated, as we toured the empty, high-ceilinged rooms.

My mother eyed inadequate closets; high, narrow windows.

"I can put shelves over the stove," father said, as we trailed through a small kitchen. "The children can sleep three in one room for a while," he asserted, standing in the center of a lightless bedroom. "After all," he shouted at my silent mother in the small, square living room, where dark woodwork looked soft and disintegrating under too many costs of varnish and stain, "what do you expect for twenty dollars a month?"

"Who's complaining?" my mother said, and walked out the door and out to the car at the curb.

But whatever anxiety and pain touched the rest of us still did not touch Jenny. She went about with her face looking like a flower with sun on it. As long as she had the kitten to be sometimes cuddled, sometimes played with and murmured to, nothing else affected her.

But I knew, if Jenny did not, that her strange impregnability was doomed. Time, which she ignored, was still inexorable. Days dawned and turned and passed into swift, forgotten nights. When six or seven more had gone, Jenny would have to abandon her kitten to his makeshift home in the empty lot, and her present happiness would shatter into loss.

On the last day of July, early in the morning, father's friend Lars arrived at the house with an old truck. Draperies were down, folded into huge cardboard cartons and covered with sheets. The rugs were rolled into cylinders. The house echoed when we spoke.

Father was furious with energy. He shouted at all of us. "Get that box out of there. Berit, open that door. Let's get that chest next, Lars. Emma, bring the hammer. Berit, get Buddy out of the way."

Everyone but Jenny hauled and shoved and carried and ran. She was not around.

It was past noon when they went off with the first load. Lars was driving. My mother sat beside him, smudged and disheveled, holding Buddy on her knees. My father stood on the crowded platform of the truck, leaning his elbows on the cab's roof. I was left behind to watch the house.

As soon as the truck rumbled out of sight, I ran to the empty lot to find Jenny. The high, covering weeds were dry. They scraped at my legs as I ran. At the far corner of the lot, the tumble of honey-suckle shimmered where sun touched it. The tiny yellow blossoms gave off light as though of sun themselves, and as I came near the lit place, the air was suffused with fragrance.

"Jenny?" I whispered, as though the place would be marred by ordinary sound. She did not answer. "Jenny?" I moved a branch, and in the deeper light, I saw her there, lying face down on the patch of ground smoothed with use. Her long hair was tumbled over her neck and face. The gray kitten jumped about her, hissing softly and clawing at the strands of her hair. The light was golden upon them, and in its dapple, they seemed private and privileged.

"Jenny!" I said harshly, although why I scolded her I was not sure.

She flung back her hair and looked at me.

"Jenny, come on home," I commanded, though when I came, I had no plans for ordering her away. The sight of that much happiness somehow made it seem necesary to save her from it.

Jenny sat up and took the kitten into her arms. It lay in the folds of her smooth arms, a soft gray bundle collapsed into comfort. The kitten's wide eyes narrowed down, and a lush rumble of purring filled the shady den. Jenny looked at me, her own eyes grown heavy-lidded with secrecy and willfulness. She shook her head. "I'm not coming. I'm going to stay here."

"Jenny, come on. They're coming back. You can't stay here forever."

Jenny looked only at her kitten. She stroked it, and her face began to assume a look of dreams and separation. Then she stopped, shook the hair from her face, sighed. "I'm hungry, Berit."

I could do nothing but go back across the burned grasses to the disordered kitchen and make peanut-butter sandwiches and take them to her with a glass of milk.

I watched while she ate the sandwiches and drank the milk. She stopped drinking before the milk was gone. She held the kitten and tilted the glass, so that he could lap up what was left. I sat and rested and did not say all the things I had already said too often. Now more than ever, she would not listen to what I said, and if I felt sorrowful and full of foreboding, perhaps by now I also envied her for being able to give so wholly what I, possibly, could never give—a desire and love so entire that it could not conceive disaster, although what it risked challenged all realities.

Perhaps I guessed, too, that for one like Jenny, so much

more possessed by what she found within herself than I, that it was not a matter of choice. Even if she admitted that she would lose her kitten and her believed-in unreality within a few short hours, that knowledge would not diminish or alter her commitment, and she would have to accept and endure the suffering which was the price of her gift.

Then I heard the truck's faulty motor clattering up the avenue, I left Jenny in the honeysuckle and ran back to the half-emptied house before father and the gloomy-faced Lars climbed out of the truck.

I ran with them from room to room, as they heaved and hauled the rest of the afternoon.

It was after five, and the hot day was dulling down toward a ruddy evening when father wearily brushed his hands on his haunches, looked around the emptied rooms, said, "Well, I guess that's it. Let's go."

He closed and locked windows and doors, strode out to the truck, and was halfway up on the seat behind the steering wheel when I grabbed his sleeve.

"Jenny. We have to get Jenny."

Surprise sent his eyebrows high up his sweaty forehead. "Jenny? Where is she?"

I pointed to the empty-looking lot. "Over there."

"Well, go get her." He pulled his leg up and settled down behind the wheel. I shook my head. "Hurry up," he shouted, and I ran again over the weeds, knowing what would happen.

After he called the third time, I trudged back to the truck. "She won't come.'

"What do you mean, she won't come? Where is that girl?" father demanded.

I pointed to the corner of the lot. "Over there. In the honeysuckle bush."

He jumped out of the cab and went down the walk and across the vacant lot, shouting, "Jenny, Jenny," in a huge voice, his long legs pumping furiously. I ran after him and saw him rummage through the tangle of branches and stand tall and momentarily arrested when he uncovered her there.

Color and weariness and anger deepened in his face as he looked. He took it all in at once—the nest in the box, the tin for food, the look of custom within the den, Jenny kneeling there on her cleared ground, her kitten against her breast, her eyes at last barren with fear. There was that moment of silence, each one looking, disbelieving, upon the other.

Then father burst into rage. "What in God's name are you doing here?"

With that shout, Jenny changed, stiffened, turned adamant with desire. In eye and mouth and uptilted chin, her will was pitted against his own. "Go away," she shouted. "Go away!"

A snarl like anguish rolled from father's throat. With flaming face and burned eyes, he bent and grabbed the animal from Jenny's arms. He held it by the neck in one hand. The kitten's body arced and twisted. It spit and clawed. Its pointed teeth yearned in the arched red mouth. The claws whipped at father's arm.

Jenny flew at father. She beat on his chest with hard fists, kicked wildly at his legs. Leaves and light shook over the three of them in a whistling, spattering storm.

The fury on father's face became a look I had never seen. That snarling sound repeated in his throat. He wrapped a large, wrenching hand around the kitten's wild, twisting form and turned it fiercely away from the hand that held the kitten's head.

The tiny crack broke through the spitting and the hissing and Jenny's crying, and, in immense silence, the kitten fell from its single, violent shudder and lay broken, looking only like a dirty rag, upon the ground.

With one long cry, Jenny fell upon it there. Father reached down and grabbed her and flung her over his shoulder. He plunged through the fragrant, blossoming branches and ran toward the truck.

We were not what we had been. What was known was gone. What was new was strange. The darker light and limited space of the place in which we lived robbed even the furniture of familiarity. But if the place in which we lived was bleak, it was less than the bleakness each of us found within ourselves. For Jenny and I could not forget. We would never forget; we knew that. And we could not understand at all.

Those summer days, Jenny sat on the chipped concrete steps in front of the duplex and looked at the paper-littered, track-scarred street and did not see what she looked at. Not even the abrupt, paining roar of the streetcars changed the flat disinterest on her face.

If father saw her there, her small round chin held on one upturned palm, unwilling or unable to play, his frown pulled blackly across his face. "Let her sit," he'd say roughly. 'She'll get over it."

But in his eyes there was a distance that had not been there before.

On a leaf-strewn day in October, Jenny and I walked home from our new school. Early evening already blended shadow to dusk. A skinny, half-wild cat darted out at us from the shelter of a low tree. Jenny screamed when she saw it and ran, terrorized and sobbing, the long block home.

When I went into the kitchen she stood in mother's arms, crying and shaking, her dropped books scattered across the floor. Mother looked at me for the explanation Jenny could not give, and father turned the same mystified and worried look from where he was, half up from his chair at the table.

"A cat. She saw a cat."

The look then that went from father to mother, and from her to him, was so stunned and so cold, so knowing and so burdened that I stood in the center of it, a prisoner in its harsh winter.

Then my father turned away. He laid his arms and head upon the table. His shoulders heaved and humped; but I would not have known those shaking sounds were sobs had he not suddenly pushed away from the chair and fled from the house out into the fallen dark. When he rushed by, I saw the tears runneling his face.

And so we could forgive. We lived through those years to years more comfortable. We knew again times of happiness and of love. Looking back, I know that if mother had needed that house less, or if Jenny had been a less willful child, or father a less passionate man, or the times easier, there would have been less hurt. But where we live and where we love, we must, it seems, bear a plenitude of pain.

Tuesdays

I park at the curb in front of the low white house set in the perfect center of its clipped yard. Patches of winter brown mar the green of the grass, but at the corner of the house, against the immaculate white wall, the camellia bush already holds knots of pink bloom in its thick dark green.

As I slide from behind the wheel, I see the curtains in the kitchen windows move. They are waiting, saying to one another, "She is here."

A small black boy, about eight, is sitting on the curb. He wears stiff new blue jeans, a yellow sweat shirt. He tosses a stone into the air, catches it, his eyes sliding toward me when the stone drops neatly into his palm. I smile, he does not smile back. He watches me go around to the passenger door and take out the packages I have brought. My arms full, I bang the door shut, try another smile, say "Hello." He stares off down the avenue, does not answer. On the cross-street, other youngsters shout and run in a game of ball. Their voices are high and shrill, and they, too, are black.

I go up the walk and the five steps to the small portico in front of the door and push the bell. The door will not be opened until the two singing tones fall away on the inside air. Why? They know it is I. Why do they make me wait? A custom of manners? A masking of anticipation, of dependence?

When she is alone, she will not answer the door. Too many hippies, too many thieves. An old couple, not far away, were tied one night to chairs in their kitchen, beaten, burned with matches, robbed. Another old woman was murdered, and somehow worse, an old woman of eighty-three was raped.

And here in their own neighborhood: thefts, beatings. The petunia pots have been stolen from their front steps. The birdbath disappeared from the picket-fenced backyard. A strange muscular boy comes to their door, repeatedly, and asks for money. They give him dimes. They tell me this, smiling as if their coins were charity. But how will the boy respond if they refuse?

They should move, of course. But would anywhere be safe? And what can they afford? And how would they manage strange bathrooms, strange cupboards? And neighbors. What would the new neighbors be like?

Here Mrs. Compton is next door and known—arthritic, long-nosed, her friendship narrow and grudging. She rarely goes out any more. Still, they know her. And across the street is Mr. Levine—humped as a camel, but his backyard full of dahlias. On a summer afternoon he hobbles over, a flower big as a dinner plate in his stained, gnarled hand. Grinning, he stays for a cup of Sanka in the secure kitchen. And down the avenue Mrs. Cavender survives. She comes, asks a widow's favors: fix a faucet, a loose doorknob. He fixes, Mrs. Cavender brings grateful pastries, hard or raw, always inedible. But she, too, is known: that broad drooping bosom, thin blue legs.

Now slowly the bell-sounds fade away and the heavy green door swings back, stops at a twenty-degree angle. Around its edge he peers out at me, his cheeks flushed over the bone, his blue triangular eyes peeky. With shyness. Or shame. Proud, he cannot bear his old age. I make myself offer cheerfulness.

"Hello, Dad! How are you? Isn't it a beautiful day? That sun! The camellias, already! Beautiful."

He touches my shoulder, his hand heavy, clumsy. His smile is small. He draws me in, closes the door behind me. She is sitting in the green plastic Barcalounger in front of the empty fireplace. The footrest of the chair is raised, her legs, the ankles thickly swollen, extended. Her fingers turn crookedly the white thread, flashing hook. Through her thick inadquate glasses, she stares at me intently. The blue light of the television screen flickers over her face. She lifts her thin voice over the melodious voices issuing from the box. "Is that you, Marcie?" she wavers.

I answer, "Yes, Mother. How have you been?" I move toward her, lean down, kiss the soft wrinkled skin of her cheek, taking in the pale, aged, delicate smell.

She spies the packages in my hands. "My goodness, Marcie, what have you brought?" she sings, a bird flute. A social smile moves her mouth. Her head dips to one side, shakes genteelly. "You shouldn't have brought anything. My goodness, that's not necessary, bringing something every time you come."

The words ring from my childhood. She offered the same phrases to her friends, neighbors, bringing cookies or cake for afternoon coffee. Yes, old rituals, old modes. Had they not been correct always? Of course, of course. But now, when so much else is lost, they seem absurd.

"I brought the custard rolls you like, Mother," I report. "And a chicken for dinner."

Behind the glasses where light moves in deep rings, her eyes widen. "Oh, are you staying for dinner? Oh my, that's nice, that's awfully nice of you."

Does she remember who I am? I always stay for dinner, cook for them. Once a week. Between us the television voices are rich with sorrow, intense with pain. "How is Charles, then?" she asks.

That, too, is merely miming convention. What I say she will not take in. But I reply. "He's fine, Mother. He's been terribly busy, there's so much flu around."

Her thin mouth turns downward, the rusty brows gather over the frames of her glasses. "I never get to see him anymore. I wish he could come over, once in a while, check my blood pressure sometimes. I have to have my blood pressure taken, you know."

"He was here last week," I remind her. "Last Sunday. He took it then. It was fine, Mother. Very low." But she will not remember, will believe again that she needs medical attention.

"No, it's been a long time," she grumbles. One shoulder pulls up toward the ear, and she looks sideways at me. She pushes a lumpy forefinger against her side, high up against the fifth rib. "I've got this terrible pain here. It hurts so I could scream. Just like a knife."

"Charlie will come soon," I tell her. "Next Sunday, maybe."

But the comfort is without function. She gives an inattentive nod, forgetting already what is being discussed. An image on the flickering screen has caught her interest. A young doctor, white-coated, frowning and tender, leans over a young woman in a hospital bed. His long fingers lightly hold her wrist. He whispers, "You're going to be all right, Melody." But the face against the pillow does not stir.

And she has moved into that fictional world, totally. Always she has loved medicine. The mysteries of disease. The magic of chemicals. Sick is more important than well. Suffering wins love. For her children she made illness a treat: a winter morning, sheets of snow outside the ice-rimmed window, snowy sheets where I lie in their wide downstairs bed. She comes with a tray: orange juice in dazzling cut glass, scrambled eggs golden on sheer, flowered china plate. Her hand a cool snowflake on hot forehead. Her voice offering music: tales of trolls, fairies, princes, magic. Who could wish to get well, princess in her caring; close, close in her love?

He has come to the archway, beckons, his crippled hand making a jerky sign. "Come and have coffee," he says. "She wants to watch her program now." Complicity gleams in his bright eye. Condescension, tolerance in his voice. The silly programs. The world of pretense.

Already he has set the table. Blue pottery dishes on the fringe flowered plastic cloth. Coffee cups, plates, forks, and spoons properly arranged. Sugar bowl, cream pitcher, paper napkins in plastic holder. The coffee warms on a low flame, giving off a dark rich odor. He is standing at the bread board covering slices of rye bread with a tuna-fish-egg-salad mix. He moves to the cupboard for a serving plate, his feet slow in brown slippers, heavy shoulders round under the blue coat-sweater. His trousers slip down past the push of paunch and are too long and fold over the instep. He goes to the cookie jar, lifts the lid, peers inside. He reaches in, pulls up a fistful of store-bought sugar cookies, drops them onto a plate. He shuffles back to the breadbox, takes out Svenhardt sweet rolls, puts them on the plate beside the cookies.

"Don't put out so much, Dad," I caution. "I'm not very hungry."

His chin jerks up, he shrugs. "You're always dieting," he answers crossly.

If there were fruit or green salad. But they do not eat those things. Nothing tart, nothing spicy. Nothing chewy, nothing hard. Not too much red meat, no fresh vegetables. Cans, frozen packages, mixes.

I eat half a sandwich, a cookie. He is offended. I give in, eat a sweet roll. We talk of weather, shootings in San Francisco, the teachers' strike. And then over a final cup of coffee I take the letter from my purse. "It's from Matt," I tell him. "It came yesterday."

Color deepens in his cheeks. He fumbles in his pocket for glasses, shoves them on. He reads the scrawled casual note. Air huffs through the high-boned nose, the glasses diffuse the angry eyes. Finished, he folds the paper, puts it on the table, runs his scarred thickened thumb over the fold. He cannot look at me. "I don't understand that kid," he mumbles.

I can offer no answer, I do not mean to sigh. His quick

glance darts at me. He pulls off the glasses, waits for my tardy comment. I mumble back, "I don't understand him, either, Dad."

The letter crumbles a bit under the left hand where the second and third fingers are gone, lost long ago under an electric saw. "He's always full of plans, he never settles down." His sharp oblique glance follows his complaint. I watch his hands, smoothing the letter now, hard, repeatedly. "What's wrong with young men these days? They don't want to make anything of themselves. He's had every chance."

It's an old complaint. I think of them together mornings of World War II: in the pale dawn he comes to my war-widow bedroom, takes the fussing baby from his crib, carries him to the kitchen. Changes him, feeds him pablum, warms the bottle. Every morning the two of them alone, chuckling, chatting, the world going up in flame. Five forty-five A.M. he comes back to my room, thrusts the baby into my sleepy arms. Get up now, he commands, take care of Matthew. Matt wailing after him in loss.

"Why does he want to be a bum?" he asks, grief in his quick eye.

"Oh, he's not a bum," I protest. "He supports himself. He's not on welfare."

He drops bits of laughter. To him it is an outrage: the clothes from Goodwill, torn shoes, shabby jackets. Vagabonding: fishing in Mendocino, carpentering in Ann Arbor.

"He needs to explore," I argue. "In another time, he would have pioneered. He would have left home, wherever it was. Just like you did, leaving home at eighteen."

"I worked. I wanted to be something, make something of myself. I didn't want to be poor." The words are sharp. He knows the ugliness of poverty. "I wanted . . . ." His hands grow still on the table, his words fall away.

And that, too, I remember: him sitting in the dining room at the round oak table he had made himself, the great dictionary open before him, paper under his left hand, right hand making the high flourishes of the capitals, bold swellings of the lower loops, practicing the foreign words, practicing sentences. Left hand pushing through the thick hair, lower lip swelling with concentration. "Be quiet!" he shouted and we children retreated. Dunwoodie Institute, blue prints, perspectives, Sunday tours of new houses. Always making. Sawing pounding gluing. Yes, always. Making something. Plans, drawings, furniture. Houses. Himself.

And now his fist hits the table. The sugar bowl trembles, the cream shivers. "You gave him too much. They don't deserve what you give them." His mouth, shaking, seals to hardness, his chin pushes back against the folds of his neck. He stares a moment at his own crippled hand stopped on the table, his blue eyes wet.

"Oh, it isn't that. It's not that he's just spoiled," I say.

His gray head shakes negatively. "I don't mean that, I don't blame you, it's not just you. Or just him. All of them, all that education. That fellowship he could have had. What does he do? Throws it away. What do they want, anyway? They've had it too good, that's all."

She has come into the room, her feet moving cautiously along the waxed floor. She stands by the table, her eyes wide, holding to my chair for balance. "Oh, Matthew," she joins in, carolling. "He used to be with us so much, remember? It was Viet Nam ruined him." She smiles, appreciating her own sagacity.

His chair rasps backward. "Sit down," he orders loudly. "Eat something."

"I never eat till two o'clock," she informs him. "My pills, because of my pills." She watches to judge whether he understands as if she has given new facts. "I have to space my meals so my pills come out right." Behind her he shakes his head, despairing. The repetitions, repetitions! "Yes," she tells us again, "it was the war ruined Matthew."

"Ruined?" he bellows. "He isn't ruined!" He lurches away, goes to the stove, gets the coffee pot. But it is there between us, her word: ruined. Those wet jungles, mines, ambushes, night-time maneuvers. A young C.O. medic, no gun. Friends killed, platoon wiped out, hepatitis. And we at home waiting without word, making our faith keep him alive. The silver star on the shelf. Ruined?

The long black stream of coffee fills our cups.

"Yah, and now that Ford." He gulps black coffee as if swallowing dark visions. "Hand-in-glove with the Wall Street crowd. He doesn't give a hoot about the poor people. And he can't manage anything. Look what happens in the U.N. A collection of bandits and murderers insulting us while they grab our aid. What they did to Israel! And what does Ford do? Nothing. Dances like Fred Astaire, bangs his head in a swimming pool!"

He cannot learn moderation. He is too old for such passions, ought to let go. At predictable times he suffers pains. His gut goes into spasm: nauseated, he cannot eat. He worries that there is something terribly wrong inside. He is hospitalized, tranquillized. Always his body's torments coincide with his grief: his beloved brother dies, Christmas bombings in Viet Nam, children starving in Africa, corruption in Washington, mass murders in California. And his stomach curdles with fury, despair.

"Dad, how are you feeling, how's your stomach?" I ask.

Red-cheeked, embarrassed, he thrusts back his chair, announces he has work to do in the garage. He is making a garden bench for a woman in Piedmont. "You visit with Mother for a while," he commands.

She is concentrating on the cookie plate, straightening the cookies, making a correct circle of them. I clear the dishes, begin to wash them. "Oh, don't bother with those, Marcia, I can do those," she says, another automatic convention. Only he does dishes now.

Then after I hang the damp towel on the oven bar we go to the living room. She lowers herself heavily into her chair. She pushes the lever, her legs ride up on the footpiece. Takes up her crocheting. "I like to crochet. It keeps my hands more limber." She does not look at me. "I've got this arthritis. My doctor says it's good to keep my fingers moving." Should I remind her I am her daughter, my husband is her doctor? No, nothing is required but that I listen. Dispute is pointless, facts have no function.

"Well." She sighs, "I've had a hard life. I had surgery twelve times." She is dreamy with old dramas. But twelve times? "Yes," I concede, "you've had some hard times."

"Have I told you about when Wendell was born?" her hands make jerky angles around the slender hook, the white chainings. Wendell, my brother.

"Yes, you've told me that story, many times, Mother."

"Have I?" Of course, she begins it again. "He thought I couldn't have children, that's why he married me. They tied my tubes, you know, when I was nineteen. On this side." Sad, negative nods. "The labor lasted three days. They walked me up and down the halls. Up and down, up and down. They threw the baby on the table. Dead." An audible inhaled breath, eyes profound with the past. "Another doctor came to help, went to the baby and worked on him. 'Forget the baby,' Doctor Schmidt said. 'Help me with this woman.' But the other one kept on with the baby. Three incisions in his head. Saved Wendell's life."

Why, out of the events of her seventy-six years of life, must she tell this story again and again? All terror, pain. When she forgets so much, why this one repeated tale? Does the deteriorating brain like our old slide projector stutter over some particular synapses, throw up a single frame, repeated, again and again?

"He." She is looking at me out of the corners of narrowed conspirator's eyes. "He never wanted children. How he yelled

at me when I got that way. Once he threw me nearly across
the room . . . ." The peaceful crocheting drops to her knees,
one knobby arthritic hand grasping the other sweatered upper
arm.

I need to stop her. "Mother, don't talk like that."

She huddles back into the chair, swift to sense rejection.
Bitter, she gives it back. "Oh, you don't know. None of you
know."

I get up, go to the television, pull the small brass button.
The picture comes wavering into focus. "Look, isn't this your
program now?"

She refuses distraction. "You don't know," she repeats
brightly.

But my own memories defend. How he came home in
work clothes pale with sawdust. His call, his laughter, lifting
us up in strong arms, the cold winter breath of him against
our faces. Turning us in somersaults, dancing us on his shoe-
tops. Nights in the basement workshop, his singing saws, his
hard hammers. Making things she needed, something she
wanted.

"Mother, he was good, too. He worked all his life for his
family."

"Ha." Her glance accuses me of disloyalty, ignorance.
"The other day, he yelled and yelled at me."

"Hush, Mother, watch your program now."

"He writes all the time. He keeps writing things," she
confides.

Yes, that is true. In his old age, he writes and writes. The
letters fly to Sweden: his sister, his nephew. To Ann Arbor,
Boston, Toledo, Hardwick—his grandchildren. To Minneapolis, his old friends. Sometimes they answer. Then he reads
the letters aloud as we sit at the plastic-covered table in the
sunshiney kitchen. Tears run down his cheeks.

"I found this letter he wrote. He thinks he is going to die."
She scoffs at the idea. *He* die? He has never in his life been
sick. It is *she* who is going to die.

"He is only thinking about you. He wants to provide for you." I turn back toward the television screen, pretend to watch. But she smiles, ironic disbelief. "Oh, he does terrible things. You don't know."

Can it be true? He is hot-tempered. She is stubborn, critical, difficult: she'd try anyone's patience. Does he yell in a frenzy of frustration? Give her a push now and then? Or is it a drama inside her head—confusion, dreams, paranoia? Why does she make him an enemy? He cleans her house, cooks her meals, washes her underwear.

I begin to talk without pause, narrate last week's small events, repeat old news about my children, her grandchildren, whom she cannot recall. Then at last the tv screen fills with a blue and green globe spinning in rich light. She smiles, wriggles back into the chair finding complete comfort, attends the screen. These are her people: these she remembers, these she loves.

I return to the kitchen and take out pots and pans, start the rice, wipe the chicken with a damp towel. He comes up from his workshop, watches. How much rice, how much onion, parsley, oregano? Salt? So: rice stuffing! How long does it bake? He found a good recipe in the paper, wants to share it. He goes through the cupboard drawer, finds the clipping. He copies the recipe on the back of an envelope. (That elegant hand, the loops and flourishes!) He hands it to me, grinning. Trading recipes! He is proud.

I am slicing carrots into a small pot. He makes that choppy, clumsy, beckoning gesture. Wants to show me something. He has taken a large black-covered book from the cupboard. A sort of ledger. I go sit at the table beside him.

"Look, what I've been doing." He turns back the stiff cover. On the pages of the book, photographs are fastened with bands of Scotch tape. Slowly he turns the pages. The photos are old, edges cracked, tones faded are mounted crookedly, clumsily, without regard for time or sequence. "I took all the pictures from all the drawers around here. I'm putting them all in here. Then we'll have them all in one place." He pushes one snapshot with a stained forefinger. "Look at this. Remember that trip we took?"

"Oh my gosh," I croon, tender over Wendell and me and him by a stone wall, the ranging high hills of pine in the distance. "When was that, nineteen-what?"

"Grand Marais, must have been 1937." He puts his finger on the lower edge of another. A color print. Of my mother. She stands before one of her rose bushes, one large peach-colored bloom cupped in her hand. The red tones of her auburn hair picked up by the ruddy, orange rose. She is plumped-cheeked, smiling. "Remember how she loved her flowers?" The calloused finger moves over the snapshot's surface, gentle. Another photo beside it, again she stands by her flower bed, several years later, a hat low on her brow. "She was a pretty woman," he mutters. "Smart, too. She sewed all your clothes, remember? Even your coats, Wendell's suits."

I study the photographs, hearing the choke in his words. I will not look at him.

"She wouldn't let me step inside the door with sawdust on my clothes, she was so fussy, so clean." His laugh is giddy, apologetic. He pushes knuckles against the wet trails on his cheeks. He finds a gruff tone. "That Wendell. Why can't he write? She looks for a letter every day." In the photograph, Wendell wears knickers, floppy cap, big front teeth. "Think, he's fifty now. At least a postcard."

The pages move again, giving irregular portions of our lives. Reminding of what we loved, of what we must remember to honor in the name of what was.

"This is a nice one," he points out. I have not seen the picture before. A young woman, small, her hair almost too heavy for the delicate head, stands in the curve of a young man's arm. Her white dress, blown by wind, curves around slender hips, lifts above slender ankles. His hair tumbles over a high brow, he is straight shouldered, lean. They look happy, perfectly confident, happy! "That was the year we got married. 1919."

In the seven o'clock evening, I lean over her chair, kiss her cheek. He follows to the door, steps out to the roofed-over entry. Dark is dropping into the dusk, and in its fall the street lamp on the corner brightens. In the antique light, he seems tired. He thanks me for coming. I say I will come next week. On Tuesday, as usual, he breathes deeply in, out, touches my shoulder. Then suddenly confesses, "Marcia, it can't go much longer, like this. With her like this."

Then we hold each other in a clumsy hug. What is there to do? The air is chilly, night has come. At home my family waits. He walks with me to the car and stands at the curb. Moving down the avenue I look back, and in the circle of light under the street lamp he is waving goodbye.

Three Against the Dark

No one called him Owl anymore. Only he himself when, in an unexpected moment, the mirror before which he hastily adjusted his tie or swooped the brush at his disordered hair became suddenly vividly objective, and the confronting image looked back at him with startling revelation.

"Owl," he said then, as if the boy who had been given that comic name could wake up there behind the heavy horn rimmed glasses where light drowned in repeating rings and shout, "Oh yes, I'm here. Don't worry about that."

In those rare moments when he stopped and looked upon his life with some obligation for measurement, Owl found it quite beyond explanation that he had become all that he had always wanted to be, and that it had culminated in this incomplete fulfillment that left him so entirely on the fringe of those things that made up usual human lives. For he had, at forty-two, no home. No wife. No children. Not even friends.

The people in his life were those colleagues who worked with him in the clean, echoing jungles of the immense hospital, and who shared with him the mysteries and wonders and worries of the lives and deaths over which he labored. But even with them his dedicated reserve made for separateness.

There were, of course, the patients. But they could, in all their multiplicity, their dependence, their gratitude, and cruel neediness, in no way be termed friends. What they asked and needed he gave in measure that was most often full, but whatever private needs he himself might have fell outside the limits of those disease-defined relationships.

So on that June night well past midnight when that old name "Owl" sounded suddenly upon the austere emptiness of the Doctors' Lounge, he was not immediately attentive. He had been sitting on the couch under the excess light of the neon tubes and had not been reading the magazine open in his hands. The light slipped off the page in a way that defied his eyes, and he was, after all, too tired to take anything in. It had been a hard day, and he knew that if he did not soon stir himself and get started on his way home, he was in danger of falling alseep where he sat. It would not be the first time he had fallen asleep there in the lounge and wakened in the greasy light of dawn to start another day in the hospital without having breathed any other than its medication-laden air. But he sat numbed, weariness almost giving the effect of pain, and he did not hear anyone else enter the room. There was only that familiar voice.

"Say, Owl," someone said, "what are you doing here at this time of night?" And Owl thought that the words must have come out of himself, from some vista near sleep. He neither raised his head nor opened his eyes. But the voice rang again, pleased, intimate, surprised.

"Owl, are you sleeping? Right here?" At that Owl looked up. A white-frocked man stood over him, leaning over as if to examine him. The face into which Owl looked wore a cast of amusement, and of kindness, but also, Owl perceived, of tenderness. An impulse to return some version of the man's fine smiling tugged at the corners of Owl's dry, sleep-heavy lips.

"No, not sleeping," he said. "Almost though," He breathed deeply, and he was immediately aware of a grip of pain high in his chest, and knew then that as he sat there on the green plastic couch he had been growing increasingly aware of that pain. Its presence made him forgetful of the person addressing him. He sat testing the sense of pressure just below the clavicle. It faded with shallower breathing, lightened. He accounted for it medically as coming from his cramped position on the discomforting couch. He lay the journal down on the cushion beside him, leaned back, breathed carefully. Once more the white-coated interested person intruded. Owl pushed his glasses up on his nose, stared at his visitor, frowned.

"I don't think I know you. Do I?" he muttered at last, thinking it odd that he did not, for surely anyone who called him Owl must come from some old intimacy he ought not forget.

The man straightened up, grinned, shoved his hands into the pockets of his trousers. The white coat shifted, revealed a broad chest, a lean, well-formed body. His response came with that peculiar joyousness Owl had first heard. "Sure. You know me, Owl. At least I know you." he said.

Irritated, resenting the necessity of it, Owl inspected him carefully. Rosy-faced, expectant, companionable. Tall. Crisp dark hair shot through with silver, deep-set eyes giving out rich light, wide brow, Grecian nose, strong jaw. Handsome. Owl hunted for the right reference. A doctor obviously—the white coat. Who? Which ward? Not one of the interns, Owl thought. Too mature for that. And not in radiology. He knew his fellows well enough to exclude that. Nor a surgeon, he thought tiredly, almost carelessly, losing interest as weariness diffused his impressions and the fingering of pain returned to distract.

"Sorry," Owl said. He pushed a forefinger under the lens of his glasses as if sleep hazed his vision and he would think more clearly if he could see more perfectly. He pushed both hands through his hair, telling himself to get up, walk the long corridors to the parking lot, get in his car, and start the drive across the city to his apartment. He wanted nothing more than to be there, simply there in his own bed in the private dark of his own place right now. But the body he commanded to move, to rise, to get on with its last chores resisted his admonishments. So he sat where he was and gazed once more at the waiting, extraordinarily friendly doctor. Anesthesiology, he thought all at once. That must be it. He gave the recognition words.

"You're in anesthesiology, aren't you?" he murmured. But this discovery had startled him into wakefulness, and wakened as well that pressure against the wall of his chest. Of its own accord, his hand lifted and lay upon his rumpled coat over the place that ached. Then the dark-haired man was leaning over him, his smile gone under a suffusion of concern.

"I say there, Owl. Does that pain you as much as all that?"

Owl dropped his hand, straightened up. "Bit of gastritis now and then," he mumbled. He had not even had dinner. His unknown friend shook his head.

"You work awfully hard, you know, Owl," he chastised. "You don't take any time off. No recreation at all. Only medicine."

Owl shrugged, indifferent to what might otherwise have offended him, wanting now only that the other go so that he would have solitude in which to deal with this thing threatening him from within his own flesh. But the anesthetist was looking at him with an expression of such real concern that despite his impatience Owl gestured assurance, and dismissal. "Tired," he said. "It's only that I'm so tired."

The man watching him straightened then, moved away. He stood by the narrow windows at the end of the room and looked out at the summer night—darkness splintered under street light, eroded by flaring neon signs. A city night, not dark, not quiet. All at once the man leaned over, pulled on the window's brass handle, raised the sash to the sweep of night breeze. He leaned his hands on the sill and breathed the cool gas-and-tar-tainted air. "Beautiful night," he said in that quiet, resonant voice. "It's a marvelous night, out there.

Look, Owl." He turned from the window, smiling again, animated. "Owl, have you ever sailed at night?"

Owl looked at him uncomprehendingly. Sailed at night. Sailed what? A ship? Him? A ridiculous question. He shook his head, watching the stranger, a dark, impressive figure against the red and amber light that flickered on darkness behind him.

"There's nothing like it, Owl." The stranger's face held an enviable energy. "The sea at night. The wind. The riding of the boat. Stars overhead. The quiet. Owl, you should hear that quiet. Immense. Peaceful. No car, not a motor. Not one human sound apart from your own. It's the most restful thing in all creation, sailing at night."

For a moment Owl felt his unknown friend's conviction persuading him. But then his great weariness, and his need to get home, and his old disbelief in the exotic denied interest. He stood up. "Guess I'll be off," he said.

But at his words the man came swiftly from his place by the window. He took Owl's arm. "Why, no, Owl," he protested firmly. "You don't want to do that. I came just to get you. We want you to come along. My brother and I."

Afterwards Owl wondered that he had not been able to resist, but it did not matter much afterward. As it was, he followed his guide along the corridors and out of the front entrance to the street's curb, where a low black convertible was parked. In it someone waited.

Owl could not see the man's face, but he saw clearly the nod and heard the clear, deep voice say, "Hello, Owl." Afterward he remembered vividly the ride down the city's hilly, night-stilled streets as he sat between the two similar, familiar, unrecognizable brothers.

But it was the voyage itself, afterwards, that fascinated him, held him, came repeatedly to his thoughts to trouble and delight him. From that recollection he could not turn, nor from that of the woman.

They parked the car at the bay's edge, where numerous boats rocked against the deep water and deeper sky. The brothers got out and strode along the piers to a large, tall-masted boat. Owl followed, not resistant now, feeling compelled, not able in his total tiredness to attend even the gathering ache in chest and shoulder.

He stopped where they stopped. When one of the two brothers already easily there on board reached out a hand to him, Owl climbed up beside him. Awkwardly, like a child, he stood wide-legged on the treacherously rocking deck. And a third voice startled him—a woman's, low, quiet, carrying a warmth and caring like that he had heard in the others.

"It's good to have you here, Owl," the woman said. For the third time that night Owl turned expecting to meet someone he would know. He looked into the face partially revealed by the night's random light. He thought that she was extraordinarily beautiful then, and afterward he could not say whether the beauty he recalled was of flesh or of person. He felt that he knew her and he could not identify her, and he could not tell whether his knowledge of her was old or new.

Beside her was a dog, a large, self-possessed animal of a color neither slate nor bronze but something between. It seemed to Owl that the dog astutely and coldly judged him. He felt that it was that massive, aloof, royal-looking dog whose judgements he had to pass. And as he stood there feeling the woman's hand lying quietly on his own trembling arm, the animal seemed to arrive at his necessary judgement. The great head dropped from inspection, swung in a low arc toward a calm surveyal of the two brothers, who leaned and bowed to tasks with lines and wheels, their motions as precise as in ritual. It seemed to Owl that the dog supervised them also.

But there was no time to pursue such bizarre impressions. Without warning, almost imperceptibly at first, the boat moved without visible cause from its berth out into the channel of water between the other berthed boats. Slowly, directed by its skilled attendants, the boat went out into the wide bay waters. There the deeper rhythms of water took her into greater motion.

Then there was a call, sudden, timely, from the taller brother. *The boom!* The woman drew Owl swiftly back. There was a sweep of timber, a sudden great shaking under the steady wind. A great sail riffled free, unfurled, spread whitely into a full, high curve, stretched taut against sky and wind.

And she moved then, the boat, no longer with that slow processional grace. With one keen quiver she swooped into the first deep trough of tide. The waters broke before her prow in an exuberant rushing. In that rush of sound the boat rose on a sleek slope of following water, paused at its crest, began again the swoop of descent. Owl clung to the boat's rail, learning the ways of that powerful motion. It seemed to him like the beginning of great music— astonishing, magnificent in risk, breathtaking in accomplishment.

Then the woman standing beside Owl touched his arm. She led him to a place near the boat's cabin. She motioned him to sit there upon a box-like projection. Then she went from him and joined her brothers in their tasks on the foredeck. Owl sat in his appointed place, protected from wind and spray, and took in the things of the strange world about him, those things he would remember.

The city's lights moved into distance. Darkness gathered around them. Over them the flocked stars swung across a moonless sky. Wind swept about them. There was the roar and splash of wave, and the cut of their journey in opposition to those waves filled the air with sound. The deck lay slick and shining under the flung spray, and surrounding them in limitless distance rolled the dark sea.

All was darkness and light, Owl thought, set in marvelous opposition—dark sky studded with brilliance, dark water laid over with dark light, the dark boat, the white sail curving like a shell against the darkness. They seemed, with the rush of wind about them, somehow arrested while in motion, held like statues in postures of perfection. Of the three, Owl perceived, it was the older brother, the darker, quieter one, who was the leader, the final authority. The other, the anesthetist, was unique in his gentleness, his beneficence. And the woman, almost as tall as they, as sure and impressively unique, seemed an embodiment of things he knew and desired and needed, and it was she who most mystified him.

But it was their freedom and authority which impressed him. They were so entirely, Owl observed, what they were, demanding nothing else of themselves than that, as sure of their self-possession as royalty might be. The beauty of the three, the beautiful naturalness and the belonging of their togetherness pleased him immensely. And comforted him. Comforted. A strange word, he thought. But right. For all at once he knew himself strangely rested there on that boat's deck. At peace. Something which he had not known he burdensomely bore was lost within him. There was a cessation of weariness, of those hungers, mute and unacknowledged, that had made his full days without reward. What he was and what he was not seemed not to matter then. What he had not mattered neither. To be there with those three on the great dark sea in a boat that rocked upon heavy waters in rhythms that more than soothed was sufficient.

He had again grown sleepy, the effect of the boat's rocking and the force of wind too much to resist. He leaned his head against the cabin wall behind him. Despite his desire to remain awake to the exceptional things of that night, he must have dozed, for unexpectedly the woman stood beside him. She leaned over him and spoke in that deeply-quiet voice.

"Would you like to go in, Owl? You may sleep in the cabin if you wish."

He could discern, even though she stood in shadows cast by the mast and sail and lines behind her, that she smiled, and

it seemed to him that her smile was edged with regret, or
perhaps with resignation. He met the look of her dark eye.
He shook his head. "No," he said. "I like it here. I don't want
to miss any of it."

She sat beside him then. For a time they sat without
talking. Wind and water took them, kept them. Within the
ceaseless sound and motion they seemed held in a central
quietness, intimate in isolation. It seemed not at all unusual,
not in the least intrusive when her questions came.

"Owl," she said, "you have always been so alone. Why
have you been so much alone, for so long?" For her, because
of what he felt she was, and because of something which the
whole night signified, he searched for a response that would
be truthful. He thought back over the years in which he had
grown from quietness and studiousness into the complete
withdrawal from which he hardly considered the word lonely or alone. It was so much in the middle of others. That was
its puzzle. And he could not, although he sat for some time
considering what events and what choices had moved him
into that extreme of isolation, find acceptable explanation for
it.

"I don't know," he said at last. The wind frayed the sound
of his words into nothing more than a whisper. "I do not
know," he repeated. "I don't even know how."

The boat dipped deeply to the water's roll. The brothers
on the foredeck swung the helm, released lines, called out,
The boom, and the great angle of white sail slid from left to
right with a great, windy shudder. The woman beside him
lightly sighed.

"You should not have been so much alone, Owl," she said.
"You missed too much of living."

Past tense, Owl thought, not present. If she had spoken the
words in the present tense he would have been certain he had
been chided in just that way before. He turned and looked at
the woman sitting beside him in the salt-fresh darkness. It

seemed to him then that the lofty brow, the compassionate eye, gave back the image of what his mother had been. He smiled at that.

"And was there never anyone, no special person for whom you cared, Owl, in all those years?" she asked.

"No one," he said, and he spoke again, letting his words fall with unusual freedom into the cave of wind. He told her how it had been for him as long as he could remember in the way of separateness. He spoke of what he had chosen for himself and of what his life had been composed in keeping with that choice. She listened to all he said as if she would keep each word for her understanding.

"I have not really needed much, you see," he said. "For so long it was enough just to do the work."

"I know," she said, nodding, and she looked up at the far clock of stars moving over them. The wind and the motions of water seemed to take up, repeat her words. *I know, I know.* And after a time Owl added that one truth he had not known and now knew and had not yet given into her keeping.

"It is only that now I am tired. Extraordinarily tired. That makes the difference," he said. "Now it all seems too much. And not enough."

I know, I know, I know. He heard the soft, accompanying sounds. Perhaps she never said them at all. Like a child who has no command greater than those of his own felt needs, Owl found himself going from her into sleep. She rose, stood over him. She laid her hand upon his head, lightly, as a mother would. The wind moved her garments about her. She spoke two quiet phrases, and then she went from him. He saw her where she stood in the cabin's passageway. She held in one hand a golden guttering lamp. The other lifted toward him as if in greeting, or farewell. "Keep you. Keep you in my memory," she said, and then was gone. And while the boat pursued its journey Owl slept.

The next day he woke at noon to the falling sounds of

cathedral bells. Sunday. He lay in his solitary bed in his small apartment, arrested by what seemed memory, but the strangeness of which convinced him had been dreams. Three people who called him Owl had taken him sailing in the dark of night, and he had known them and deeply cared for them and he did not now know their names. Incredible, he said aloud. But the aspects of that voyage came to him in vivid detail. The recalled experiences and none of the obscurity had none of the fragmentation of dreams.

So he watched, in the days that followed, for that anesthetist. He observed each white-frocked person striding the hospital corridors, each one leaning over microscopes and lab counters and diagnostic equipment. He watched particularly the masked men who stood in the operating rooms watching over patients and medications. He never saw the tall, rosy-faced person who had befriended him that night.

And more than he knew, he watched for the woman who had sat beside him on the boat's deck and heard the insignificant revelations of his life and found them valuable. Now and then, at odd places, he found himself stopped by some stranger's walk, by the lift of a chin, a gesture of hand. The person he paused then to observe was never the woman who stayed so vividly in his memory.

One day several months later, Owl sat at the desk in his office and looked down at the X-ray plates which revealed the pattern of irreversible disease. He had now to give the disclosed news of no hope to the young woman who sat in tense restraint on the chair in front of his desk.

"Your mother," he said, keeping the distance and quietness in his voice which he had learned allowed best the listener's defense, "has carcinoma of the lung. The X-rays indicate that there is already diffuse metastasis to bone. See here, now." Owl paused and moved the X-ray plate across his desk so that the woman could herself see the empirical evidence of inevitability.

The woman listened quietly to his statements. Only the tremor in her voice as she asked the necessary questions betrayed her composure. At the end, when she rose to go, she looked at him with sudden compassion. Something in her eyes seemed to convey her understanding of what it meant to be the bearer of such unhappy facts. The look was at once familiar.

"Say," Owl demanded abruptly, "do you sail?"

The woman stopped in her going, looked back at him. The solemnity of her face changed as she looked at him to puzzlement and then to a gentle delight.

"Why no," she said. "I don't. Do you?"

And beyond the fumbled explanations of his rudeness, his curiosity, past the clumsiness with which he tried to mitigate what might have appeared unkind, Owl recognized sufficient ground for what later grew between them. Six months later they were married.

Then to Owl's life things were added which took his attention fully—a son who inherited his mother's easiness and his father's solemnity; a daughter whose vivacity was accountable to neither. And with the children came other facets of experience which Owl had once thought not possible for him, or even desirable. Neighborhood barbecues, ball games, involvement in the minor catacylsms of school and home and community.

He ceased to watch for the three with whom he had sailed. With the passage of time he thought of them only rarely. They became only an image in his mind, three forms against the dark, a recollection of beauty and of peace which was only momentarily present.

But on a night twenty years later, he drove down the steep slope away from the hospital, thinking vaguely of the case he had watched over that night, of his daughter's graduation dance taking place at that very moment, of his wife waiting patiently in the now familially historic house on the

tree-lined street of the city's surburbs. The avenue's slope
went toward the bay, and on that night the glinting bay water
seemed particularly beautiful. For reasons he did not analyze,
he did not keep to the avenue circling the bay as he usually
did. He turned from the street and drove down to the piers
where rows of sailboats dipped and swayed in the sheltered
water. He parked.

When he heard the voice, he was not surprised. He realized
at once that it was the reason he had come.

"Owl," someone said. "Say there, Owl." Owl waited,
listened. He felt the lurch in his breast. "Come aboard." He
heard that warm, companionable voice tell him. For a moment the invincible pain cleaved flesh from thought, and then
he heard that other low, remembered voice, the woman's,
murmuring, "Remember me. Oh, keep you me."

Owl saw her then, on the boat's deck, and she reached
toward him with that singular backward gesture of hand he
had never forgotten. Beside her stood the brothers in their
remarkable authority, waiting. The large dog lay on the
moon-whitened deck, quite motionless, silver and blue under
the wash of dark light. Only the roll of watchful eye marked
his knowledge of Owl's presence there.

Hardly knowing how he moved, his chest aching with
need, he went to them. He stepped into her arms like a child
returning home. The boat slid past the docks. "The boom,"
one brother called. The great sails snapped to white towers.
The boat leaped like a swan to the rolling sea. The dog lifted
a blue head, howled.

Only then did Owl regret. He saw as if his eyes had new
power the lit room in which his daughter tugged crossly at
the sash on her green gown and his wife ran to help while
their tall son laughed.

"No," Owl cried out to the whistling sails, the imperious
wind, the endless sea.

But the woman's arms held him. She lay her cool cheek

against his. The vision dropped into darkness. The child, the wife were nothing. He saw only the woman's face, felt only her breath, sharp as chrysanthemums in the deepening night. The brothers, silent and calm, gazed at the distances toward which the ship sailed and the blue dog, unmoving, kept watch in the prow.

The Middle Place

The tan thermos is filled with iced tea and the battered green gallon-sized thermos jug with cool tap water. Victoria carries them, her straw sunhat, two terrycloth towels, and a bar of soap down to the car where Aaron is putting his tools in the trunk. As they drive past the Ross Valley Savings and Loan, the electronic sign on the building's face flashes 98°, 12:03 P.M. Yes, the middle of the day. August. Hot. It is Aaron's "afternoon off," and they are going to the vineyard.

On Highway 101 the concrete lanes shimmer under sheaths of light. Flashes of chrome from speeding cars dart against the eye. Air flowing through the open windows is warm, dry, dusty.

Aaron drives intently, his head thrust forward a little, his shoulders moving with the rhythms of long curves. He likes to drive. His square strong hands hold the steering wheel firmly. His face appears both attentive and relaxed. But, of course, Aaron likes all doing and demands of himself that he do all things well. He is so easily graceful, it seems, having no awkwardness of body. And no inefficiencies of mind, either, Victoria believes, perhaps because he gives precise concentration to whatever task or problem faces him.

A sigh drifts from her. She shifts a little on the sticky plastic passenger's seat. She has always envied Aaron a little. She is erratic, absent-minded, her head doing one thing, her hands another. And so she falls into foolish error. Just this morning she had turned the stove on high, intending a quick cup of coffee. Then she had gone out to water the potted plants on the patio. Only when the dark stench of burning dregs stained the outside air did she remember. She had burned the pot! Of course such mishaps irritate him, though he is accustomed to them.

She is just home after four months in England where her daughter Elise has borne their first grandchild. And while there, she decided to travel the continent, see everything she could. Now, though they have been married forever, and Aaron was well cared for in her absence, she feels she has been gone too long. For the one traveling, time goes too fast, but for the one at home, it absurdly lengthens. Victoria feels a strangeness in Aaron, a growth of something new which she cannot identify. Of course, in new situations persons shove out newnesses, unobserved and unattended sproutings, that when discovered startle even themselves. And hasn't she also set out strange tendrils, traveling alone, stretching herself, or restraining, to accommodate foreign ways? Yes, the four months apart have pushed them into difference, and Victoria watches Aaron, listens intently to what he says, studying him, trying to perceive how he is changed. She observes a darkness in his look, a shadow lying under his familiar broad smile. What unshared thought lies beyond his words? What does the change portend?

It has been a beautiful summer, he has said. *A perfect summer.* It is a statement he repeats, not realizing, she sees, the repetitiveness. He seems to be explaining something, or offering excuse. But the summer seems to her like all other California summers. The days since her return have been, like this one, identically clear of sky, warm of mornings, hot of afternoons. Each evening comes with suddenness and is cooled by the breath of fog sifting over the tanned hilltops. Yes, California summers are always equable—long, pleasant, and predictable. What then, in all this, is *especially* beautiful? What is the particular perfection Aaron marvels at?

She looks at the passing land, the tan flanks of long high

hills. The grasses are dry now and the slopes no longer golden, but dun-colored, almost gray. The runnings of live oak in the folds of land look tarnished, in the brilliant sun the green crowns blackened by the deep shadow lying under leaf. This is not fertile land they are driving through, range county, and the scattered cows droop in the trees' aprons of shade.

Beautiful? England had been lush with summer green, the fields flowery and fruitful, the summer skies dappled with billowy cloud. Ripeness, rich growing, summer bounty, blue and green, moist and fragrant. Yes, that was beautiful. But this, this time of long dusty sameness, the perennial stasis of California days—can this be called beautiful?

The car is slowing. On either side of the highway, orange and yellow machines roll along the great hills, moving in their toothed scoops great mounds of earth. The cut slopes are ragged with stone and dry soil. Clouds of dust rise from the machines' heavy treads, fly out in sheets with the hot wind. Aaron closes his window, Victoria hers. They stifle in the small closed space, and the construction project forces them to drive slowly.

Bernie found leafhoppers last week, Aaron is reporting. *He thinks we'll have to spray.*

Bernie is the farmer who tends the vineyard. He is a vigorous, positive man, but long experience gives his robust enthusiasm a cast of wisdom. Victoria wipes the sweat from her forehead, asks, *What are leafhoppers?*

As Aaron talks, she watches for clues, extends intuitions. Something deep in Aaron's primitive self, something unknown to him in his earlier years, comes with great joy to the tending of his land. A nature lover herself, she does not find it hard to take pleasure in his weekly trips north to the small vineyard: the hour's drive through this countryside, the spread of prune orchards in the valley flatlands, the small cattle ranches in the sparser soiled, partially wooded hill-lands, the apple groves near Petaluma, the charming acres of orderly vineyards around Healdsburg. Yes, all these delight her, ring the closed circle of her daily living with a fine earthy connection. And she likes working in the vineyard with Aaron, tying vines to stakes and wires, pruning suckers from the ropy stalks, pulling the wiry tenacious morning glory weeds from the powdery earth, exchanging slow talk as they move down the rows of fruit, sharing silence under a cover of nature's quietness. But she knows the vineyard does not signify to her what it does to Aaron. For her the connection is a loved finery; for him it is a root thrusting more deeply that he had known it would, feeding the very center of his existence. Yes, for him, it is a connection to a life source. The artery, the heartbeat.

Where the large green highway sign reads DRY CREEK ROAD, Aaron takes the off-ramp, drives under the overpass and then along the two-lane macadam road bordered by small houses with fenced ungardened yards. Beyond the last pasty pink house he makes a sudden left turn and bumps along the unpaved roadway to the field's gate. Aaron stops, sets the brake, slides out. His faded blue workshirt sticks damply to his back. He pulls the key from his jeans pocket, opens the rusty lock, swings wide the long gate. He returns and drives through to the edge of the field.

Hot, Victoria murmurs. *It's going to be terribly hot.*

Wear your hat, Aaron cautions.

She climbs out, settles the cheap Mexican straw hat on her head. She stands in layers of heat, feeling suddenly and strangely small. The vineyard lies before her, the vines, Johannesburger Riesling, hanging voluptuously from the wires, their broad flat handshaped green leaves coated with a thin film of dust. The green looks slightly reddened under that dusting of earth, as if slowly rusting. Set precisely eight feet apart, the vines stretch in straight green rows, and from where she stands at this end, it seems that the rows close together at the far end, making a great scalloped oriental fan.

In the near rows Victoria sees the thickly crowded grapes hanging in pendant clusters under the shelter of leaves. They are silvery green, each globe round and tight, the skin's sheen milky and luminescent, like opals. On the left side of the narrow roadway, the neighbor's fields are also heaped with leaf and fruit. Those vines are spur-pruned, without wires, and at this time of year they seem a wild tangle of untended growth. To the eye moving the distances of the field, they look like round green huts crammed close together, hundreds of them, no space visible between one green hump and another. Victoria crosses the road, leans close to examine the grapes. These clusters of Pinot Noir are blue, a pearly deep sapphire blue, and they smell of sun and sweetness and must. She reaches out, pulls one perfect blue globe from its stem, puts it in her mouth. It lies warm and smooth on her tongue. When she crushes it between her front teeth, the liquid spurts out tart blue and sourly sweet. She shivers, grins.

Aaron has opened the trunk of the car and is hooking to his belt the yellow plastic pail which contains a pumpkin-sized ball of thick yellow twine. He pushes over his thumb a metal ring with a small protruding blade, a miniature scimitar. Victoria particularly delights in this small fifty-cent tool, designed to meet so special a need: freeing the hands to hold vine and string while a motion of the ringed thumb cuts the needed length. Aaron lifts his shovel to his shoulder and moves along the edge of the field to a center row. He enters the green-edged aisle. Victoria follows after him, simply observing. It is so long since she has been here! She missed all the spring, the flowering of the valley's prune trees, the burgeoning of the life-less looking crooked vines, the first miraculous growth!

It's a good set. Aaron lifts a leafy branch to demonstrate. *It should be a good crop.*

Yes, there is so much fruit that the strong vines are strained to bear it. Aaron bends to chop a sucker from the base of one thick woody trunk, rises to tie a wind–loosened branch. Victoria watches his hands: the motions of winding the cord twice around branch and wire, the looping for the knotting, are perfectly precise, without waste. Boy Scout, Navy man, surgeon. Order, deftness, economy, control. Gardener now, scrupulous farmer, he works with the vines with as much absorption and skill as he brings to a medical problem. Victoria laughs at him, admiring his absurd industry, loving him. But she continues to stroll the aisle like a tourist, makes no pretense of working.

Grapes! She remembers blue heaps in a blond wooden basket, a crimson border around its edge, a wire handle for carrying. Bought at the Farmers' Market Saturday morning, cool and dewy. Her tall father. Her mother ambling in slow pleasure along wooden platforms heaped with bushel baskets and crate boxes of corn and beans, tomatoes and apples, potatoes, and, yes, grapes. Overalled, sunburned Minnesota farmers, tightmouthed with shyness, eyes evasive with fear, their short–sleeved shirts showing the odd whiteness of their arms, making them seem peculiarly vulnerable. The 1930s. Those grapes in that place were purple, deeply fragrant, all you wanted to eat. The grapes slithering under the teeth, released from their thick papery skins, the green seeded pulp still round and whole. Tiny seeds spit out. Grapes crushed under the potato masher, hung in an old thin flour sack to drip their red (how do purple skin and green fruit make *red?*) juice into the blue and white enameled pan. The boiling jelly, thick, lilac colored, chuckling hotly to the deep pot's very rim. The steaming glasses, wax whitening over the darkening sweet.

But these: Johannesburger Riesling and Pinot Chardonnay, wine grapes, will hang on the tough, sunbattered vines another two months, Bernie and Aaron checking the acid and sugar content, watching the ripening for the finest moment. Then amiable Mexican farm workers will move along the rows plucking the heavy clusters, carrying their boxfuls to the waiting bins. The bins will be lifted on the fork, the grapes dumped by the ton into the gondolas of large trucks and taken at dusk to the winery where they will be crushed through large rolling cylinders, pumped into vats, coopered, and later bottled . . . the fermented fruit. Differences, yes. California and Minnesota, childhood and now.

How long ago. How far she has come. How changed. That child she remembered, who now seems in Victoria's mind innocent enough to pity, who read the Bobbsey twin books and wept that she could not see oceans—could that child have dreamed that she would become a middle-aged woman walking a summer vineyard in California? Ah, no. What child ever imagines middle age or the ordinary lot that will be his?

Aaron has checked the thermometer hung from a stake. He reports that it reads 104°. He is pleased. The heat will raise the sugar content. He works now without his shirt, hatless. His body is lean and muscular and the skin browned by such hours in the sun. He is dark as any farm worker. He is extremely fit. *Fifty-five, I am fifty-five*, he has said several times since she arrived home. She thinks how he says those words. Is he teaching himself, trying to overcome disbelief? Or disappointment? How is she to interpret his low, tense tone?

It's taken me twenty years, he said last week, *to really love California. But how I love this place now!*

Twenty years? Twenty years to learn love of this place? And even then Victoria heard the timbre of sorrow in his voice, as if what he declared a gain robbed him of something. And he had been, then, discontent those long twenty years? He had never said so. Of course, California was not his home, and his family, unlike hers, was far away. Yet he had often declared that he could not live in his small hometown of terrible weathers and provincial interests. He needed freedom, newness, and change, the larger pond.

But now his avowal of finally achieved contentment

throws all into question. And Victoria finds herself guilty and
puzzled and a bit estranged. How much has he disguised, this
willfully cheerful, practical, disciplined man? And has the
disguise been kept up to benefit her? Has he secretly sacrificed
for that, for what he believes she needs? But if that is so, she
has not been allowed to perceive his sacrifices, nor to refuse
them. And where was the justice in that?

How many desires bloom in his secret head which he
weeds out from fantasy, even from dream? In the early hours
of the night, when he sleeps most soundly and she lies awake,
she hears him laugh, often, in his dreams. In the morning,
curious because her dreams most often give life to her fears,
she asks, *What did you dream last night?* He pauses in his reading
of the news, frowns, but is not interested. He cannot remember. And he is honest; he does not recall. Why does he turn
away from such knowledge? Even on those rare nights when
he mutters aloud, begins to thrash, struggling in nightmare
against some immense dream force, and she wakens him,
crying, *What is it, Aaron? What is the matter?* Even at that
moment he cannot recall his dream. Only the shake of breath
and the beat of heart mark the edited message of the dark.

Love, Victoria thinks, stooping to drag up the long involved root of a morning glory weed, ripping open the shallow skin of dry earth. Love becomes so complex. Suddenly
she knows that she feels pity for this accomplished man, her
husband. Pity? Yes, though it surprises her, it is pity that is
shooting new growth out of the tough stalk of her love.

Why should *she* pity *him? He* is better in human exchange
than she. He is more knowledgeable about the demands of
living than she. He does more of import in the world, and
governs more of it, than she. It is he who is needed by many
people and also deeply loved. Why *should* she pity him?

Victoria tugs at other flat gray persistent weeds, chastises
her judgment. It does not shift. She is hot. Sweat drips from
nose and chin, smarts in her eyes. She stands straight, hands

on hips. She looks at Aaron, unpausing in his work under the glaring sun. He is far ahead of her now, pruning, tying, inspecting. It seems that from the act of work he takes in energy, rather than expends it. His vitality is everyone's marvel.

She thinks of his life: out of the house at 7 A.M. , home again at 7 P.M. , patients filling all the hours of his day; calls in the middle of the night from people who have been sick three days and choose to demand help—penicillin or flu shots, nembutol or antihistamines— then, at that sleep-robbing time; the friends who dash over on Sundays for a quick, friendly consultation; the cranky aged, the anxious careless teen-aged girls, the impudent agressive young jocks. Everything they put on him, he accepts. He refuses anger or impatience. For years it has seemed that he gains stength from the burdens the desperately ill or neurotic place on him. The paradoxes of getting and spending.

Yes, he has been strong, stronger than she, surely, stronger than most. Of course, gray hairs thread through the dark brown now, and the laugh-lines in his cheeks are permanent creases. But still it seems he will never tire. He continues the rhythm of work, the stride, bend, smooth rise. Clippers drawn, used, returned to his belt, a lean downward to lift a heavy sagging branch, a pull of twine, the neat tie: oh, he is full of grace and vitality. No, pity is out of place.

I am fifty-five, he has said, with sorrow. She laughs a little, appreciating absurdity.

Aaron, she calls out. *Would you like some tea?*

Great! he calls back and moves without pause to the next vine.

She walks the long way back to the car, conscious of the damp film all over her body. She gets the thermos of iced tea and returns. He stops when she reaches him, straightens, waits as she pours the amber liquid into the clumsy wide plastic cup. He has pulled the blue handkerchief from his pocket, wipes his wet face. He pulls off a glove, takes the cup, drains it without pause. He stops, grins, and she fills his cup again. He stands sipping, his eyes roaming the vineyard, lifting to the ringing hills. She perceives that his happiness is whole, without qualification. *It's beautiful here, isn't it, Tory?* he comments. *Look how the burn is almost grown over.* Yes, the hills were blackened last summer under a sweeping week-long fire. But now the burned areas show a green scrub, and the eye must take special care to discern the blackened tree trunks thrusting upward in the green. *But it's coming again,* she says. *The dangerous season.*

She has alway hated the threat of September and October. The dry earth crackles under the heat of the day and the cool of night. Over all the California hills, the dry grasses invite flame. In their town sirens ride the air daily, riding also the paths of wary nerves. Grass fires. Children playing. Spontaneous combustions. The rich, fruity, lush, dry, terrifying autumn. While the great valleys give up their grains and fruits, supplying the world from that richness, the mountains burn, the hills sear. Bounty and danger, hand in hand. Paradox. Yes, we teeter on such razor's edges, chance, autumn, September, October. Still, it is only August.

We need a long hot fall, Aaron says. *The sugar won't be up until October.* He hands her the empty cup, stretches, pulls his glove back on. *If it doesn't rain, we'll have a tremendous crop.* He begins again the bend and rise of his labor.

Victoria finishes her cup of tea. She decides to leave the thermos there beside a stake and pick it up on her way back. She leans down to set it in place. A momentary darkness flickers over her, a blink in the eye of the sun. She looks up. A falcon is taking the wind on spread wings, the wing-fingers distinct as printing against the blue. She watches its flight, the elegant veering, the sudden spring upward, the swift slide away toward the hills. And then, as if taking up a warning theme, a rabbit leaps over the field, small, gray, swift. Its ears are peaked, the hind legs pump a strong rhythm. It stops momentarily, looks back at her with wide eyes. Tenderness for the creature's beauty springs up in her. But it is the rabbit, is it not, that commands pity, not the falcon? In any parable what pity is offered the strong, the untrammeled, the self-reliant?

She pulls weeds and ties vines, then, until she feels herself slowing with heat and tiredness. Far ahead of her, Aaron shows no sign of stopping. She pulls the hat from her head. Her skull is damp, her hair flat and wet against it. She runs her fingers through the wet strands, lifts them out to the drying air. She decides to stop, to wait for Aaron in the shade of the prune orchard to the west of the vineyard. There are old fruitboxes there. She will, as she has done before, set one of them against a tree trunk and rest till Aaron is ready to leave.

She has not brought a book or even a notebook. She will be idle then, letting sensation and thought move in willess motions. Inexplicably, in the midst of the grove of tended prune trees, stands one old apple tree, twisted, unpruned, obviously too old for fine bearing. Nothing is done for it. But it still bears not altogether perfect but abundant fruit. The apples are ripening; some have already fallen. They lie on the earth, their redness growing golden and the soft bruises of their fall turning a mushy brown. The opulent lush fragrance of their ripeness mingles with the tang of those still green. She sits under the umbrella of green, gazing sometimes up through the cage of leaf, sometimes over the patterned fields fanning in all directions. She feels an immense stillness under the circular roofing. The winy air stirs with the beginning afternoon wind. The small motions of leaves cast wavering shades through the lemon light. Thrumming bees spin around the fallen, decaying fruit, their wings a dazzling blur. Such calm, such stasis: Victoria feels what has been coming to her the entire day. She is in the center, the middle place.

Far from beginning, far from early ambitions and angers and desires, here there is no great threat, no awesome demand, only this nowness, this halt in moving, this balance. Sitting there, she understands her completeness and is happy. This is not ecstasy: this time in her life has neither such height nor such swiftness. But it is the fruit, ripened, guarded over through long early seasons, fruit grown full, round, ready. Has she not waited for such a time all her life, a time when she would say, *This is it, I am happy, I want nothing more?* Has she not nurtured her days to grow into this most perfect time? Smiling, she envisions herself: a woman of middle years under an old gnarled apple tree in the middle of ripe fields in the middle of a summer day, happy, contented—in the center, the heart of being.

The vine shadows grow long to the east of their stakes. The wind begins to pull strongly across the valley. Swallows fly in great numbers along the creek, over the fields. It is growing late. She sees Aaron making his way back to the car, still tending plants as he walks along the row. She watches him a little while, thinks of the falcon's shadow over her surprised face, thinks of the darkness in his eye, the shade behind his smile. The air is cooler now, and gooseflesh briefly runs along her arms. She rises, dusts off her hat and puts it on. She gathers a few apples, making the tails of her shirt into a bag for them. She enters again the golden sunlight and walks slowly toward the car.

Then in the dusty tan furrow at her feet a small object catches her eye. Curious she leans over, sees that the thin wee gray thing is an animal. A mouse? A field mouse. Stiff, two inches long, sun-dried, a mummy.

She leans down and takes one curled paw between thumb and forefinger, plucks up the corpse, looks at it closely. The large wee ear, closed delicate eye, wiry stiff brown tail. How tiny, how perfect. A week or two old, perhaps, just lying there, shriveled in the brutal sun. How had it died? Attacked?

Poisoned? Or simply inadequate, too weak to survive? The baby mouse mesmerizes her. She feels peculiar grief and almost she cannot let it go.

Then Aaron whistles, and she sees that he is standing beside the car, beating dust from his jeans. She recalls the thermos. She still must pick it up. She lets drop the compelling insignificant corpse, moves quickly over the hillocks of earth between the rows of vines, retrieves the thermos, and hurries to the car. Aaron has stored his twine and tools in the trunk. She offers him the last of the tea, tepid now, but wet.

We'll stop for a beer, Aaron says, *I want the newspaper anyway.* They buy the beer and the paper at the cluttered roadside market and then agree to stop by the river. Already it is six-thirty and the chain is across the parking lot driveway, the bathing beach empty. There is a sign posted forbidding swimming after 6 P.M., but they strip in the shelter of shrubs and slip into the water.

The cold current shocks delightfully, sweeps away sweat and dust. Aaron ducks his head, rubs his scalp. He comes up spewing spray, laughing at the luxury of coolness. He reaches for her and holds her close. They look into each other's face. Victoria sees no shadows beyond his pleasure. Yes, they are content, and very happy, this moment. Now. Weary and refreshed, comfortable and middle-aged and sensuous. Yes, they have everything. She thinks again of centers, fulfillments, perfections. Lucky, they are, happy and blessed.

That night after making love, calm and at ease in the cool evening dark, with the bedroom door opened to an angle of August stars, they murmur small declining thoughts. Bernie doubts he can sell to Couvaison this year. . . . Your father's birthday next week. . . . Must write Arnold. . . . Invited to the Nashes. . . . Surgery at seven-thirty. . . .

She falls asleep and does not know how much time has passed when she wakens, feeling along the backs of her arms the shivers, knowing the startle in her mind. What has wakened her? She listens to the night: the crickets' wild chirrs, the cry of the small owl, the almost inaudible whirr of the electric clock, Aaron's long breaths. She finds nothing out of place, turns to her pillow, readies herself for return to sleep.

But in her mind shapes the image of the small dead field mouse, locked by curious process into the form of his living. She holds the tiny creature before her, compelled to attend it.

And yes, now in the dark she knows, knew all the time perhaps what it is that darkens Aaron's eye and quietens his smiling. He has gotten there just one step ahead of her. The perfect summer, the perfect center. It will turn her, of course, to another time. Oh, certainly the center is beautiful and may seem secure, but that is, of course, only illusion. There is no stasis ever. There is never that. She turns to Aaron, holds his warm body close to her own, wanting now to comfort him as well as herself for what he does not confess he knows.

A Season For Going

Outside the narrow window the October sun lay its thin light over a stirring, wakened world. Ardys stood before the curved front of the large dresser that was made of oak and painted white. She pulled the brush through her fine, pale hair and did not look in the white-framed mirror on the wall she faced. On the top of the dresser lay the single page of blue-lined paper covered with the black scrawls of her father's hand. She looked down at it. She could not be at home for her birthday. She would have to write and tell him that.

At dawn Ardys had heard the honking of geese. She had wakened abruptly, her eyes wide open to darkness, her ears straining after that far, lonely sound. She had listened with a sense of great expectancy, as though she had slept with that sound as her sleep's goal. But awake she could not hear it and thought perhaps she had, out of her desire for it, dreamed it.

And then she was lonely, as if not hearing the geese had left her deprived. She had lain in that high, narrow bed in the flower-papered room off the kitchen which was the only place in the dark old house that was hers, thinking back over other autumns when the downward drift of leaves and the wild cry of flying geese brought the year's cycle toward the day that was her birthday. Every one of her past eighteen birthdays had been spent in the town in which she had been born. That small town was set in lake country where the comings and goings of birds and weathers were the signposts on which all days were hung. Here in the city it was not the same.

It was three months since Ardys had come to the house of that strange family. In those three months things had changed for her. She had grown used to the old house with its clutter of dark furniture and shining, worn brocades. She lived in its large dimness with less sense of ghostliness than once she had. She was used to David's inexplicable sorrows and humors, to his wife's quick laughters. Stephen's cruelties did not bother her. She expected that from boys, and if he had not surreptitiously made faces at her that day she had come for the interview she would have not stayed. Her brother was like that, and even her own father was sometimes cruel. Ardys understood well enough what it was the male hid beneath his cruelties, and tolerated that. Ba–Ba, the grandmother, was dear and if not less mysterious, she was more lovely than all the rest. For her, Ardys could stay there.

But there was Belle, the old aunt. Belle was a tall wraith of a woman. She had a wide, wrinkled mouth, a fierce, high-boned nose, ardent eyes. She tyrannized them all. Always she spawned more anger or fury, more enthusiasm or impatience than she could contain, and in a variety of passions she spilled her excesses over them all. The others endured her, soothed her, pampered her. They suffered her follies and furies with a gentleness Ardys could not understand. Ardys could not like her, not at all. And it was because of Belle she would not be home for her birthday.

Two weeks before, David had come home from his work, sauntered into the walnut-paneled living room, and lifted the soft green hat with the narrow, turned brim from his head. He dropped into the great leather chair. His arms dangled over the armrests. The hat hung carelessly in his drooping hand. His rosy face was taken by his sorrowful, crooked smile. He said, in his slow ironic voice, that he had gotten promoted. He was Barton and Fried's newest vice-president. Ba–Ba, Stephen, and Nannette went to him, stood before him, demanding explanations. Belle flew up from her place at the piano, opened her mouth on a giddy laugh, shouted for a party.

"We must have a party," she had cried, flapping her wrinkled imperious hands in front of her chest, summoning Ba-Ba and Nannette and even Stephen to attention. "Certainly we must have a party! Vice-president! That calls for a party!"

The others turned from their surprise and their smiling, looked at her, interrupted, frowned their skepticism. David renewed his weary grin and groaned.

"Oh Lord, Belle," he said. The words issued on a negligent fall. "It's only a promotion. Money," he sighed, setting the green hat on the back of his head. He let his eyes slide nearly closed. "If it were all as easy as that."

Under the mellow light of the high, brass fixture of the dining room where she was setting the table, Ardys watched, listened, wondered. She did not like David when he said such things. He seemed to her then cynical and selfish. She knew too many for whom lack of money was the barrier to needed comforts, the cause of futile efforts, the source of despairs.

But Nanette stood behind David's chair. She brushed the foolish hat from his head, wrapped her slender arms around his neck, leaned her cheek against the brown up-springing hair.

"Why would they make a blockhead like you vice-president?" she cried, laughter shaking like leaves in her voice. "Such fools they are! They'll pay for that decision, David, my lad. Much more than they bargain for, they'll pay! Vice-president!"

And Ba-Ba, squat and solid as a loaf of bread in her skirt like a sack and the close brown sweater, kept Stephie quiet in the circle of her arms. She nodded her large gray head at her son and his wife. Her smile was warm and steady as summer sun.

But Belle quivered within the shimmer of her shawl. She fluttered in circles around them, crooned and sputtered her private joys. She stopped in front of David's chair, leaned over him, put her grimacing yellow face close to her nephew's, and pleaded.

"David, sweetheart, we must have a party! Such a fine thing it is, could we not have a party? We must celebrate what's good, David! Friends should come and celebrate! A party, David! A nice party!"

Ardys, apart and separated there in the dining room felt that she watched a play. She saw David glance at his mother. She saw the change in Ba-Ba's look that did not change her wordless smiling. She saw David's quick glance up at Nannette, and Ardys understand that were was something the three of them considered and agreed upon. But it was Nannette who stood suddenly upright, flung her arms wide, spun in a small circle so that her yellow skirt wheeled about her knees.

"Oh yes, let's do have a party, David," she laughed. "A big party. A week from next Saturday, David, how's that?"

"I get to come," Stephie shouted, breaking from Ba-Ba's arms and leaping upon his father for an evening's tussle. "I get to come!"

Right then, at that moment, Ardys should have said that she could not stay that weekend, that she had to be home. It was not that she had forgotten. She had not. It was, instead, some interior thing that kept her from speaking, that made her hesitate until it was too late and the party was already planned. It was the feeling that if she said that, if she refused to be there on that Saturday night, that the refusal would also bring from her the final decision to go from them entirely.

She should not be staying there. She knew that she should not. She had come to the city to find a different kind of job. She thought that she should work in a bank, or in a telephone company office. That was what she had planned to do. When she had first come to them in their foreign-seeming house, it was with the understanding that it was temporary. Now it was time to go. She must go from them to other things, go from their strangeness and her difference, from her help-less bondage to them. But she did not say that to them then.

She had let the party be planned on the Saturday of her birthday. Her father and her mother expected her home, and she herself wanted to be at home. Aunt Bertha and Uncle Paul would be there, her brother Richard, and her three boy cousins. There would be the angel cake and the array of presents wrapped in gaudy colored papers and bright curled ribbons. There would be the one huge ornamented box which would open upon a smaller wrapped and ribboned box which would open upon a third box, on through all the foolish stages until the final small box was there, holding perfume or pin or lipstick or whatever small gift Uncle Paul would have chosen this year.

Ardys sighed. She went to the small table beside the bed. She took from its single drawer her pen and a sheet of paper. *Dear Mom and Dad,* she wrote, *I can't be home on Saturday. We'll have to celebrate on Sunday instead. It's all because of Belle who insisted on a big party on that Saturday night. It's all Belle's fault. She's an old goose. I'll catch the two a.m. bus. Love, Ardys.*

Ardys sealed the note in an envelope, addressed it, found a stamp in the small jar inside the drawer, pasted it on the envelope's corner, and propped it up against the mirror. She made a face at her own narrow, sad-looking face and went out her door through the small hall to the kitchen.

She fixed the coffee pot. She went into the sunlit, chintz-curtained breakfast room.

She set the green table with yellow mats and white plates. She arranged the yellow halves of grapefruit and placed them like flowers upon the plates. Then she sat down on the stool beside the sink and sipped at a cup of coffee. It was seven o'clock.

At home her father would have gotten up in the dark of five o'clock. Her mother would have risen with him, cooked his breakfast, packed his lunch in the blue metal box, and started her wash. By this time she would have the white things out on the line. Her father would be bustling around the rail yard checking the cargo of incoming freights. Here the great house stood in sleepy silence.

But Nannette, at least, was up. She was always up at the first light. She came running down the steps in jeans and a heavy sweater and tennis shoes and went, breathless and laughing softly, out into the back hall. There she pulled on the coveralls made for carpenters and the great clown-like gloves and went outside. With a kind of frenzy she would work there in the garden. Ardys could see her out there now, running burdened and awkward from shed to garden bed with hoes and spades and rakes, digging the earth free around the base of some plant and scooping up the dark crumbly soil in both gloved hands and holding it to her face as though its damp darkness gave off a lovely perfume, bending her face down to some flower or plant and breathing of it as though she consumed something of its green growing. Whatever she did out there, pruning or spraying or planting or raking, she did as though it were some glorious celebration. Her small face was, beneath the wisps of her disordered hair, lit with color and smiles. It was, Ardys knew, a somehow private thing for Nannette. She gardened alone, always alone, full of that secret pleasure. Even looking out on her, Ardys knew that she intruded and she turned precisely away from the window where she might see the bobbing, bending, rushing figure in its loose flopping gloves and pants.

But when Nannette came in this morning, Ardys would tell her. While Nannette sat by the counter bending her face to the warming fragrance of a cup of coffee, Ardys would say that she had to go home this weekend. She would explain that there was a two o'clock bus out of the downtown Greyhound depot and that she wanted to catch it so that she could be home for the family breakfast. Belle's party would surely be over by that time. Surely they would not mind.

But when Nannette came in, she did not stop in the hallway. She did not take off the coveralls and hang them on the hook in the basement stairway. She rushed into the kitchen still wearing them, the large stiff-fingered gloves still on her hands. She went to the coffeepot and splashed coffee into the mug Ardys had set out for her. Grit sprayed from the gloves into her cup, over the cupboard and upon the floor, and where she walked a trail of fine damp dirt fell from her clothes. Nannette did not notice. Her face was without light. None of the usual weary pleasure was there. There was whiteness around her lips and around each eye a delicate rim of redness.

"Ardys," she said, her dark curly head drooping over the dark steaming cup, "Ardys, my Chinese azalea is dying. It's dying! Think of that!" Her voice was a low, abstracted murmur. Her mouth was fallen to a queer scallop. "I watered it and fed it and nursed it for six years. And it's dying! I don't know what's wrong with it!"

She looked at Ardys then, helplessly, as if Ardys might explain. In the hazel eyes with the spray of laugh-lines tilting up from the corners, tears stood and caught the pale intruding sun.

Ardys felt that her throat was dry. She could not think whatever it might be that Nannette thought she could say. She did not know how to comfort someone for the loss of a garden plant. How could you share the grief for a peculiar love that was not your own?

"But Miss Nannette," Ardys offered at last, her words coming thinly, uncertain. "It's just a plant. You can order another one just like it. Can't you?"

She had seen all the catalogues Nannette read. She had seen the dozens of them filled with pictures of glorious high-colored growing. But Nannette looked at her with widened eyes. Her mouth frozen and stiff.

"Oh, no, Ardys." The whisper was surprised and bereft. "No plant is ever just like another."

She left the mug on top of the stove and ran from the room. She ran out into the dining room and through the living room to the front stairs. She was going up to David, going in her coveralls without the cup of coffee she always brought him after she had drunk her own.

Ardys sat alone upon her stool, puzzled and unhappy. She wondered what other things she could have said. She wondered again at their strangeness and whether she would ever understand them at all.

Then Stephen burst into the kitchen, startling her. Water dripped from his flattened hair down onto his blue sweater. He slapped his geography book down upon the table.

"Ardy-smarty," he yelled, "Hurryup-or-I'll-be-tardy!"

He sat down, dug his spoon into the shining round of his grapefruit, shoved his mouth full, grinned. Ardys started his eggs.

One by one she served them as they came—David, shaved and fragrant, sleepy-looking, his newspaper occupying him entirely; Nannette, showered, impeccable in white blouse and pleated skirt, quiet; Ba–Ba, calm, serene, making lists of the day's duties. Fed, they bustled away, preoccupied and efficient with the plotted motions of the day to come. And then it was time to take the tray to Belle.

Belle was a poet. She slept late. She had to have breakfast in bed. Each morning she had been in that house Ardys had brought to her, at nine o'clock, the tray set with a glass of orange juice, very cold; one egg, boiled, very soft; one half of one English muffin toasted slightly, buttered, set on the blue plate with a mound of currant jelly beside it. And tea, the small blue and white pot filled with boiling water, the leaves of Jasmine tea hung in the small metal basket from the pot's bamboo handle.

Each morning Ardys went up to that room uncomfortable

and apprehensive. Sometimes Belle would be propped up on several heaped, disordered pillows, her yellow face weary and exposed, the eyes red-veined and shadowed.

"Didn't sleep well, Ardys, my love," she would mumble, the deep voice full of its foreign accent. "Hunted all night for one elusive image!" Other times when Ardys came to that room at the end of the hall she would have gotten up, hidden the ravaged face under powders and rouges. She would be sitting then at the large table in front of the windows of the south-facing room. When she was working there she scarcely lifted her head at Ardys's knock. "Put it down, put it down," she would mutter, waving her ringed hand vaguely, and Ardys would find a place for the tray somewhere amidst the books and papers that littered the whole room.

· Though she had regularly dusted and polished the knotted, fat legs and the long, curved trestle of that great table where Belle worked, Ardys had never seen its top. It was covered over every square inch of its surface with the books and papers, pencils, pamphlets, clippings, notebooks among which Belle scribbled and stirred. Belle sat on a high wicker stool in her multi-colored robes and shawl and scrawled words in large letters on papers of all sizes and colors. There seemed to be no order to it all, no way one could tell what belonged to what, what was first, middle or last, what was her own poem and what was a poem she had read somewhere and written on whatever piece of paper she could find. Ardys did not see how anyone could write poetry that way.

But on one of the shelves lining the inner wall of the room were the slim, high, elegant volumes with the name Belle Lehman printed in gold upon their backs. One morning soon after Ardys had come there, Belle had taken one of those thin books from its place, showed it to Ardys.

"I've made my little place, Ardys, you see," she crooned. "All this scribbling and studying and burning out my eyes over words and words and words comes to something after all. Nobody expected that, you know. Nobody." The large eyes rolled in their rounds of white. Her red mouth opened wide, and all the large, perfect yellow teeth shone out of the old, rouged face. Her bony head with its smooth cap of slick black hair bobbed up and down. "Look at it," she had cried, and thrust the tall, narrow book into Ardys's unready hands.

Ardys had opened the book. She looked at the small blocks of print placed impudently and imperiously in the small center of each pure, heavy page. She looked steadily and hard at the printed words. What she looked at she could not read.

"Yiddish," Belle shouted. She pulled the book back into her own hands. She flipped the pages in her long crimson-tipped fingers. She held it open in the back and gave it to Ardys again. "Start in the back. You start there," she laughed, "and go the other way around. It's Yiddish, Ardys, and no one can read it any more. The most beautiful language in the world. A shame. A shame. So beautiful. So old."

She peered at Ardys out of wide, mournful eyes, the thin, black brows arched upward on the wrinkled, bony forehead. Ardys had no answer to make. Belle leaned close to her, looked down at her book.

"But scholars know it," she had whispered. "It's the scholars who read my poems. They study them and they write criticisms of them and they write to me, too!"

Ardys had looked blindly down at the book with its indecipherable backwards secrets.

"Like Chinese," she had murmured, and at Belle's look she had blushed so painfully that tears sprang to her own blue eyes.

She had seen some of Belle's scholars come to the ancient house, sit in the brocaded chairs grouped on the complicated Oriental carpets of the living room. They were not the rheumy-eyed, bearded old men Ardys had envisioned. They sat in their firm, fine manhood and talked excitedly and passionately with Belle, offering her a respect and admiration that astonished Ardys. All the poems Ardys had known and loved spoke of desire and beauty, of rose-lipped maidens and light-footed lads. What had Belle to do with those? Nothing, thought Ardys. Old Belle could have nothing to do with those. And sighing she picked up the tray and started once more up to the room in which she would have to face that fierce and helpless Belle.

In the hours that were her own that afternoon, Ardys walked to the library. The sky had grown gray. The air was heavy with moisture. The trees were now quite barren of leaves, and from the lawns and leaf-strewn gutters rose the dark, sweet odor of decay. Ardys dropped her letter in the blue and red box on the corner. Tonight at dinner she would explain how it was she had planned to go home.

But at dinnertime they sat around the large, linen-covered table involved in the headlong chatter that permitted no intrusion. Other families Ardys knew spoke of weather during dinner, told the chronicle of the day's small events, discussed plans for the morrow, were quiet. No one else she knew shouted and argued like these five did. At first it had seemed to her that disaster threatened them every day of their lives. At any moment one of them would bang out of the house and, propelled by his anger, never return. Belle might fling herself up too suddenly and upset the whole table, tumbling china and glassware, gravy and creamed peas all over the carpet they treasured. David would sweep his arm too wide and send the arched and elegant candelabra off in a flare of destruction. Nannette would say the final, unforgivable thing and plunge them all into intolerable despair. But none of those things happened.

Ardys took up the shallow, almond-shaped gravy boat and the basket of biscuits and pushed her way through the dining room door. She crossed the rug patterned in blue and red and green and gold and stood beside David where he sat at the table's head. He paid no attention to her.

He leaned across his plate and stared at Nannette with high, astonished brows. He held his fork in one hand, his knife in the other, both cocked like weapons and forgotten in his hands.

"Unfair?" he shouted. "What's unfair about facts, Nan? You forget it's a document, not a treatise."

"Those are terms, David. Meaningless terms! Even a document has its choices and its omissions! And its tone!" Nannette's small head shook up and down on her frail neck. The dark, cropped curls shook upon her forehead. Her cheeks were red, and under the whipping light of the candles her eyes blazed with yellow fire. "It's slanted, I tell you. And it's unfair! More than that, it's treason. A betrayal. Against us all."

"Emotional, Nannette, you're being emotional. She simply assigns responsibility where it belongs." David lowered his head and his tools, shrugged, smiled helplessly and absently at Ardys, and took the food from her hands.

"Since when, David," Nannette persisted, her voice suddenly low, her small perfect teeth closed together over her words, "is emotion equated to error? One has to care, David. Haven't we learned that?"

She leaned farther toward David, leaned so that she was in front of Stephen, in his way. Stephen pushed at her shoulder.

"Stay in your own place, for God's sake," he yelled, red-faced and furious. "I gotta eat."

No one corrected him. Not even Ba-Ba. The adults were heedless, each caught up in the thing that so greatly angered Nannette.

"David, she betrays us," Nannette repeated into white teeth. She held David captive in her fierce gazing. "She gives them the means to absolution!"

Then Ba-Ba put down her fork. She raised her braid-crowned, gray head from its quiet listening. She looked at them all with her eyes that were like David's but richly

different with her wisdom and her age. She put her elbows
on the table in front of her half-emptied plate, set her hands
together one before the other as a sleepy cat sets its paws. She
looked at them one by one, Belle, Ardys, David, Stephen, and
Nannette. Nannette last of all. The softness in her eyes was
far from smiling, yet it comforted.

"I feel it too, Nannette. The shame. The sadness. But
Hannah Arendt tells the truth, Nannette. It is the truth, and
so we must accept that, too. Not deny. Not judge. Accept."

Then something strange came between them where they
all sat with darkened eyes at the white-clothed table under
the sheen of the trembling candle flames, and it grew tall
among them and shook its cold and silent winds over
them—regret, pain, anger, sorrow, held them all.

It was Belle who finally moved. She flung down her spoon.
It fell on her plate with a rude clatter. She stood up. She raised
her rouged face and both arms toward the ceiling. The striped
shawl fell from her shoulders to the chair behind her.

"Great God of Abraham," she wailed, her voice choked
and low. Like a statue she stood, like a carving on the prow
of a ship, the thin, breastless body arched backward on its
despair, the long throat stretched and corded, the wide mouth
a cavern for grief. "Why," she cried to the far, dim ceiling.
"Why must we expect to be braver—stronger—holier than
any other creatures? We are human." She glared at them all.
"You forget. We are only human. He created us—human.
How should we be perfect? Who would not wish to save
himself from death?"

Suddenly the yellow face went vague under streaming
tears. She pushed herself free from her chair and the table and
fled from them. The wide sleeves of her Chinese robe spread
like wings on the air behind her

With stiff faces the others looked after her. With bleak,
barren eyes they turned and looked at one another. What had
they done to Belle? they mutely queried of one another. How

could they let themselves hurt her so? their stricken faces asked.

"Ah Belle, poor Belle," Ba-Ba murmured at last. "She will forgive us our failures."

She looked at them with gentle eyes, the beautiful, low brow calm. She unfolded her arms, picked up her fork, led them back from terror and guilt to ordinariness and dinner. Ardys, eating there with them, was slow and awkward in her eating. She wondered again at them all, at their anger over Hannah Arendt, who she understood was someone in a magazine, at their hatred of "them," of whom she knew that she was one; at their prolonged unforgivingness and need for revenge; at their pride and anger and love.

Suddenly Ba-Ba stopped eating, put down her fork and drew a slim, flat envelope from under the edge of her plate. "Look," she said. "Today a letter from Rosa."

Then, as she did every night, Ba-Ba offered the news she garnered from the letters that flowed into the house on the tides of the mailman's comings and goings. Every night someone's aunt or cousin had broken a wrist, or had a gallstone removed, or gotten mononucleosis. Every night there was news of someone's lost job or awarded honor. Sometimes there was news of someone's death, and when there was, Belle, with tender eyes and preposterous statements, eulogized whoever had died.

Ardys had never heard anyone keep track of commonplace human events the way Ba-Ba did. She was historian and bookkeeper. The accounts of illness and death and marriage and birth which came to her from what seemed every town and city of the world were entered in the tall birthday book she kept on the spindly desk in her orderly room. Most of those she kept news of she did not even know. It was enough that it was cousin of a cousin, or nephew of her dead husband's friend, or grandchild of some scarcely remembered person she had gone to school with in her distant childhood.

The rest of them who listened to the detailed, impersonal accountings there in the shadowed circle of the dinner table were fascinated and repelled by what they could not bear to hear and what they could not refrain from listening to. For them all that vast collection of change and progress, of failures and triumphs, of beginnings and endings, bound them to places and times they neither knew or understood, and filled them with the terror and the wonder of human frailty and human glory, and left them at last, each of them, even Stephen, humbled and grieving and cheerful, according to what it was that Ba–Ba had given them that day from the ongoing stream of her innumerable letters.

So now they turned their faces toward her, the four that were left in the candlelight at the table, waiting for the new page in the saga, waiting for some addition or subtraction of the burden Hannah Arendt and Belle Lehman had laid upon them on the simple Tuesday evening of a gray October day.

"Twins," Ba–Ba said, her voice like a bell, her eyes like deep water. "Twins." She opened a sheet of sheer airmail paper from its folds, turned the page over, found the place. She looked around on them all, waiting for their disbelief and expectation.

"Twins!" It was Belle who shouted. "Think of that, twins!" She whirled in on them in a cloud of added perfume. She floated to her place and dropped down upon her abandoned chair. She flung the wide kimono sleeves into graceful folds upon her skinny thighs. "Who, Ba–Ba? Who had twins?" Belle's smile was full of teeth and rejoicing. Her eyes denied all earlier despair. "Rare, you know," she cried to them all. "Terribly rare."

"Hey, Belle," Stephen shouted, flopping his napkin in front of his nose. "Boy, do you stink. Eau de Old Bones, whew!"

Belle's laugh fell freely upon the sweet, dense air. She rearranged the flowing sleeves. She turned again to Ba–Ba.

"Come, Ba–Ba. Do tell us. Who had twins?"

It was hopeless, Ardys thought. Even her one small need, the one thing she needed to say and wanted to say, had planned all day to say, was lost in the tumult of their usual confusions. It seemed that they could not exist for five minutes without crisis. Ardys longed for the clean and orderly and calm existence which was the freedom in which she had grown up. She thought of the composure and discipline that was her Swedish heritage, and she wanted it then as one must greatly want in the thick tangles of tropical jungles, a time in the space and distance of grassy plains or of wide seas. She stood up.

"I must go home. This weekend," Ardys suddenly loudly announced.

They stopped all their exclamations and arguments over the phenomenon of twins and looked at her where she stood trembling and taken by anger. In that immediate moment, they were to her, after three months of seeing them and hearing them and talking to them every day, strangers she did not know at all.

"Home?" Belle said, the narrow face swinging around on the long column of her neck. "But the party, Ardys. You know we're having the party."

All the others looked at her, questioning. Ardys placed both hands on the edge of the table, looked down at her knuckles, breathed deeply of the glancing, odorous air.

"I won't go till after the party," she said. And then on a falter of explanation she did not intend to make, she murmured, "It's my birthday."

"Your birthday?" shouted Belle. Her eyes stretched wide for wonder.

Nannette leaned through the flickering candle light, earnestness soft on her face.

"Why Ardys, you should have told us," she said.

Stephen pounded the table with both fists and shouted, "Oh

ye gods, a historical event!" and both David and Ba-Ba looked at her as though no one else had ever thought of having so marvelous a thing as an ordinary birthday.

Ardys suddenly smiled at them, could not keep from smiling. She rushed to clear the table, carrying emptied platters and cluttered plates to a rhythm of happiness that sang forgiveness of their foolish ways.

Except for Belle, high-handed, arrogant, demanding, she thought, putting apple tarts upon thin, scalloped plates, she could be happy there, even as the maid.

She went among them carrying the canapé tray. The sandwiches were arranged in patterned rows. The triangles and circles and squares of bread, frosted with cheese and eggs and herring and caviar, were shining and colored like valuable jewels. Ardys looked at all the guests in astonishment.

The women were high-blooded, warm-eyed, audacious. Their bosoms were full and high under bright, bare dresses, their legs slim and shining in lacy hose, their feet narrow and long in lizard and suede. Even the old ones, with shadows beneath their eyes and thin, flat hair, were mascaraed and lacquered, girdled and perfumed.

The men were wearier, more dapper, than men she had known. Something in their long, arrogant noses, their drooping, fleshy mouths, their groomed, fleshy shoulders and clean, flashing hands made them seem full of power and hunger and love.

The women talked like men, assertive and argumentative. They acted as though they were valuable objects, displayed for the watcher's pleasure. The men spoke in weary, wooing voices. They listened to the women with tender smiles, differed with them in amused tolerance, leaned over their stylish heads and exposed bosoms like lovers.

And their words, their words. They made so much of words, all of them. They flung them like weapons, handled them like jewels, tossed them on air with reckless abandon as though they scattered confetti.

"Zionism is provincialism," the woman in red velvet shrieked indignantly.

One with bleached hair and dark skin looked at her cruelly.

"Then provincialism is identity. Identity is strength. Strength is survival," she said, and turned away with authoritative disgust.

None of that made sense to Ardys. She moved on.

"Bellow. Bellow is magnificent," declared a man with a body shaped like a long, arched bow and white hair flinging itself over his ridged brow. He grabbed a circle of cheese from Ardy's tray. "Superb craftsman. That letter to Pulver. Marvelous, wasn't it? 'A herd of peasants driven to nihilism!' Beautiful."

"Ah," the short man next to him, who leaned with cocked legs and one raised elbow against the dining-room arch, objected. "Bellow can't match Malamud. Can't match him at all. So Bellow has style. Malamud has soul!"

"But I am tired," cried the laughing girl for whom they debated, over whom they bent their sweet, flushed faces. "I am tired of Jewish writers." Her free hand swept through the smoky air. "If we only could forget, just for a moment, that we are so special. If we could belong to the simple human race! My God, give me Ken Kesey. No style, no soul!"

And all three laughed as though whatever they said so positively, so earnestly, could thus be blown away like a frail tower of cards.

Wherever Ardys moved through the crowded room with her filled and emptied trays, it was the same. In her place, in her home town, the women were quiet and shy as birds. They fluttered in the presence of men, hid their bodies and their souls in sedate dresses and inconsequential chatter. At dinners together those women sang brightly of recipes and children and bargain sales, and the men sat silent, dour with the obligation to be sociable, impatient to eat, impatient to be through, impatient to be home again in old clothes and comfortable shoes.

Here no one seemed hungry. No one wanted to turn from the joy and fury of their cocktails and controversies to bother with food. Out in the kitchen, the white-uniformed caterer fussed over beef getting too well done. In the study off the living room the sour-faced bartender examined his watch and muttered complaints. It was past ten.

Ardys went, carrying the nearly emptied tray toward the corner where Ba-Ba sat in the gold brocade chair. She looked like an ancient island queen. Her body was awesome and grand in its loose cover of blue satin. Ardys passed Nannette, absorbed and laughing. She passed David, who lifted his fine groomed head, winked, bobbled his fingers at her as though he drummed on air, and bent again over the narrow-boned, smooth-faced blonde and listened, his handsome face mocking and serious, to what she said.

Surrounding Ba-Ba were the old ones. Belle was there, shouting her positive notions at a frail, violent old man.

"That rendition was strident, Belle," the old man roared in a quavering voice. "Simply intolerably strident." The finger he shot out at Belle quivered like a twig in wind.

"Bartok demands stringency." Belle bellowed. "It has to be tart. Pain. It has to pain. It was a perfect performance. Perfect."

"My God, Belle," the old man shouted. His eyes were wet and furious. "The string section sounded like cats in heat. Intolerable, intolerable. How *can* you defend that?"

"You're getting old, Isaac," Belle croaked at him, shaking her shoulders, her head, her hands. "Too old for Bartok. You won't stretch anymore."

"Belle," he muttered, his pocked and reddened nose almost touching hers, "I should put you over my knee and spank you."

But Ba–Ba had seen Ardys waiting there and understood what it was she wanted. She pushed herself up out of the soft cushions, took the old man's arm.

"Come, Isaac, Come, Belle. Now we shall eat." She took them in a slow, wayward parade off toward the dining room.

And then at last they all ate. They ate as rapidly and furiously and ardently as they talked. Ardys ran between kitchen and dining room replenishing the platters of beef and turkey, the trays of rolls and relishes, the bowls of vegetables and potatoes.

Then, suddenly, when Ardys rushed from the kitchen through the dining room door, bearing for the third time the silver platter mounded with thin slices of pink and brown beef, a wall of silence confronted her. Halfway to the table where glassware and food and flowers and silver stood in brilliant array under the shine of the branched candelabra, she stopped. All about the large and crowded rooms, faces turned toward her. All stood in their places, the plates in their hands ignored. They looked at Ardys. She stood with her fair hair fallen over her damp forehead. The stiff, white uniform hung like a board on her young, soft body. The tiny apron was wrinkled and spotted. Her helpless hands trembled with the burden of the platter of beef. No one moved.

Then they broke into sound. *Happy birthday, happy birthday to you,* they sang. The whole strange, unknown crowd of them sang in one dissonant, disorderly voice. *Happy birthday, dear Ardys, happy birthday to you!*

She stood stiffly under that shower of song. Stiff as a scarecrow bearing the frozen fall of snow she stood. She wanted to hide her simple, colorless, unready self from all their joyous watching eyes. She wanted to run from where she stood. She felt the deep red blood sweep her throat, her cheeks, her temples, her brow. She would fall. She would die.

But David came and put a strong arm around the curve of

her shoulders. When the last discord stopped, and their raucous cheering, he spoke out in a loud voice.

"To the loveliest girl in the room," he said, and lifted his
glass and smiled down into Ardys' face.

They cheered again, and Nannette came and took the
weighty platter from her hands, kissed her cheek, laughed.
David put a hand on her shoulder and turned her so that she
faced the living room.

There Belle shook the flame from a match and stepped
aside. Mounted on a silver plate on the black piano for all to
see was the high white cake. The light of a cluster of candles
broke from the top of the cake and made over its whiteness
a golden tower of burning.

"Look," Belle cried, spreading her bony arms on air, the
beak of her nose hunting from face to face. "Nineteen candles! Think of only nineteen candles!" She turned again and
smiled her yearning smile at Ardys, held out her arms as
though Ardys would fly into them. "Our flower, Ardys. Our
girl. Think, only nineteen!"

Someone at Ardys's right spoke and the whisper went like
smoke into the quickened, resumed confusion. *That Belle,*
someone whispered, *how brave she is.* And Ardys saw that
Nannette was suddenly unsmiling and that she rushed away
to the kitchen as though to escape anyone's seeing. She saw
that David shipped a swift, watchful look from Nannette to
Belle and then on to Ba-Ba. And then Ba-Ba, always so calm
and slow, hurried to the piano and stood beside Belle and
called aloud for plates, for a knife, for Ardys.

As she was commanded Ardys went, went to the piano
where Belle waited under the tower of shining. She did not
know what it was they knew, and she could not guess what
worry they hid. She had to cut the cake.

She slept after a while. Not even the lumpy sway of the
roaring bus could keep her from sleep. She stumbled out into

the cold gray dawn, clutching her coat about her. Her father was there, his face ruddy from the brisk air, his shoulders hunched toward his ears. He squeezed her against the roughness of his plaid Mackinaw and took her quickly to the clean, small warmth of the house in which she had grown up.

She had breakfast in the tidy kitchen ringed by the strangely innocent faces of those she loved. Her brusque, round mother made her sit like a lady and be waited on. Her brother Richard called her skinny-bones, as he always had. Her father suffered from smiles that pulled at his wind-chapped lips, his weathered face.

Together they went to church in the square brick building where she had gone to Sunday School every Sunday of her childhood. She sang the hymns in the company of those who had sung them all those past Sundays. Here the organ's melodies were comforting sounds. Here no one would talk of stridency or pain. The minister spoke and chided their lack of charity. Ardys thought of David. *Your God is a God of renunciations, Ardys,* he had said. The minister chastised their selfishness. Ardys thought of Belle and her imperious ways. The minister warned of fleshly sins. Ardys thought of the party and of the picture she had seen in Stephen's drawer. It was hidden under the tumbled piles of underwear and had been torn from some *Playboy* magazine. In it a pink-skinned, balloon-breasted girl lay with cocked legs and a knowing smile on a disordered, inviting bed.

Through bright noon-softened weather they all walked home. They had dinner of fragrant pot roast and mashed potatoes and thick-crusted pie. In the kitchen afterward her mother and Aunt Bertha shared dishes and insignificant gossip. Her uncle and her father dozed over the Sunday paper. The television offered a forgotten football game. Outside, her cousins and her brother tumbled and chased their way through their own wild games. After a while Ardys put on her jeans and joined them.

Then late in the afternoon there was the special angel cake with frosting piled on it in snowy abundance. There were nineteen candles and one to grow on. These, her own, also sang Happy Birthday in loud, uncertain voices. They brought out of the closet in her parents' bedroom the secret, predictable presents.

Then Bertha and Paul and the cousins went home. It was dusk. Ardys sat with her father at the kitchen table for a last cup of coffee.

"Well, Ardys," her father said, frowning at her from where he sat with his elbows leaning on the table top. "Have you had enough of the city yet?"

Ardys laughed as though he were joking. But she knew that he wanted her home, that he had not yet been won to the idea of her being away from them all in a place that might lead her to things he did not want her to have.

"I've been there only three months, Father," she said.

"Those people, Ardys." Her father looked down at his calloused, stained hands. He spoke as though shy of what he was saying. He looked at her out of clear eyes. "I'm not so sure you should be there with them."

"They're nice people, Father. They're nice to me," she answered. She said nothing of Belle.

"They are not like us, Ardys. They are different from us."

Ardys looked into his plain, troubled face. She did not answer that. She could not answer. She knew what it was he meant and she knew that it was, in large part, true. Perhaps he was right. They looked at each other, and neither of them turned away. They faced one another in the warmed, gleaming kitchen, each letting the other see the hungers and needs and worries and unspoken love that bound them in their blood, in their lives, in their age and youth, and separated them.

Then suddenly that sound broke upon them. Geese. It was the sound of geese.

Both of them thrust their chairs away. They rushed from the kitchen out into the dim, cold evening air.

The geese were rising from the lake on the edge of town. They burst upward in a clap of motion and high honking, sprang up in swift disorder against the sky's last, yellowed light. They mounted high on the strong, swift beat of their wings and came into the remembered shape of their flying. In the sky overhead they came, high above the heads of Ardys and her father where they watched. The long necks were stretched like ropes before the smooth, strong breasts. The tumult of honking dropped to a single occasional cry, echoed, repeated, passed from one fleet bird to another.

That calling. That marvelous calling. It hollowed the ear and soul of the hearer. Ardys heard again how that cry spoke of ecstasy and longing. The brush of the birds' wings on high air was like a wind upon her flesh, felt, not heard.

They flew, those haunted, hunting geese, in wonder and in woe. They flew on a dark necessity of seasons from what was known to what they did not know. They went in beauty, without choice, and they called out the glorious need of their going, praising the place in which they had been, and mourning, as well, its loss.

They had veered, the geese, into the southern sky. Already their wavering line grew small. Then suddenly, as she watched, it seemed that another wing touched Ardys. It drove its icy breath over her. Flesh and bone was pierced by its fierce tip. She stood with her face lifted toward the cold sky, and it was as if she stood in the center of a great wind. The sky into which she stared was a blinding darkness. She heard a call. A long, mournful call. Did she not hear it? Someone's call? Ardys looked into the sky that kept her from seeing. Was it Belle who called? Why would Belle call that way, as if in danger, as if in need?

"Ardys?"

She heard her father speak. She turned and looked at him

across the chill-darkening evening. But she saw that his face, in the gray air, took from her own a look of grief. She flung herself into his arms and stood trembling against him, taking from his strength comfort and courage for herself.

And when she returned to that high old house, walking from the bus in the windswept dawn, the car was there at the curb. As she drew near, she saw the black-clad man carrying a compact bag shaped like a small trunk leave the front door and go to the car. By the time Ardys reached the yard, the stranger had driven away. But Ardys had recognized from his costume what he was. A doctor. Someone was sick. And as she went up the walk, preparing to turn to the narrower walk that led to the back, the front door opened.

"Come in, Ardys. Come this way," Ba-ba said. She held the door open, standing away from the wind. Even so her flannel robe flapped about her thick legs. Ba-Ba took Ardys into the circle of her arms, held her against her full bosom. "It's Belle," she whispered. "Ardys, our poor Belle is sick."

But Belle was more than sick. She was mortally ill. All those rituals of pills and rest and sleeplessness Ardys had observed, and the solicitous indulgence of the others, and the strange remark she had heard at the party (*Poor Belle, poor brave Belle*) came into meaning. They had known, all of them, and she had not. They had kept the secret as if from her. Belle would not live.

Daily Ardys carried the trays. Daily she saw that ugly yellow face sink toward its bone. The dark eyes looked out from caverns of shadow like candles glimmering within a cave. "Ardys," Belle croaked, an old, hoarse bird. "Ardys. Thank you, darling. But I can't drink that broth."

But still she would imperiously ring. Each hour Ardys ran up those stairs, answering the summons of the chiming ring.

"Ardys," Belle would say, and stop. The old eyes fogged, and the mouth fell to a strange shape without words. She gasped then, as if she pulled strength from the intake of air, and found then something to demand. "Ardys, straighten up that pillow, will you, my love?" she croaked in one swiftly given-up breath, and then the old emptying eyes shut down, and the gaunt yellow face lay blind and naked under its ravages. "Ardys," she sometimes rasped, "give me that book, that one of my poems." And when Ardys took down the slim, fine volume, Belle opened her fingers to the touch of the leather, but she did not open her eyes, or more than lightly touch the book where Ardys placed it upon the bed. And sometimes she found nothing at all to ask. She would look at Ardys out of dim, dark eyes and mutter, "Nineteen only nineteen can't remember now nineteen," and Ardys stood helpless beside the bed and found nothing to say to those impossible sounds.

Never, now, did Belle perch at her table, flicking her way through the scraps of writings. Never did she sit as if caught in a far flight of thought, unmoving, unseeing, while she made up her poems. The bed held her prisoner now, and her decaying flesh locked her from visions. But still she would not let Ardys clear off that table. She demanded neatness and order in all the rest of the room, as if anything the least bit awry spoke of a large, looming chaos. But she wanted nothing on that table touched. It seemed that it was a kind of altar, kept there, presided over by the poet who had made it herself a shrine.

And then one day in late November, Belle's call chimed like falling ice through the afternoon quiet. Ardys ran to answer, quickly, quietly, anxiously up the stairs and down the high dark hall to that sunny room at the end. Belle was alone.

She did not even turn her head when Ardys entered. She lifted one claw where the rings hung like hoops and waved vaguely toward the chair by her bed. Ardys sat where she gestured. For a long moment Belle lay there without looking out. Then the heavy, oily lids opened, and dark light glinted faintly out. "Ardys," Belle gasped and sighed. "Ardys, it's time to do it now.'' She closed her eyes, sighed, gasped, spoke again. "Take all the papers, Ardys, love. All the papers on my table. Burn them, Ardys, now, right now.'' And Ardys's face must have shown refusal, for Belle's little claw grabbed her hand. "Ardys,'' Belle said, and leaned from her bed, a hunched-up, robe-covered lightness of bone. "Do as I say. All those scraps. Burn them, Ardys. Now, right now.'' There was no way not to obey.

Ardys swept all the loose, black-embellished papers—the little torn edges of newsprint where Belle's hieroglyphs ran, the pieces of paper napkin on which she had scribbled, the backs of envelopes and programs, and even three squares of fine, flower-printed lavender toilet paper on which three lines of poetry were written—into the large, wicker waste basket. She pushed and shoved at all the scraps and packed the basket full. Belle supervised her cleaning through scarce-opened eyes. "All of it, Ardys. Burn every bit.'' And she watched Ardys go from the room, carrying the packed waste basket in both arms.

Out in the bitter November day, in the obscure corner beyond the garage, Ardys poured the papers into the incinerator. One lone piece escaped on a thrust of wind and went whirling away into a low gray sky. To the rest of it, Ardys laid a single struck match. The first fine flame moved yellow at the papers' edge. Then caught, and the orangeness leaped up. The parts of poems gave themselves up to the snatching patches of ash. But as Ardys watched the burning, one word on one scrap of paper caught her eye. *Season.* English. That was what made her want it. The single word *season* on a lined paper. She reached down, grabbed a stick and fished for the paper in the gathering flames. She poked it, caught it, pulled it out. Blackness and glitters of orange consumed its edge. Ardys dropped it to the frozen ground and stepped on the place where it burned. Then she picked it up and read the few words written there. And read them again.

Leaves fallen
the black oak reveals
its truth.

In sharp wind
the garden gate creaks
open.

Wild geese weave
across the bleak sky,
calling.

November.
Winter come, the season
for going.

Was it a poem of Belle's, Ardys wondered, staring down
at the char-edged scrap of yellow paper where the dark, tall
letters leaned as if to the autumn wind. It was her writing,
surely, but was it a beginning of one of her own poems? or
was it a fragment she had copied somewhere? But that didn't
matter, Ardys thought. Its words seemed written to her and
for her. The only piece of Belle's writing she had ever seen
which she could read could not have spoken more directly
of the things she now knew.

For she stood under the bitter November wind, breathing
the bitter smoke of the incinerator's fire, and she knew that
winter had come. Winter was there, immaculate and without
comfort, for Belle. For her, it was, despite the warmth and
fury and joy that had so long held her there, a season for
going. A bitter season of going. And Ardys stood holding that
ruined scrap of paper and shook with a sudden surfeit of grief.
It was a season of change and loss for her, too; for what she
now knew, after the months of being there, that it was for
Belle only that she had stayed. When Belle was gone from

that dark old house, Ardys would go too, would then find it necessary to go. She would not stay for Ba-ba with all her histories, nor for Nan with her ready drollness. She could not stay for David with his sophistication, nor for Stephen and his brashness. Belle, Belle only, had held her there.